In Memory of Hawks
&
Other Stories from Alaska

Dec. 1998 –

For Eileen & Steve –

To help you think about
colder weather – since
you're so spoiled!

Jack

In Memory of Hawks

&
Other Stories from Alaska

Irving Warner

Pleasure Boat Studio

PUBLISHED BY PLEASURE BOAT STUDIO
802 EAST SIXTH
PORT ANGELES, WA 98362
TEL-FAX: 888.810.5308

E-Mail: pbstudio@pbstudio.com
URL: http://www.pbstudio.com

Design & Compostion by Shannon Gentry
Cover Photographs by Irving Warner

Several of these stories first appeared in the following periodicals:
The Cape of Saint Gregory, *Colorado Review;* A Journal from the Bay of
Islands, *The Stand Magazine* (U.K.); Fever, *Karmic Runes;*
Weather, *The Montana Review;* In the Islands of the Four Mountains,
The Cimarron Review; One Wing Falling, *The Montana Review.*

Library of Congress Number: 98-066089
ISBN: 0-9651413-4-9

Printed in the United States of America by Thomson-Shore
First Edition

For

Madge Clark, Jim Wolf, Bruce Swanson, Bob Tamburelli

Now gone,
but friends always

Contents

*For I am a stranger with thee, and a
sojourner, as all my fathers were.
O spare me, that I may recover
strength, before I go hence,
and be no more.*

Psalm 39:12-13

Drums

When they rounded Mission Point, Paul squinted and saw a brigade of uniformed soldiers floating back up, their blue tunics glistening. His sexton, Alex, brought the skiff to a halt and they both studied them: iron clad, with two blue rings across their middle.

Father Paul Orloff struggled to remove his glasses from under his raincoat, gave them a quick wipe on his shirt sleeve, and put them on.

"They're oil drums!"

"Yes, Father. Must be a hundred of them."

Alex motored into the flotilla of drums; each one floated low in the water. The blue enamel paint was clean and shiny, and it was obvious they'd been adrift for only hours. After coming alongside one, Paul bobbed it over and saw a stenciled label that read, "80/87 Avgas." They went to several more drums and each had the same marking. Alex whistled. "Aviation gas. That makes good kicker gas."

Paul, only having come to Port Herman two weeks before, reminded himself that *kicker* was the villagers' term for outboard motor. When his wife Alicia first heard the term, she'd unfortunately chuckled in front of several parishioners.

"Alex, why are they out here, floating?"

"I don't know, Father."

Paul was somewhat disconcerted when Alex, without consulting him, began towing them two at a time to shore. After all, it was an Orthodox Diocese's skiff and they were on church business.

"Alex, perhaps this isn't legal."

Yet Alex continued working, mentioning that at sea it was finders' keepers, and in fact he turned on the CB and radioed the village for help. A dozen villagers arrived in four skiffs within a half hour, and they worked for the remainder of the morning towing the drums into a nearby cove and pushing them up the beach into the grass.

There were 117 drums, a little more than six thousand gallons of gasoline.

Δ

The drums were the talk of the village, for it was indeed lucky to simply find thousands of dollars worth of gas. Despite what Paul said, none of the villagers concerned themselves with how the drums came to be floating off Mission Point. When he joined the elders in their discussion about the drums, he felt more an intruder than their priest. He'd waited for his turn and said, "Certainly there must have been a major sinking."

But several of the elders said they'd heard nothing about a sinking, and they listened to the radios all the time. In the Bering Sea anything could happen and several theories were developed to explain the drums' presence, most of them, Paul thought, quite unlikely. But Billy Arthur, a sly Yupik Eskimo with one arm, pointed out that St. Basil's Church was certainly in line for some share of the gas.

Paul soon saw that his concerns about the drums were superfluous to the villagers. The annoyed, self-conscious glances of the villagers all meant the same thing: "Your duties are in the church."

Paul's wife Alicia saw the issue of the drums as unimportant and instead talked about the poor response her weaving class had received. Only three Yupik women had participated from the two hundred villagers.

"Alicia, don't you think there must have been a terrible accident for those drums to be floating free?"

"Yes dear, but you see, that isn't the issue. The issue is, the gas is theirs. It's a tribal thing."

Paul resented his wife's two years in the Peace Corps. She'd spent it among a tribe of Indians in Paraguay, and she always lectured him on aspects of native cultures despite the fact he'd been her lecturer at the university when they'd met. After her declaration concerning the drums, Paul was tempted to mention the continued low turnout at her weaving classes, but did not. They would have certainly quarreled.

Δ

"Father, tell me about Jews."

He and Alex were in the cupola of the church strengthening the

2

mount for the bells when his sexton raised the question of Alicia's ethnicity. His initial resentment disappeared when he saw the innocence in Alex's eyes and remembered the warnings about the candor with which Yupiks approached many issues. Paul stopped, threw his leg over the edge of the small bell alcove, and smiled. Relieved for the temporary escape from the controversy about the drums, he'd explained Judaism briefly and simply, and concluded by saying, "My wife's not Jewish, but from an orthodox Jewish background. She's from Philadelphia."

Though he'd expected Alex to ask what a Russian Orthodox priest was doing being married to a woman of Jewish extraction, Alex simply lowered himself down the ladder to fetch the new pull line. It was good he didn't ask since Paul did not have a ready answer.

He found it exhilarating in the cupola. St. Basil's was built on the only hill in Port Herman and was easily the highest structure in the village. From his present vantage point, the advent of late spring was everywhere.

Swallows had arrived precisely on May 30th; the salmonberry bushes had begun to sprout intensely green leaves. At the mouth of Sitkin River, terns and black-hooded gulls fought for nesting space on offshore islets. These faced the small bay, and Paul turned and peered into the sharp onshore wind. He took a handhold on the bell's rim and looked beyond the bay onto the open sea. As the earth approached its summer solstice, the land and sea were warming, and the green tinge evident on the hillsides and bluffs elevated Paul's mood.

Towards the river he saw the doors of the community house swing open and the elders file out. Another meeting about the drums had concluded. From what Alex and others said, Paul knew the first two meetings had ended in no agreement. Family factions, old grudges and vague issues crept in from the dark fringes of every friendship and family. Worse yet, in the midst of the second meeting, it was disclosed that someone had already begun using the gas. Since the fuel was several miles from the village, any of the families could be suspect.

While he helped Alex rig the bell pulley and line, Paul cast an occasional glance towards the community house and noted that most of the elders remained standing in the lee of the satellite dish apparently arguing. Alex smiled along with Paul when they saw Old Moses throw up his hands, then shake his head and walk away.

"The old man is against everything."

"Well, Alex, in the case of the drums, I don't blame him."

Alex looked around the pulley at Paul, and they finished the job in silence.

The bell tolled beautifully for evening services.

Δ

Alicia was irritable during dinner because her coffee grinder and case of connoisseur coffees from France had arrived damaged. Perhaps this was the reason, Paul thought, she was especially brittle with him when he attempted to discuss the drums.

"Listen Paul, the drums are the villagers' concern. They don't need spiritual advice on the drums. I hope you aren't getting involved."

He put on a new CD of a Mozart string quartet, and the music made the ensuing silence easier. Evening services: Paul smiled at the term since this far north there was barely any night or evening. In fact, evening services were held when the sun was quite high on the horizon. He'd had trouble concentrating during the celebration of the Divine Liturgy. After services one of the dozen old women who attended took him gently by a corner of his cassock and advised, "Father, that young wife of yours, she's gotta have babies. She's young and strong and has too much time."

After he closed the church, he smiled and considered sharing her advice with Alicia, but this wasn't the day for it. When he was locking the front door, Paul again felt guilty, but he remembered Bishop Neimoff's warning about vandalism in the villages. When he turned away from the doors, he saw the *Bering Victor* entering the bay. It was a large steel ship, black and awkward. An anchor tumbled from its bow creating a great splash.

The gulls and kittiwakes circled the ship, crying out for morsels of food. He knew that no ship was scheduled to arrive, and as he walked away from St. Basil's towards the beach, he knew instinctively that the owners of the drums had arrived.

Δ

Paul sat in the front row in the community house when Captain LaBeau of the *Bering Victor* completed his story. Except for the elders, the villagers listened spellbound.

"So you all see, it was the work of a lunatic. Now we've sent him off to Anchorage, but he threw every barrel overboard on the night watch. We didn't even know until four hours later, and by that time we'd covered forty miles."

The irony was that Captain LaBeau had listened keenly to the radio and had overheard villagers gossiping about the drums. He'd reversed his course and returned to Port Herman for his gas. Paul and those not on the elders' committee were excused for the first private meeting with Captain LaBeau. Outside, they mixed with a half dozen of the crewmen off the

Bering Victor and heard numerous accounts of the lunatic who had pushed all the drums overboard. Knots of villagers surrounded each crewman and listened to his narrative, each one slightly different in details but identical on general items.

Paul was about to return to the rectory when one of the elders came out of the hall and approached him.

"You'd better come inside."

A bitter dispute had arisen between Captain LaBeau and the elders. The captain shrugged his shoulders and suggested calling the state troopers and turning the matter over to them.

"The law's on my side. This isn't a question of salvage. We lost the drums as a result of a criminal act, and that isn't salvage."

The elders weren't certain of their legal ground and asked Paul to mediate strictly in the interests of order. He thought momentarily and saw Captain LaBeau sitting at the table, tapping his finger.

After considering the situation, Paul agreed.

Δ

They negotiated for five hours. Captain LaBeau was sure of his ground, and the elders were less sure of theirs, except they had possession of the drums. Only twice did shouting erupt, and that was in Yupik, which the elders resorted to when they wanted to talk among themselves. Captain LaBeau did not seem uncomfortable with the situation and waited patiently for each offer and counter offer.

Finally, the chairman of the elders stood and made the group's final offer to Captain LaBeau.

"You pay the village community fund $5000.00 and wages to those helping you tomorrow to move the drums. The money is to be in cash."

Captain LaBeau thought about this: The elders knew he was a cash fish buyer on his way north and that he needed the gas to operate. Buying more would be expensive and cause delay.

Paul was unsure of what the law might say, and as the session drew on, he suspected that Captain LaBeau was too. The mariner stood and paced the floor, biting his finger and glancing towards the Council which awaited his reply. He looked at Paul and groused, "This is tough business."

"Yes, yet their offer is not unreasonable."

Captain LaBeau looked out the community house's only window and put his fingers to the glass. He had huge, globular eyes that seemed to express constant outrage. Outside it was dusk, and Paul knew it was past midnight. The captain took out his pocket watch, tapped it firmly several times, then nodded as if agreeing with some inner voice. He moaned sadly.

"OK, you got me. I agree."

Everyone was tired, and the elders arranged to meet at the *Bering Victor* at mid-morning and join the ship's launches to fetch the drums. The $5000.00 would be paid then and the wages at the end of the day. Paul insisted that the Chairman of the elders shake hands with Captain LaBeau "to show everyone that there are no hard feelings."

A single crewman slept in the small launch that awaited the captain, and the elders watched as the despondent captain motored towards the *Bering Victor* . Paul began the trek up the road towards St. Basil's rectory but one of the elders stopped him by saying thanks. When he turned, most of the others nodded and smiled, even waving good night to him.

He walked uphill towards the church feeling tired but good. The heavy dusk gave Paul a sense of privacy that one lost in the prolonged daylight. There was even a light dew on the bushes, and it had become decidedly cool. He was surprised to feel that there was no wind.

On the bay, the *Bering Victor's* lights shone creating a circle of illumination that encroached upon the deep shadows of the bluffs. At the beach, the village and bay were joined by a timid, peaceful surf. It was extraordinarily quiet.

Δ

Paul was awakened very early by Billy Robert; he held his one arm out, pointing towards the bay.

"The ship is gone and so are the drums. He lied!"

He stopped, his mouth biting at empty air, his eyes twisting right and left. He turned and stomped away down the road, his short stout legs thumping against the ground. In back of Paul, Alicia shook her head and sighed. Although she didn't reproach her husband, she quickly put on Levi's and sweater with nothing underneath, something he'd requested her *not* to do in the village ("What if somebody called suddenly?") and retreated to her loom.

At the community house villagers gathered. Paul joined the others who listened to Billy Robert describe the vanished drums, the ship not even on the horizon, and the initial feelings of outrage. The elders looked at one another and simply shook their heads, and some of the villagers openly criticized them for not posting a guard at the cove. Paul wondered if anyone would question why Billy Robert was paying an early morning visit to the drums, but the matter wasn't raised.

No one really said anything to him, and since everyone must have known that he only mediated to keep order, Paul hoped no one in their frustration would in any way blame him or the church.

By sheer chance, a Village Peace Officer arrived by plane for a routine visit while people were still gathered at the community house. After pleading for everyone not to tell the story at the same time, he listened, shaking his head sadly. It disconcerted Paul that after an unfriendly glance in his direction, the elders switched to Yupik, pointedly excluding him. Still the officer, a rotund Yupik born in a nearby village, answered in English in deference to the priest.

"He'll have an invoice for the gas to prove he purchased it. The law will say he can't steal his own fuel. It'll be tough. Did you have him sign anything?"

Everyone began to realize they had little recourse, and the officer's pencil stopped in mid-word when he heard the captain's name. He scoffed and closed his eyes momentarily.

"Not Captain Claude LaBeau! My God, up north he owes half the villages fish payments. He's a crook. Hadn't anybody heard of him?"

But no one had, and soon everyone returned home after the officer said he would report the incident to the state troopers, but he wasn't optimistic.

Paul hiked dejectedly up the hill towards St. Basil's, regretting his involvement in the entire affair. It saddened him that Captain LaBeau had been so methodical in his deceit, and stopping to look back at the bay, Paul recalled LaBeau's glance at his watch, the sigh and the words, "OK, you got me. I agree."

To the priest, LaBeau had seemed thoroughly resigned to his plight. Unlocking the church, he entered and prayed in the quiet of the old wooden building.

Δ

That Sunday four villagers attended service. Afterwards Alicia sat across the lunch table and made no attempt to mitigate the effect the fuel episode had on Paul's ministry. He drew a sharp breath and said, "They blame me."

"Yes they do."

"But I was only there to keep peace. I specified that."

He began to live each hour with a heaviness, and he wasn't surprised when Alex did not show up for duties on Monday morning. He resumed the refinishing work on the communion rails himself on Tuesday. He received a note from Alex at midweek reading, "I had to go to Holy Cross to help my brother," but Paul knew it wasn't true.

In the late afternoons he sat on the steps of the rectory and watched the swallows build nests in the eaves of St. Basil's. From the edge of a large puddle near an outbuilding, the birds gathered mud for their nests, often fighting over choice areas. On the power lines, the swallows would rest, brown-vested aerialists in neat, disciplined lines. Now, no one came to Alicia's weaving classes, and when she went to the store, only a few of the older women would say more than a few words.

Late one evening in the rectory, Paul put his book aside and removing his glasses noticed that Alicia had fallen asleep on the couch. Her right hand was cupped to her mouth, and the sweater she wore moved slightly, keeping pace with the rhythm of her breathing. When he thought how she'd supported and trusted him when he resigned his faculty post, following him four thousand miles to Port Herman, he felt a fresh onset of despair.

The whole idea had been a horrible mistake.

His colleagues at the university had furrowed their brows when he announced his intentions to go north and assume the responsibilities of a parish priest. Though most faculty members knew he was ordained, in the last ten years they had come to view him as a academician. And now, realizing his ministry was clearly crippled, he began to fear that failure was becoming a part of him.

When Bishop Neimoff called him the next morning about his visit, Paul knew it was the end. In the three weeks since the incident with Captain LaBeau, he and Alicia had become virtual maroons. Except for a few elderly women, no one came to church and Alex remained in Holy Cross. When he told Alicia about Bishop Neimoff's plans, she aired what he knew was inevitable.

"He's relieving you. I wonder where you'll be sent?"

Δ

Paul felt a twinge of envy when the church filled for the evening services offered by Bishop Neimoff. A former priest at St. Basil's, the head cleric was clearly overjoyed to be shut of administrative duties and back in the village. There were many home visits and two baptisms. At each function, the Bishop laughed and greeted all by name. Paul tried to not be envious, but it was difficult.

After the special salmon bake for the Bishop on Monday, they finally went to the rectory and talked. Asking permission to smoke his pipe, Bishop Neimoff studied the walls while digging out tobacco from his pouch and stuffing it into the bowl with a short, stubby finger.

"Well, circumstances have not been fair to you, Paul."

"They asked me to help, and I consented, Your Excellency. I had nothing to do with the details of their agreement with Captain LaBeau."

8

Between puffs on his pipe, Bishop Neimoff explained his decision to move Paul to Anchorage where he'd serve as a circuit priest. He would have Father Ravil at Holy Cross fly into Port Herman once a month until another priest could be found for St. Basil's.

"With your distinguished academic credentials, you'll be doing some teaching in Anchorage, I'm sure. And Alicia will like it. It has a very active cultural life."

Δ

After seeing the Bishop's plane off at the airstrip, Paul went into the church and prayed, but he felt somehow unrefreshed by it. He stood at the doorway to St. Basil's, then on a whim climbed into the cupola and looked out over Port Herman and the bay. In truth, a day hadn't gone by without his ascending to this vantage point, especially after the incident with the fuel drums.

Though his father, the only son of a Tsarist Minister, had been dead for twenty years, it was in the cupola that his long forgotten words returned to Paul. On many evenings long past, he had watched his father refinish furniture in the shop behind their small five-room house. The old man would smile at him over the top of the furniture and say in his heavily accented English, "Paul, this is my only solace." His father would dampen a suspect area with a sponge, feeling with the pads of his fingertips for possible flaws, driving the wood to a finer point of perfection.

In the fifty days Paul had been in Port Herman, so short a time, the land had become seized by a madness of green and fertility, and it awed him to witness this simple but perpetual renewal. A plain tundra hillside that a month previous had been disfigured by patches of dirty, half-melted snow was now richly decorated with tiny flowers. The berrybush thickets were dense and inhabited by small excitable birds that had paired and then begun building tiny nests nonstop.

The near-constant sunlight drove all things at a pace Paul had never seen before. Pairs of great swans and flocks of cranes cruised over Port Herman. The swans flew in stately lines without fanfare, while the cranes chattered noisily, rising and falling like sheets of gossamer in the onshore wind. Both turned upriver, flying towards their nesting grounds, vast wings pumping at the masses of air to maintain their impressive bulk aloft.

Because of what he'd seen, Paul refused to be excluded from scenes such as these. He would return to the city, but only temporarily. If he were patient, another opportunity would present itself; there were dozens of villages that required priests.

Something had happened to him here that was similar to the quiet, subtle drive that had urged him to leave the university and come north, but he couldn't define what it was. Looking over at the river landing, he saw villagers loading a scow with iced boxes of salmon. As the men shoved the containers down a ramp, the fish's metallic scales glittered in the diffused sunlight that struggled through the overcast. The men and women of Port Herman worked as they always had, and Paul didn't feel bitter about any of them.

Looking towards the beach, he saw Alicia walking up the path towards St. Basil's, head bowed, hands stuffed in her pockets. Why couldn't he take her in his arms and explain how he felt? Paul had never been able to do that with her, but he wanted to, now more than ever.

He held onto the edge of the bell and stood; at the mouth of the bay, gulls swarmed in funnel-shaped swirls, feeding frenetically on shoals of fish. At this distance, the birds formed impressive spirals at which Paul marveled. The birds, like time and the seasons, turned into themselves, coming around again and again, until they all became one creature that held itself white against the sea.

Pilgrim

He arrived in Fairbanks in late winter on the mail plane from Fort Yukon. Reeking of wood smoke, eyes alight with fervor, he told any who would listen about God. Alone in the wilderness since September, he'd learned about the essence of God's will through reading scripture and contemplating the vastness around him.

So he came to town early because of the urgency to communicate his visions. It had been a 118-mile ski trip to the closest human settlement.

He understood why people in cities and towns were locked in terrible moral dilemmas, just as he had been. But when someone sought enlightenment through the scriptures, he announced, these thorny pitfalls melted away.

Late one night, during the winter's last cold snap, I saw him round a corner, huddled into his patched, stained parka. Two others, who stood in the doorway waiting for a bus, immediately sidled away. He came up to me and talked about God's infinite wisdom and the potential for Mankind's redemption. The joy of these possibilities made him weep.

The Whale

i.

When the whale came into the bay everyone sensed it was close to death, but for the first few days no one would say so. It hung beneath the gray water, a shadow, occasionally fracturing the surface with its nostrils to blow a thin watery plume. Fat gulls circled above it, eventually settling on the water or nearby rocks. Through the long days and short nights, except for emerging to breathe, the whale lingered a few fathoms down, waiting.

On the dock, men watched the whale while theyunpacked staves and assembled barrels for herring season. Occasionally, as the mystery of its presence persisted, they stopped and looked toward the middle of the bay where the huge animal rested. King slapped his hand against a barrel and growled, "Hey! Work to be done here. This isn't a zoo."

But there were no herring yet and assembling barrels and moving salt from barges was busywork, so eyes returned to the whale when King climbed up the stairway into the gear loft.

In the evenings men came from the bunkhouses to sit on the dock and speculate about the whale's presence. This activity consumed the hours until sundown. After this, a night wind moved down from the mountains and brushed ripples across the bay. The watchman on his rounds listened for the whale, but its breathing was inaudible because of the wind. Only the mist of his blow was visible, but that would rapidly be swept away.

The watchman stirred cream and sugar into his coffee and studied the bay from the cookhouse. The coffee got cold as he thought about the whale.

The Whale

ii.

The land around the saltery was ugly: The bay hung gray from silting and the low, rolling tundra that surrounded it stood treeless. Rocky outcroppings were covered with crusty lichens, and small bushes clung bravely in tiny cracks and fissures. A few miles to the southeast a range of naked mountains met the prevailing sea wind with forbidding brows.

On the tundra were strewn many ponds and small lakes that in spring were used by nesting waterfowl. Since it was late July, the birds moved with their young to richer grounds to the west. A few loons stayed, singing their song to the rocks and tundra.

iii.

King was angry with the whale. He had been coming to the saltery for twenty-five years and had been superintendent for fifteen of those years. He liked each season to follow an identical pattern: In midsummer the boats and barges would arrive and they'd open the saltery. The women would arrive from the Indian villages and fishing would start; the processing would begin and the season would continue for eight weeks. By the second or third day King would have put a proposition to the best looking of the new Indian women, and she would live with him for the remainder of the season, being assigned light duty and extra overtime hours. Breakfasts were at 6:00 a.m., lunch at noon, dinner at 6:00 p.m. Coffee breaks at ten and three. If there was no work after dinner, the crew would play cards in the dining room until bedtime. Once a week there was a movie, a western.

Each year King would make out the schedule, typing the new from the old, then making six copies. The bookkeeper tacked up each copy after writing ATTENTION at the top. Saltery rules were simple: No fighting, no gambling, no drinking, no fraternization between male and female employees. Anyone breaking the rules was fired.

At the end of the season the Indian women would go home to their villages, and the men to their cities in the south. A ship would take the barrels of herring to Asia. Lastly they'd prepare the saltery for winter, and King, Isaac the mechanic, and a small crew of laborers would be the last to leave. It was always that way.

In twenty-five years the bay had never been visited by a whale and King wondered why one appeared now, this season. It was a shallow bay and he'd never noticed any marine life except for seal when the dock workers unloaded herring

Several times a day he had to reprimand the men for not working because of the whale. It distracted them. When the women arrived, they would be worse.

If the whale died here, it would wash up on the beach and cause a terrible stench. Workers would sneak down and try and remove teeth or baleen, depending on what sort of whale it was. Huge bears that ranged in the nearby mountains never came near the saltery, but a dead whale would change that. A sick whale was bad, but a dead whale was worse.

From his office, King looked out on the bay, squinting to see the vast silhouette sinking and rising under the water. Maybe it would simply go.

iv.

Isaac began to read excerpts from the Old Testament to the whale the day after the women arrived. Isaac was the only person who had been coming to the saltery longer than King and everyone respected him.

He read to the whale for about thirty minutes in the evenings. Everyone became embarrassed and left the dock when Isaac came out, sat down, pulled his mechanic's hat low over his eyes, and read aloud. He'd follow the lines with a greasy, spatulate index finger, pronouncing each word with difficulty. After he was through, he closed the Bible and put his spectacles away, giving them a gentle, reassuring pat. Only then would people drift back onto the dock to watch the whale.

No one dared ask Isaac why he read the Bible to the behemoth. The day before the first delivery of herring, King commented that he'd never known Isaac was religious.

v.

They had been salting herring for a week when a summer storm struck.

People ran around the saltery tying things down; fishermen secured their boats to the dock with extra lines; the boat masts swung east then west with the force of the wind. The water in the bay steamed angrily when the wind raked across it; the spray rose in the wind, then whipped toward the cannery giving each wooden building a sheen. The gulls squatted low on the rocks, their flat webbed feet planted firmly.

In the office the storekeeper and the cook played cribbage and watched the storm. They listened as the buildings moaned; sometimes a can or box would be blown loose and go clanking across the boardwalks. The smell of curing herring permeated everything and the men exchanged cursory complaints about it.

Between plays, they glanced out the window and tried to see the whale but couldn't. The waters of the bay were hidden in an angry haze.

The Whale

vi.

After the storm the whale was gone. King climbed up to the top of the gear loft and surveyed the entire area with binoculars, and he was glad to see it hadn't washed up dead on any of the beaches.

Soon, he knew, people would stop talking about the whale. At breakfast he said nothing, but during lunch he pointed out that such a huge beast had no business in such a small, shallow bay.

"There are other bays, and we've got work to do."

The boatwright gamely kidded Isaac about reading his Bible to the whale. "You drove it away, Isaac. You drove it away."

Isaac said nothing, but for the remainder of the day the boatwright's words were repeated, gaining dimension upon each retelling. The boatwright, the folks all admitted, was a helluva fellow.

At dinner the bookkeeper brayed loudly and said that the entire incident with the whale had been a fluke of nature. Few got the joke and fewer laughed.

King suspected that the bookkeeper had a bottle hidden somewhere and decided to alert the watchman.

vii.

King let himself into the cookhouse and made a sandwich after the Indian girl told him he was almost as old as her grandfather. She'd laughed about that.

He wrapped his bathrobe around his legs and sat close to the huge oil range. Only the night light in the exhaust hood illuminated the kitchen, and King was surprised when his mind wandered back fifty years to when his grandmother would fix him a sandwich and talk about her childhood in Norway.

The compressor in one of the large freezers started up and he studied the fan through the ventilator screen, its blades a blur.

The watchman fractured his reverie, stammered somewhat, and apologized. He was about to leave, but turned and rested a freckled hand against the door jamb.

"The whale's back, King. I can hear it blow. It's pretty quiet out there tonight and I can hear it blow. There's a loud rattle to it now. Sounds bad."

He left King alone.

King threw the remainder of the sandwich away and shuffled off to his quarters, a large apartment in the west extension. When he'd first come to the saltery, the elderly superintendent had lived there with his wife.

When King settled into bed, he told the Indian girl that the whale had returned, but she slept soundly. It was a problem for him to fall asleep.

viii.

Old Thomas and a dozen other Eskimos arrived a week after the storm. They lived on a rocky, inhospitable island twenty-five miles offshore. Their skin boat was powered alternately with a sail and an old outboard motor that coughed and smothered itself in its own exhaust.

The Indian men that fished on the boats and the women who worked in the saltery watched the Eskimos with half-hidden smiles. They considered the Eskimos old-fashioned, but it was because of this quality that King liked them.

Old Thomas was ninety-three years old and nearly blind. His sons, grandsons, and great-grandsons helped him up to the dock, and they all went to the store and bought supplies. King always invited them into his quarters for coffee and sweet rolls. Through a son who spoke some English, King asked Old Thomas about the whale. His leathery face twitched as he smoked his pipe, finally speaking his ancient tongue. "He says you can't know about whales, except when they want to die, they die. Can't do nothing about it," his son reported.

Old Thomas puffed for a while longer, then added a further comment through his son: "But the old man says not to eat the meat when the whale dies. It could kill you."

Like always, Old Thomas and King exchanged gifts: This year it was a new pump shotgun and a case of shells for a beautifully carved set of walrus tusks. King turned the tusks over in his hands, wondering at the workmanship.

"Tell the old man this is too much. I gave only a shotgun."

One of Old Thomas's sons pointed out the window; the wind had come up, and they needed to depart at once since their fish camp was ten miles down the coast. They would return to their island in several weeks with a winter's supply of fish and other staples.

While King walked them back to their boat, Old Thomas stopped and took him firmly by the forearm. As was always the case, the old man carried on a conversation begun a dozen seasons before. It was so familiar to King a translation was hardly necessary.

"The old man asks what's wrong that you still don't have a wife?"

King managed a smile and shook his head. "Tell the old man I'll be a bachelor all my life."

Old Thomas muttered something that no one translated, but kept hold of King's arm until he was helped down the ladder. His grip still had the remnants of great strength. All the Eskimos laughed when their motor wouldn't start, and as they sailed from the bay they passed near the whale as its dark back broke the surface and it sighed a misty cloud into the air.

Since the saltery crew was working, King and the storekeeper were the only ones to see them sail from the bay.

"You know, King, they're way behind on their bill."

"I know they are."

He walked away from the storekeeper, who stayed behind to watch the whale. King had wanted to watch the skin boat sail until out of sight, but he wanted even more to get away from the storekeeper.

When he got to his office he looked out the window but could no longer see the boat. Slowly he reexamined the walrus tusks, following each line of the carving with the pad of his finger.

King remembered years before when his grandfather had taught him to carve cedar decoys. They would be alone in his shop. He could still see his huge arthritic hands rubbing linseed oil into the grain of the aromatic wood.

Suddenly he heard a loud splash and a hiss.

Looking out the window he saw the whale's flukes just before the animal snorted and slipped under the water. King had never seen it show its flukes and make such a splash. He was standing at the window watching when the cook's helper brought him coffee.

"Isn't this a godawful lonely place to come and die, King?"

He was a college student whom King rather liked. He took the coffee and shrugged.

"I never thought about it much."

After the cook's helper left, King felt a mood of melancholy come on, so he returned to his work, attacking a backlog of pack reports and payroll ledgers.

ix.

They found out the bookkeeper was drinking when he chained and padlocked himself under the dock at low tide. Around midnight the watchman had heard the intoxicated man giggling and talking to himself.

After putting on hip boots, King checked the tide book and was grateful to see they had plenty of time.

"OK, get a bolt-cutter and let's get him loose."

When they climbed down the ladder under the dock the bookkeeper was asleep. King leaned against a piling, avoiding the softer portions of muck and giving each boot top a tug while the boatwright lighted a cigarette; they waited for the others to fetch the bolt-cutter.

The bookkeeper slumped against his chains, snoring loudly. The boatwright studied him with disgust.

"Did the drunken bastard tell anybody why he wanted to

kill himself?"

"He told the watchman he was going to die with the whale."

The boatwright had a good laugh on that. King studied the undersides of the dock and wondered at the hundreds of red and purple starfish the low tide had exposed.

As they struggled up to the dock with the bookkeeper, the rain started coming down in icy dollops. He was tied face-up on a stretcher, and when the water struck him in the face, he awoke and began to weep.

They put the stretcher on a wagon and pulled him towards the saltery. Suddenly there was a watery slap, and they all turned in time to see a great splash and giant flukes, and, despite the noise of the rain, they clearly heard the roar of air rushing from the whale's nostrils. The foreman cursed.

"When is it going to die?"

But no one guessed, instead just kept on pushing the wagon in a silence punctuated only by grunts and the bookkeeper's muted sobs. The frigid rain worked its way through King's coat, causing a shudder. How many times had he gone out without rain gear and gotten wet? Fortunately the mail plane was due the next day. The bookkeeper would make that plane.

Though the drunken man would have done something stupid in any case, the reason for his mawkish suicide attempt would get around by tomorrow. What seemed asinine, even funny, under the dock would gain credence. By the time the man was on the plane, people would feel sorry for him and wonder even more about the whale.

King recalled what Old Thomas had said and knew there was nothing anyone could do. There could be no predicting the whale.

x.

The quartet of ravens leapfrogged each other on the railing of the dock, clucking and looking out at the whale. Each of the large birds would vie for the best vantage point, occasionally stabbing at each other with their black, down-curved bills. Gulls resented them, but the ravens were fierce and wouldn't relinquish their favorable positions. King watched the birds from his office with binoculars. Ravens were common around the warehouses and in back of the dining room but had always been driven from the dock by the gulls.

The whale had taken to lying at the surface for many minutes breathing lightly. Its great back was slick with water, and even without binoculars King could see many scars, some deep and crusted. One or two of the ravens would push off from the dock, swoop down low to the water, then climb sharply when they flew over the whale. Spreading their wings and wheeling, the birds returned to the dock, usually finding their former perches occupied by gulls. After intense pecking and scuffling, they would sit and continue their vigil.

"Why don't I shoot the goddamned things. They're just waiting for it to die. They're black from the outside in. Worse than vultures."

King was surprised when the storekeeper said this. An ordinarily sedate man, it wasn't like him to shoot things, and in any event King didn't allow shooting near the saltery. There was no need to remind him of that, so the storekeeper scuffed at the boardwalk and sighed.

"It's annoying, is all. Just annoying."

That evening while writing in the log, King decided to mention the whale. The log was a place for business, he knew: approximate pack figures, personnel changes, the arrival and departure of boats, and of course the weather. These were all entered daily. Despite this he wrote, "Whale still present in the bay, this date."

Immediately he felt stupid. King remembered the company headquarters with its waxed floors and bright offices. Who there would be interested in reading about a whale? He located a gum eraser and rubbed it out, sweeping the rubbery residue carefully away.

xi.

The Indian girl would sit up in the middle of the night and talk. The first time she did this King woke her immediately, reaching up and taking her by the shoulder and shaking her awake. But the second time it happened, he listened.

She talked about her village, not talked so much as stated things that weren't connected.

At other times she babbled. Only the individual words had meaning; together they were a jumble. After that, King would go into the other bedroom. He could hear her rambling despite the thick door.

After a pause of about a week, she resumed by sitting up and speaking Indian. King had never heard any of the Indians speak their language, and he sat quietly and listened until she began trembling and striking out at the air with both hands. When he caught her wrists she woke, her eyes black, huge, and frightened.

"You were speaking Indian."

"No. I can't speak Indian. It was nothing."

She curled up and went back to sleep.

But King felt certain it was Indian. Dressing, he thought about the girl, wishing he occupied the superintendent's quarters alone. He wandered onto the dock.

The crew had not worked late and the saltery was quiet. King knew the watchman would be in the top story of the warehouse cradled in a herring seine, asleep. He dragged out his pocket watch. It was three forty-five and still dark. The nights were getting longer.

When King looked out onto the bay, he saw the whale at the surface. It lay still, and in fact the portion of the animal above the water seemed dry. King studied it.

When there was no blow, he knew it had finally died. He was just beginning to feel remorse when he recovered his senses and shook his head so hard it hurt.

Don't be dumb.

It was dead and that was that. King admitted that the season was becoming strange and the whale was part of whatever made it strange. The tide was incoming, and he looked down at a skiff tied to the dock. He had an urge to row out to it, but when he put his foot down to the first rung he heard a tired, slow sigh followed by a familiar rattle. Gradually the whale submerged, so slowly it seemed the water itself reached up and concealed it.

It took King several moments to realize his error.

King walked quickly off the dock. Coming to a snap decision, he sneaked up the stairs and caught the watchman asleep. When he poked him awake with a boot tip, the watchman shot to his feet, flaying at the air for balance, but instead he fell back onto the net, blinking. King's words were terse:

"What if there was a fire?"

King left him sitting there. His question was punishment enough. By the time he reached the kitchen, King realized he'd overreacted. Despite the watchman's error, it was an infraction long tolerated. There had been other ways.

King studied the kettle of water as it drew to a boil. Steam curled from its spout, reminding him of Aladdin's lamp. He tried to recall who read him that story. His grandfather? Yet in the end he couldn't remember.

When the cook came in it was 4:00 a.m. and King was drinking coffee. After pouring himself a cup, the rotund man began preparing dough for biscuits. King watched the waddles of fat sway under his arms as he kneaded.

The cook shaped the dough into a giant mound; he punched a beefy fist into its soft middle then paused.

"That whale still alive?"

"Yes, but it's weak."

They sat together in silence until a heaviness came over King's shoulders. He stood; with luck he'd get a couple of hours sleep before breakfast.

xii.

Herring catches were high and the crew began working twenty-hour days. With such volumes of fish, King had constant concerns about supplies, spoilage, and his crew.

There was a pushing match between two warehousemen late on the third long day. King and his foremen tried to decide if this was early in the season for such problems. All of them seemed to think it was.

On the fourth day of the rush it occurred to him he hadn't slept in thirty-six hours. The storekeeper, who had himself been up for twenty-eight hours, sat on a pallet of unopened sacks and sgroused about what he'd do with his money. It was the first time King had heard that this year.

All the bins and hoppers were filled with fish, and cascades of them poured into the curing vats. Each fish was big and fat and would bring a superb price.

King took pride in all his decisions and moves; they had been perfected over a quarter century. The massive worn planks that formed the floor of the saltery felt certain to King, more certain than anything he'd known. Everything that rested or moved across those floors had its place.

During the late evening of the heaviest day he retreated to the dock. From there the saltery was a fortress in the midst of a siege: The clanking of machinery beat regularly, with each sound identifiable; the rumblings of barrels being pushed across wooden decks formed a tangible backdrop. The lights of the saltery cutting into the dark created a web that, for King, formed the hub of a wheel whose spokes were the stillness of the bay, ponds, and mountains. The rigorous, clean smell of curing herring blended with the sea and was not unpleasant. Only a newcomer's nose would wrinkle.

He watched and listened, quite hypnotized. Already King felt less tired.

Yet a familiar resentment took hold when he heard the whale's rattling blow. King turned suddenly. The flood lamps on the dock favored the bay with some light, and King saw the whale at the surface. A stiff onshore wind swept the vapor from its blow towards the dock, and King noticed it was extraordinarily voluminous and black; when he looked down at his jacket and trousers, they were spattered with droplets of blood.

He reached out and gripped the handrail.

Another blow erupted, even blacker, and King knew he was watching the whale die. The dock and several skiffs were soon sprayed with red; King wiped his face, and his hand came away red and slick.

Though common sense told him to retreat, he stayed and watched it all. Finally, the beast rolled once on its side, righted itself slowly, then rolled over completely. The deep grooves on its belly gleamed in the light and it was still.

King walked from the dock and hurried to his apartment. When he entered, the Indian girl was leaving for the dining room to prepare rolls and coffee for break. She gasped and slapped a hand across her mouth.

"What happened!"

"The whale died. Just now."

He removed his clothes and stepped into the shower. While the hot water ran over him, he leaned his head against the wall. Through the curtain he could see the outline of the girl.

"King, are you okay?"

"I'm okay."

She went to work and he was alone. He wrapped himself in his robe and sat in a chair, staring out the window. The whale had died at the worst time. What could he do?

King leaned back and fell asleep at once.

When the Indian girl returned after break, she put a blanket over his shoulders, tucked in another around his legs, and let him sleep.

xiii.

The whale drifted ashore barely three hundred yards from the saltery. When King, his tradesmen, and his foremen walked to the carcass, the birds lifted off from it at the last moment, but landed close by, watching jealously.

The boatwright and one of the foremen measured the whale, speculating on what kind it was.

"It must weigh forty tons."

Others discussed how best to dispose of it; they agreed that with four weeks of season remaining, the situation would otherwise become intolerable.

King sat down on a chunk of driftwood and looked on as the discussion became intense. He took off his hat and studied the circle of men: Arms enacted movements with imaginary pulleys and hypothetical lifts suggesting networks of lines radiating in all directions. Rubber boot-tips dug impatiently into beach gravel. Occasionally someone would spit, look up, then squint as they all reappraised the whale. Puffs of tobacco smoke drifted across the whale, its skin draped over its wasted form like a vast, threadbare blanket.

Isaac folded his arms in back of him and paced back and forth the length of the whale, shaking his head, occasionally throwing his arms in the air in frustration as he passed the group. Voices implored Isaac to agree with one of several prevailing methods for removal.

But there wasn't complete agreement.

Finally one of the foremen reported to King. "Most are for burning it, using fuel oil to get it going. A few others, mainly Isaac, are for towing it off with boats and taking it out to sea."

King looked at the tide book and announced that they'd try to tow it off.

He'd made the controversial decision in a moment, and when he headed back toward the saltery his most senior foreman followed him. When they were out of earshot the foreman said, "Jesus, King, we'll have to call in all the boats. We'll have to stop fishing. It'll bring the place to a standstill. Even then, we aren't certain if they can do the job."

King asked him to draw up the duty list for the coming evening's labors, for high tide would occur at 4:00 a.m. They returned to the saltery without discussing it further.

As he walked down the boardwalk toward the office, King looked back at the whale. It was speckled again with white gulls; toward its mouth and eyes the ravens worked, their calls coming in short excited bursts.

When King opened the door, he resisted looking back again. He became anxious to drag the whale from the beach and have it towed to sea.

xiv.

By midday the first of the boats arrived. The fishermen took the opportunity to pick up mail, take showers, and have a warm meal. Yet they weren't happy. No money resulted from dragging a whale off a beach and the shoals of herring had been vast and catches high. The fishermen's complaints spread to the saltery crew.

Even with the partial loads brought by the boats, they would be out of herring by early afternoon. Only a few workers would be used to help that evening. This had been the peak of the season, and it would soon pass.

By late afternoon everybody agreed that burning the whale was the best thing to do. Even as skinny as the whale was, fuel oil would take up where nature failed. Attempting to pull the whale from the beach would simply waste time; in the end, they'd have to burn it anyway.

King spent the afternoon in his office and when he took dinner there was little talking. The boatwright joined them late, and when he sat down he sarcastically remarked, "Well, we're out of herring."

Nobody discussed this further. King opened a newspaper he'd received in the mail and began to read; he offered sections of it to others, but soon he was left alone doing the crossword puzzle.

He always considered crossword puzzles a waste of time, and he was about to mark his activity off to boredom when he remembered that, decades before, his mother always did crossword puzzles. He'd fetch her the evening paper, she'd take off her shoes, and he'd rub her feet while she worked the puzzle: "What would be a six-letter word for *hypocrisy*?" she'd ask.

He had been too young to know about such words, but she'd smile and say how nice it was, his rubbing her feet. How old had he been?

He stood abruptly and stuffed the paper into his back pocket. The cook's helper looked up from his mopping and nodded a greeting. The acrid-smelling cleaning solution rankled, and instead of talking with the lad, King left the dining room and went to his apartment. It would be wise to get some sleep before the early morning's activities.

The Indian girl wasn't in yet and at first he was disappointed, but this turned quickly to relief. There would be no responsibility to talk about anything.

He crawled into bed.

Outside, he heard the cook's helper mopping the corridor, the bucket rolling across the wood floors as he swabbed, dipped, and wrung out.

There was nothing else to hear but the near-silence of old buildings.

xv.

King dressed in the dark, careful not to awaken the Indian girl. Boots in hand, he crept to the window and saw the new moon. The tides would be at their peak.

When he turned he saw the Indian girl sitting up in bed; she embraced her legs, tucking them into her. She said several words in Indian while weaving gently, side to side.

King decided to leave her there sleep-talking and had nearly sneaked by her when she spoke again.

"That was my Indian name. It means 'Shining Crane.'"

It took him aback when he realized that she wasn't asleep. She looked down at the bed and swept away her long black hair, laying it across one shoulder.

"I thought you didn't speak Indian."

"Just a little. Isn't that a dumb name for a girl?"

"No. It's a good name."

To see her by the light that came in through the window was strange. King left her, walked in stockinged feet to the kitchen, and sat down to put on his boots. The cook's helper was unscrewing the caps on a half dozen thermos bottles.

"Nobody thinks the whale will float, King."

After King stomped each foot down to secure the boot's fit, he took an offered cup of coffee and sighed. "I'll take the thermoses down to the beach."

"No, that's okay, King. I'm going to watch. There's quite a few down there."

After putting on rain gear, King walked onto the dock. Down the beach the floodlights from the half-dozen fishing boats created a naked, harsh brightness. The men who threw lines over the whale were tiny next to the hugeness of the whale. Beyond this the moon climbed higher: big, cold, and steady.

xvi.

King stood above the high-tide line several dozen yards. It was a familiar pleasure watching Isaac work with lines, pulleys, and winches. Even twenty-five years before, Isaac had been an established master of his trade. The others were confused but did their best to follow his directions.

Though the tide had come in around it, the whale still remained grounded, and the workers slogged about, passing lines back and forth with difficulty.

When Isaac came up to him, he took off his mechanic's hat and wiped the sweat away. Isaac handed King a flare pistol. When fired, the boats would all start pulling. Taking out his pocket watch, he looked at the time.

It was seven minutes until high water.

King lowered the watch and looked at the elderly mechanic. He had never seen him so weary. A question struggled outwards, but he hesitated; Isaac looked up at King and nodded, anticipating it.

"It'll move."

King counted almost fifty saltery workers up the beach. They had made a fire from beach logs and had surrounded it, looking on blankly, hands tucked into pants or coat pockets. The women all sat together, but King noticed that the Indian girl was not with them.

When he fired the flare, the boats drew the lines taut, then pulled with all their power. Sterns squatted down into the water; the bows rose, straining. The whale's body lay unmoving. King and Isaac looked on as the boats' combined prop washes created an angry froth at the waterline. The engines united in a frenetic scream.

Down the beach, the saltery workers stood, backing away. The power of the boats, completely frustrated by the whale's bulk, caused the vast network of lines, cables, and pulleys to vibrate ominously. Someone behind King shouted, "Stop them! Something's going to give!"

At that moment, a line parted with a sharp crack. Men dived for cover with panicked shouts. King dropped backwards, but managed to grab Isaac by the belt and pull. He rolled over on one shoulder and, when he struggled up, he saw the whale's body glide sedately into the bay. Beach gravel rattled under its mass.

The boat operators began blowing their air horns, and, after the fright and astonishment passed, everyone cheered.

Isaac winced with annoyance as the foreman and boatwright pounded him on the back. King brushed gravel and dirt from his pants and walked to the waterline.

The whale floated a few yards away. Though its skin was wet again, in no way did it resemble a living animal. The carcass bobbed slowly back and forth. King was contemplating it when he became aware of Isaac standing beside him.

One by one, the air horns quieted, and the cheering ceased. The workers and tradesmen walked to the waterline and joined King and Isaac; the boats' crews stood at the rails, looking on.

"Okay, there's work to do."

After saying this, King forced himself to walk toward the saltery. Ascending the bluff he hesitated to catch his breath and saw that everyone remained by the whale. In an approximate circle formed by the shore and boats, the animal floated serenely, dark and dead. Despite the coming of dawn, the moon shone brightly, and this plus the boat lights created a type of illumination King had never seen. It was silver outwardly, so people and boats gleamed like zinc or aluminum. Yet the whale was no longer dark, but black, so black, King thought, that it was like a deep night had left some of itself behind.

Everyone was quiet, and King walked several feet down the bluff and joined in the vigil. The gulls flitted in and out of the light, their shrill cries echoing over the sea.

xvii.

The other boats returned to the fishing grounds while one towed the whale out to sea. King went with it. He intended to have the whale towed down the coast six or seven miles.

Outside the bay, the sea was like the land, gray and cold. The beaches were straight and wide. At low tides, offshore shoals curled the waves into whitecaps. On the flood tide, the black volcanic sads were beaten by an imposing surf that washed over them and up to high bluffs topped by dry, yellow grass.

A mile offshore, King watched the line of foam stranded by the falling tide. A shroud hung over the shoreline, created by mists rising from the miles of tumbling, breaking surf.

Hundreds of gulls followed the whale, some peeling off to sprint downwind towards the beach. Shading his eyes and squinting, King could see a dozen ravens slowly paralleling their course along the apex of the bluffs. They played in the wind that curled over the bluffs; undoubtedly they were cawing and hooting, but the din of the surf silenced them.

The whale towed easily, flukes first. King stood on the stern of the boat and shrugged deeply into his coat. Someone handed him a cup of coffee, but regardless of the cold he looked first at the whale then at the surrounding panorama. He could never tire of it.

Despite the business at hand, King's attentions returned to a notion he had been trying to identify over a period of days. It had come to him like pieces of a strange puzzle. Only this morning had it become recognizable.

The fact was, he had a desire to stay at the saltery all winter. The company would allow it, being desirous of having a winter watchman, yet people would wonder about him. The winters at the saltery were long, unrelenting, and extreme. When he was younger, he'd almost wintered several times, for it had seemed a challenge. But he never had.

In the winter he would be alone and that could be an advantage. He valued being alone.

The boat slowed then stopped.

He watched the whale as its swaying from port to starboard ceased. Their wake had left a residue of white spume along its crest.

"Is this far enough, King?"

They brought in the towline until it was close to the whale's flukes and they cut it loose. Freed from its burden, the boat wrapped in a tight half circle and began the return trip. The bulk of the whale rose on the crest of a wave, then fell from view in the following trough.

He stuffed his hands in his back pockets and recalled that morning's scene when he'd looked down the beach and had seen the whale floating quietly. There seemed nothing more final than the whale.

Yes, he was staying the winter.

He took a sip of coffee, but pulled back when he felt the cold on his upper lip. Tossing the remnants away, he looked out and saw that the whale was almost out of view. Birds turned overhead, falling occasionally to the wave tops, seeming to reassure themselves of its presence.

"Shining Crane."

He startled himself by pronouncing the Indian girl's name. King recognized her as a possible flaw in his plans. Certainly he could conceal his decision to overwinter until all the Indian women had left, but he wouldn't. He'd simply let his plans become known via rumor; then she could decide for herself. She was quiet and never talked much; hence, King didn't perceive her presence as an infringement upon the luxury of solitude.

King looked forward to walking across the old plank floors and hearing only his footfalls. There would be no sounds except those he made. He could brew coffee and sit up late in the big kitchen with no cook to disturb him, no sudden change or strangeness to confront.

The docks would have no boats arriving or departing; the gear lofts and warehouses would be quiet.

If he wanted to look out a window all day, no one would be there to think him strange or different. He could, if he wanted to, think about seasons gone by, or those more recent. King would most certainly think about the whale.

He strained to see the whale, but except for the tiny white specks of gulls that spiraled overhead, it was gone from view. The wind was cold now and his coat was too light. Reluctantly, King turned and went inside.

Reports of Disappearances I: Wes Ingram

Wes Ingram was flown north to the Colville River delta by a famous bush pilot and guide. Wes had read the pilot's book on living in the Arctic, had corresponded with him, and was hired sight unseen for the pilot's fish camp. By June, he was netting whitefish in waters he'd only dreamed or read about.

In the Arctic, the sun really did shine twenty-four hours. From the south, snow geese arrived in hordes, their black-tipped wings flashing like leaves against a sky of washed cotton.

But soon, Wes began having problems. When he radioed his employer about lack of food, equipment, and various other matters, nothing was done. Soon, the pilot became so disgusted, he didn't respond to Wes' frequent calls.

On a flight in to pick up fish, Wes tried to quit, but the pilot reminded him there was airfare to repay, and for that, he needed to catch fish. The next time in, the pilot found the camp abandoned. A note explained Wes had rafted across the narrow stretch of brackish water to the mainland. He intended to hike the fifty miles to Prudhoe Bay.

Since his fishing operation was an experiment, the pilot just struck camp, little more than a Sears and Roebuck tent, a cook stove, and a sleeping bag. And two nets.

The pilot was angry because Wes had taken with him a pack frame, several articles of clothing, and even a pair of excellent boots belonging to the pilot's son. This made Wes a thief, and the pilot didn't care if Wes made it to Prudhoe Bay or not. Ultimately, no one went looking for Wes since only the pilot knew he was missing.

Wes' parents reported him missing on the second day of September. By then, the Arctic coast was getting true nights, and low temperatures went down to eighteen degrees. Wes had told his parents that in the Arctic, mail was irregular, and staying out of contact was part of the lifestyle. To complain about it, well, only a city person would do so, not someone used to Arctic living.

By the time the pilot was contacted by the authorities over fifty days had passed since Wes had rafted off the islet. Most of us speculated that he didn't survive the raft trip across the quarter mile stretch of water to the mainland.

Within a week, a trooper on a special flight to collect the body of a murder victim in Barrow diverted to the Colville River to have a look. That night, there had been a dusting of snow, and the temperature had dropped to eight degrees.

Wes evidently never made it to Prudhoe Bay, or anywhere else. He joined those who had gone north for discovery and never returned.

The Second Chamber

The trawler set anchor a mile from the beach at midnight. Massive combers raised and lowered it as they glided towards their inevitable collision with the shore. The boat's mast swayed first port, then starboard.

The anchorage was little more than a cove tucked perilously into the south side of the island. It offered poor shelter. From the dimly lighted interior of the bridge the captain watched. He drank coffee, checking first one radar then the other. Occasionally, he lifted binoculars and scrutinized the beach. Even through the dark, he knew that only a lunatic would attempt to land a small boat in surf that high.

If it was like that by morning, they would have to wait.

Δ

Corwin came out onto the deck and strained to see beyond the deck lights into the dark. Save for the imposing luminescence of breakers, he saw nothing. Because of the boat's generator, he could not hear the driving roar of the surf.

In the brilliant deck lights, sea birds bobbed about the boat, maneuvering with an occasional paddle of their webbed feet. They looked sleepy and annoyed at the constant need for effort. Corwin supposed that Robert would have known what sort they were.

He tucked his hands into his coat and faced seaward; the onshore wind quickly chilled. Corwin could go to the bridge, but in the voyage north from Seattle he'd tired of the crew. Their talk didn't interest him.

On the rare occasions that they did discuss Robert, it was in barely concealed negatives that certainly would have been stronger if Corwin wasn't paying money each day to charter their boat. It reminded Corwin of his grandfather's expression, 'rice Christian.' The old man would settle back from his gardening and smile, explaining, "Yes, give anyone enough rice, and they'll pray at your altar. Rice stops. Praying stops."

If Corwin's money suddenly ran out, which it would not, the crew would gladly set him ashore alongside what everyone most certainly assumed were the bones of his son.

Δ

They had a late dinner. The crewman tried small talk, but as always Corwin remained silent. Early in the voyage his routine had become established: After meals he did exercises on the stern, then he would check with the captain on their progress before retiring to his stateroom.

The captain: arrogant bastard.

The engineer had complained to the captain, who remained silent on the subject of their patron. But now the crewman looked at Corwin over his coffee and persisted: "You must have reason to believe your son is alive, Professor. I mean, they declared him dead a year ago. Have you had a sign or something?"

He put ironic emphasis on the word *sign*. The captain shifted and looked nervously at the cook. Corwin pushed his plate away and declined a refill of his coffee by crisply cupping his hand over his cup.

"I've had no sign."

He then rose and returned to his stateroom; the door's brass latch emitted a soft click as it snapped shut behind him.

Δ

Corwin wedged himself between the small writing desk and his bunk. He was writing a paper on petroleum exploration by the light of the small lamp which the engineer had improvised over the desk. Yet his efforts bored him, and the crewman's insolence still stung. He put his pen down and watched it roll back and forth with the constant motion of the boat.

Constant motion.

He slid into his bunk. Corwin felt no need, desire, or reason to explain his venture. The romanticism of his deathbed promise to Jason's mother would remain private. All anyone, including relatives, needed to know was that he was going to Krilof Island to look for a dead man. His son.

Only Alice's brother, vigilant for reasons, had guessed. At the reception following the funeral, he had studied Corwin over the top of his wine glass.

"You're a man of science, Corwin. A geologist. A slave to facts. You wouldn't spend a dime foolishly. I suppose the only reason you're doing this is because you've promised Alice?"

Corwin abruptly swung his legs out of the bunk and placed them flat on the deck, bouncing his legs angrily. He'd never liked any of his in-laws, Alice's oldest brother least of all. Certainly least of all.

He stood, but an unusually large roller swung the boat even further to port, forcing him to brace himself, straight-arm style, against the bulkhead. Was the surf getting even rougher? Forming his hand into a fist, he thumped it softly against his leg.

In the morning, would he be able to get on with his hapless charade?

Δ

During the night the surf had subsided somewhat, and in the morning, after a meeting in the wheelhouse, the captain gave permission to land. As Corwin started below, he overheard the engineer mutter, "Well, I hope no one gets killed landing in this stuff. It isn't good. Everyone knows the crazy bastard is dead."

At breakfast Corwin could see the captain was not happy about his decision, and after getting a refill of his coffee, he observed, "Glass is falling. Satellite weather has a couple of hellacious northers heading this way. Major lows." Corwin made all the necessary associations within seconds: Storms meant higher winds and perilous surf; the boat would be forced from anchorage onto the open ocean. He allowed himself a rare second cup of coffee.

"I'll have to camp on the beach."

The captain sat silently. The engineer went below and when the crewman continued to sit, Corwin noticed the captain cast an impatient glance at him. He excused himself, to be soon joined by the cook who went aft to feed leftovers to the birds.

The captain stirred cream and sugar into his coffee and gestured topside towards the wheelhouse.

"Professor, what you're doing is damned dangerous. Damned dangerous. You're sixtyseven years old, no spring chicken."

"I appreciate your concern."

"It's damned dangerous, is all. We could be blown out of here for a week, ten days. A sixty-seven-year-old man slogging around in that weather. Then there's those goddamned wild-ass cattle."

"Sixty-five. And I have fine equipment. I'll land plenty of supplies. As a petroleum geologist, I've camped in all sorts of country most of my professional life, including a stint in the Aleutians after the war. Corwin nodded his head confidently. I'll be all right, Captain."

The captain stood and went to the steps that led to the wheelhouse. Lifting his gnarled hand to the rail, he looked back at Corwin.

"Then is then, and now is now. I'm worried about the now. I still don't like it, Professor. But I've said my piece. It's your nickel."

Δ

From the wheelhouse the rubber raft looked like a buoyant mat of reeds upon watery dunes. Behind it, the small outboard raised an almost indistinguishable blue froth. The day was gray and rainy, and an occasional squall swept across the cove as it drifted landward.

In the raft Corwin clung to a waterproof bag that held the radio and spare batteries. The cook, a stolid, cheerless man who talked only about retirement investments, looked fearfully at the surf. "Jesus, I don't know about this."

The crewman steered straight towards the beach; his usual self-assured smile steadily faded as they drew closer to the angry breakers.

The surf created a mist that hung above the coarse volcanic sands, shrouding the cove in a fog. Flocks of kittiwakes and gulls clamored just outside the line of white foam, folding their wings as they dived headlong, feeding frenetically on tiny fish. Corwin forced himself to look beyond this to weird palisades formed from columnar basalt, making the faces of the cliffs seem sculpted by a macabre, otherworld artist. From the tops of these, streams spilled, creating waterfalls that combined into a single cascade, tumbling several hundred feet onto the beach, their force throwing up earth and gravel. The waters formed rivulets that emptied into the surf.

Beyond these cliffs, mountains loomed: naked, irregular crags that looked to Corwin like toothed jawbones frozen forever in dark rock. The crewman looked up, then shook his head rapidly.

"This place gives me the goddamned creeps."

Yet Corwin experienced a strange sense of excitement stirred by the bizarre geological formations. The crewman held up a hand of caution, motioning towards the beach.

"OK. Get ready!"

He braced himself as they followed the swells into the shallows where the ponderous waves rapidly curled and burst into white, menacing breakers.

Corwin was impressed with the degree of skill the crewman demonstrated as they approached the surf. At the precise moment when continuing ahead would have broached them, he veered left and ducked behind a shallow reef that functioned like a breakwater. Timing the approach to take place between the waves, the crewman ran the rubber raft firmly upon the beach while Corwin and the cook jumped out and pulled it from reach of the breakers. Their feet spattered foamy blotches of white spume as they ran up the beach's slope.

Once they'd unloaded the equipment, the cook radioed the boat that they'd landed successfully. While he did this, the crewman offered cursory instructions to Corwin on how to use the hand-held radio. Just before relaunching the rubber raft, the crewman gestured towards the surf.

"If it gets any bigger, we wont be able to come in and pick you up. You'll have to camp. And watch the cattle. They're mean."

After he helped them launch, Corwin watched the rubber raft grow smaller until it was only intermittently in view as it was lifted up by the oncoming rollers. A mile beyond this, even the mast of the boat was barely visible. He remembered the captain's warning: "If any weather at all comes up, it'll blow us from this damned cove and out to sea. If that happens, well, you have a radio. Keep in contact. We'll pick you up when it settles down, Professor."

Corwin felt foolish for thrusting himself into such a vulnerable situation. After all, Alice passed away a month ago. For her, the issue of Jason was thankfully over. Corwin was the only one left now, and perhaps that was the final ironic twist to their family history.

Δ

He saw the first of the cattle after he followed a cleft in the bluff into a small valley. Near a small lake a herd of a dozen grazed on the chest-high growth of grasses now burgeoning in the long daylight of late spring. Their tails flopped about randomly, creating an odd pattern above the top of the grass. Corwin knew that the crewman's warning hadn't been idle. In Seattle, federal biologists had suggested a firearm. Though backpacking with a cumbersome weapon would remind him of the misery of Korea and the military, he took their advice.

Seeing the cattle, Corwin moved the rifle up somewhat on his shoulder, but the beasts continued feeding, ignoring him. They looked unlike beef cattle he'd seen before: They had very long hair, longer horns, and an exotic red and black coloration.

Corwin followed a cattle trail along the shoreline until he came to a stream that fed into the lake. There he put down his rifle, slung off his daypack, and took time to reflect after his sanity.

He had seen the case reports from three different agencies and they all concurred: Five winters ago, while crewing on a fishing trawler, Jason had gotten into a disagreement with the captain and, subsequent to that, the crew. He had gotten violent and had commandeered the launch, going ashore on this island, a small unpeopled blotch of land sixty-five miles from the closest landfall. When last seen, he had only a sleeping bag and rifle.

"He couldn't have been violent. Jason was never, never violent."

The image of Alice as she spoke once again in Jason's behalf was, even now, almost too real: She sat on the den floor, the official reports scattered about her. She wasn't then, and never had been, convinced about their veracity.

"But Alice, you once said Jason could never use drugs; then he was arrested. So, he did use drugs. Marijuana."

"That isn't really what I'd term a *drug*."

"The report said the disagreement was drug-related, and it wasn't marijuana, Alice."

And it became like all their discussions about Jason since their son's birth: A cold anger developed between mother and father. Their disagreements had been conducted without words, typical for them. He had slept in his office at the university for nearly a week.

Corwin opened his pack and took out a thermos of tea. He poured a cup and was about to take his first sip when he heard a loud, ragged snort. He froze in mid-sip: A line of cattle had come around the shore of the lake, and a stout bull studied Corwin with dumb, ambivalent eyes. His face and head were deeply gouged from many fights; one eye socket had been overgrown by scar tissue.

Corwin put his tea down carefully and picked up the rifle. Unlike Alice and Jason, who admired and romanticized animals, Corwin recognized them for what they were: stupid and consistently self-destructive. This creature was no exception. The bull snorted again and pawed the ground several times, tearing up moss and dirt. The spring air had a chill to it, and the vapor from the bull's breath spurted out in visible clouds. Corwin shook his head. He loaded a cartridge into the chamber and lifted the weapon to half ready. And he shouted: "Get out! Shoo! Go!"

The powerful creature just stood there, snorting, unmoved. And an odd quirk came to Corwin.

He shouted "Get out!" again, but this time in Homeric Greek. The bull's head immediately jerked upwards, as if an unseen rider had yanked back on its reins. Then, after yet a louder snort, it bolted upslope taking its half dozen followers with him.

Corwin moved the cartridge back to the magazine, and put the rifle down. He picked up his tea and resumed his reverie. Almost anyone would have been impressed with his composure and of course surprised at his action. Except Alice. In fact, she would have expected it.

He had met her in fourth year classics while at the university. During their first lunch together, Alice had trimly crunched up a bit of cellophane, stuffed it in a milk carton, and furrowed her brow.

"Why is it that a grad student in Geology is taking Homeric Greek?"

"My father was a minister. He taught me quite a bit of Homer and Hesiod before University." She smiled while shaking her head impatiently.

"That isn't an answer. What I mean is that you've almost got your Ph.D. It's strange a science type would be interested in Homer."

"Really, you think so? I don't."

And in their thirty-five years together, that was the last they talked about Corwin's unlikely zeal for the classics. When, after their marriage, her friends and family complained about Corwin's unbending, colorless personality, his endless love for data and facts, she allowed him the ironic privacy he enjoyed in practicing his strange hobby.

Since before their marriage, he especially enjoyed reading aloud translated passages of Homer to her, and later, Jason, though the boy soon became impatient with the practice. That had hurt Corwin.

"He doesn't disrespect you, Dear. He simply doesn't enjoy Homer. Certainly you realize that it is a peculiar taste."

Yet Corwin expected that a young boy should naturally take to stories of stirring struggles and battles, epics about the world's most renowned heroes. How could any intelligent youngster possibly be bored by Homer?

Had that been the beginning of the unpleasantness?

Corwin picked up the pack and rifle and continued around the shore of the lake. He hadn't gone a quarter mile when he saw a pair of swans fly low across the tundra, landing on the opposite shore. Across the span of water he heard low hissings and squeaks that he'd never associated with swans.

As he was about to head inland, a school of smolt scattered, creating dozens of ripples across the surface as they retreated to deeper water. Hitching up the rifle, Corwin scanned the slopes for grazing cattle. The highest of the mountain peaks reached into the overcast, parting schools of fat rain clouds that sailed inland with the steady onshore wind. The weather front was here.

Δ

"We're two hours from another anchorage."

Corwin had asked them to repeat the message twice before he could understand. Since the closest anchorage to this island was sixty-two miles away, Corwin felt a distinct pang of loneliness. It might be several days before they returned.

Below him in the lee of a rising slope, a column of cattle wound their way downhill. The beasts were several hundred feet below him and threaded their way through a mountainside of green grass that bounded about wildly in the rising wind, as if attempting to uproot itself and fly away. The animals huddled as they walked, keeping nose to tail.

The whole island was dominated by the wind, and its unheeded wildness impressed Corwin.

By late afternoon he was forced to huddle between two large out-croppings of rocks. The noise of the constant wind had attained a low, forbidding cadence. He remembered old stories about greenhorns driven mad by the wind. Like most such tales, they were quite likely untrue.

Huddling down, he opened a pack of trail mix and poured a cup of tea; when he burned his lip, he became proud of his thermos. It had been keeping tea good and hot for almost twenty-eight years and was his best companion in the field. Alice had always packed it carefully whenever he went afield.

In fact, she'd been cleaning the thermos when she'd told him about Jason's educational plans:

"Jason wants to attend an art institute in London. It's renowned for illustrators of natural history."

"There aren't a half dozen people who make a living drawing birds."

"He could stay with my brother in London. It wouldn't be that ex-pensive."

Corwin seethed inwardly when he imagined his son, just out of high school and impressionable, staying with Alice's younger brother, a self-centered libertine.

"But Alice, he couldn't earn a living."

"His talents are in illustrating birds."

Silence. Finally she dried the thermos, packed it, and, as it always seemed to Corwin, looked down at him, finally extending both arms around him, burying her face in his hair, moving her lips to one side and talking in his ear. At the age of forty-two, Alice was at the peak of her beauty: tall, auburn-haired, with gentle blue eyes that usually had their way.

"Corwin, why don't you let the boy do what he was born to do."

"I was born to read and enjoy Homer, but there's no money in it. There's money in finding oil, Alice, and in teaching other ambitious indi-viduals how to find oil."

In the end, Jason had gone to the institute and matters resolved them-selves in their usual way: Jason would have his way with his mother, and she would have her way on Corwin.

Corwin drank tea but put away the trail mix. He was suddenly not hungry.

The Second Chamber

By late evening Corwin made camp inland from the beach where he'd secured his supplies. Within the lee of the somber-faced palisades that faced the anchorage, he'd secured his dome tent with extra care, and by dark, the light nylon settled into nervous tremors with the williwaws that forced their ways over from windward. A great roar of breakers became the continuum behind the frenetic voices of the wind. At midnight, the wind blew harder than he ever remembered it, harder than it had along the Tierra Del Fuego or even during that terrible spring in the McDonald Islands, half a degree within Antarctica.

Those who were familiar with Corwin would not think he had a keen appreciation of irony, but he always did. Listening to the storm, he thought of a father dying on the same uninhabited island as his prodigal son had, a father steeped in common sense and logic, looking for a deceased son whose entire life was conducted on whim. The unknowing might romanticize Corwin, the loving parent searching for the son.

"You've never loved the boy. Never. Or you wouldn't believe this stupidity!"

Alice glared at Corwin when she'd first received the official summaries concerning Jason. She held the envelope tightly across a bosom already irrevocably altered by surgery. She'd confronted him in his office at the university, an unusual appearance for her. In all the years since the geology faculty had refused to endorse the antiwar petition, she'd never forgiven his colleagues. Though her voice was soft, and she kept glancing nervously over her shoulder out his open door, Corwin knew the discussion was escalating into a scene.

"Alice, this isn't the place."

And she'd swiveled, lashed a final parting look at him, and left. Later that night, the talk ended in disagreement and the inevitable coldness against which he was always so helpless.

By morning the most severe front had moved through, and winds were reasonable. He was actually comfortable outside his tent, and, over tea and biscuits, considered his plans for the second day. The next place to look was the island's only noteworthy point, where the focal point of the search for Jason had been. He calculated that Krilof Hot Spring lay six miles east of his camping site. In Seattle, he had consulted the Coast Guard officer who had conducted both searches for Jason:

"Not much of a hot spring as I recall. Small; water's bad; foul; stinks, as a matter of fact. Nothing there. Even the cattle avoid it. Put twenty men on it first time, thirty the second. Had 'em looking under rocks. Nothing. Not even a footprint."

The officer leaned back in his chair and looked out at the Puget Sound, squinting to remember back over the three-year interval since the two searches for Jason. After only fifteen minutes, the officer had confirmed Corwin's thoughts about both searches: They had been methodical and thorough.

"After all," the man had reminded him, "the whole damned island is only fifty-two square miles. Right out in the middle of nowhere. There were 4,300 man-hours and 475 fixed-wing and rotorcraft hours invested in the searches." The official pursed his lips while replacing the lid on a fishing reel he'd been repairing when Corwin called. "So I'll be blunt, Professor. Though I admire your dedication and love for your son, I feel you're wasting both time and money. Also, it's dangerous, even to a man of your background."

Corwin thanked the officer for his time and had taken coffee at a waterfront cafe. He mulled over the idea of putting Jason, himself, and *love* in the same sentence. No one even vaguely aware of his relationship with the fickle Jason would have done so. It had been years since Corwin honestly could say he loved the boy.

Corwin had left the cafe and caught a taxi to Fisherman's Terminal. On the way the driver had discussed baseball for several minutes before realizing his fare was interested in things beyond the confines of his vehicle. The information just gleaned from the Coast Guard was nothing new, and Corwin would continue with his original intentions and charter a boat north. The essence of his situation was unchanged.

Δ

On his approach to Krilof Hot Springs he emerged from the lee of the mountain, walking into the face of the wind. It pressed his rain gear flat against his chest and legs. The tall grass thrashed, flattening with the higher gusts. The rain that was blown almost sideways by the north wind was so cold that he almost expected it to become slush. Wet and exhausted, Corwin shrank into his rain gear. The pungent sulfur aroma and level terrain told him he was very close to Krilof Hot Springs.

He stopped to rest and have tea in the lee of an outcropping. Around him was smooth, bare igneous rock. Pouring the tea from his thermos, he cupped both hands around it, hunkered down behind the rock, and sipped by lowering his lips to the rim of the cup. Enjoying the old feeling of the tea's warmth spreading inside him, he stared into the rising vapors of the liquid and fell into a reverie recalling the morning he learned of Jason's disastrous marriage. Alice had reached him at his lab from her sister's home in Connecticut where she'd been visiting. Corwin had startled his two grad students by uncharacteristically exclaiming, "Burkina Faso!"

During a tour in the Peace Corps, Jason had married a native woman, choosing to surprise Alice with his new bride at Kennedy Airport. Alice was excited over events and considered it cute that Jason's bride thought the toilet in her sister's house was a well. Corwin saw nothing good resulting from transplanting the poor woman to North America. He'd sulked into his office, lamenting how Jason, and oftentimes even Alice, seemed to think that *willing* something to be was sufficient to guarantee success.

Corwin's reverie was broken when he noticed that the ground was warm beneath him. Standing, he concluded that subsurface geothermal activity was somewhat more extensive than he'd judged from the maps. His interest rose. He picked up and continued on, glad to have his thoughts drawn away from the almost comical plight of Jason's marriage.

The wind began a strange dancing motion, moving to the southwest, then easterly. Which way would it settle on? Corwin was just walking into the hot springs proper when the wind switched another forty-five degrees and steadied from the southwest. This sudden activity, Corwin knew, indicated the advent of another weather front: raw, angry, recently birthed on the open ocean.

Corwin understood the officer's views about the hot springs. They were small and typical of their kind. A half dozen mineralized outcroppings were the core of the springs: hot water seeped from viscous mineral deposits forming small hot-water streams. The beds of these were slick with various drab yellow fungi. High concentrations of sulfur had killed most of the vegetation in the area of the outcroppings. Corwin admitted that to a layman, the hot springs would be less than impressive.

Occasional snippets of steam rose from each outcropping along with surface water. Corwin ran across several dozen rusted tins of military rations left behind by the search parties. Disturbed by such irresponsible behavior, he was about to bury them when a slight tremor caused him to stiffen.

An explosion several hundred yards behind him sent Corwin stumbling backwards. He looked on as steam erupted in a giant plume-shaped cloud, then expanded until it cloaked the entire area in steam and he could see no farther than a half dozen feet. An angry yet dying hiss marked the end of the eruption. Within minutes, the wind cleared away the rank sulfur-infused steam.

A geyser!

This discovery excited Corwin. Naturally, he'd read the available geological information, but there had been no mention of any geysers. Since they formed spontaneously and could erupt at long and irregular intervals, he wasn't surprised at this omission. He approached a small fissure from where the geyser emanated. Corwin could tell from recently displaced vegetation that this geyser either was new or erupted rarely. Immediately several invitations from journal editors for submissions came to mind, and this geyser would at least make a decent note. Returning to his pack, he retrieved a hundred-meter tape, a compass, several tools and a notebook. Wherever he went, he was never without them. After quickly burying the old tins of military rations, he began work investigating the geyser.

Corwin was not aware of time passing until he heard the first deep, unearthly moan. It could have been the sound of an animal in torment or perhaps the foulest of demons waking from slumber. He dropped his pickax and stood. Each hair on the nape of his neck vibrated.

He resisted the urge to run, but instead he looked in the direction it seemed to come from. What in hell could cause such a sound? He walked to his pack and picked up his rifle, loading a round into the chamber. Standing there with the weapon at ready, he immediately felt foolish. How often had he showed open contempt for jumpy field assistants? He ran his hand across his mouth, thinking of rational explanations.

Could it be a huge bull, perhaps wounded in a fight?

Corwin moved in the direction of the sound. When he heard the moan again, it was different. This time it seemed less ominous, not eerie but mournful, nearly a lament.

When the explanation suddenly came to him, even Corwin wasn't able to resist an ironic smile. Lowering the rifle, he walked on and within minutes located the source of the mystery: A small opening in the earth betrayed both the entrance to a cave and the explanation for the moans. Often, caves in areas of geothermal activity moaned, the deep sound actually caused by the expansion of cold air entering them. He remembered an entire system of such caves in Northern Japan predictably worshipped by local villagers.

Lowering to one knee, he saw that this entrance was large enough to admit a small man. Since no caves had ever been described here, Corwin knew his find at the hot springs could yield more than a mere note. Quickly he returned to his pack and fetched his flashlight, some spare batteries, and a half dozen candles. Lowering himself back down, he held the flashlight, looking downward. It might be nothing but a small mineralized cul-de-sac; it might be more. His hopes rose.

He eased into the entrance on his back, carefully taking handholds before twisting about, then taking out his flashlight and switching it on.

The Second Chamber

Wiping dirt from his eyes, he didn't like what he saw. Geothermal fluting had created a steep, narrow passage downward. The light illuminated the pinks and reds of oxides and minerals. At best, the passage was a tight squeeze. His body nearly took the entirety of the entrance, and cold air forced its way past, chilling him.

Corwin backed out cautiously. In the light, he leaned against a rock and reminded himself that skinnying down such a passage was dangerous work and he was alone. Yet he couldn't allow this discovery to go uninvestigated, and at least he could try and make a preliminary survey. Resolving that he would use every degree of experience and caution, Corwin turned and began his descent.

In places, it was all he could do to force his shoulders through, but soon the passage down began not only to widen but to level out. Corwin scraped his elbows on the rough mineralized walls when he twisted around to aim the light straight ahead. His uneasiness gave way to excitement when he saw a large chamber. At the same time, the acrid mineralized smell, dominated by sulfur like everything else at the hot springs, began to give way to another. Resting while looking ahead at the chamber, Corwin decided the smell was of organic origin.

"Fetid."

Corwin's voice died away in the passage. His breath erupted in short bursts as he inched forward. Since he emerged head first into the chamber he was forced to shut off the light, secure it in his pocket and ease down onto the floor. His feet splashed water, creating a strange echo. He was tense, and he struggled quickly to remove the light, turn it on, and play it up and down.

As he surveyed the chamber, Corwin realized that despite a great sense of anticipation, he was exhausted. The chamber was smaller than he'd hoped: Perhaps a little over six feet high, it extended for about a dozen feet, then narrowed down again into another tunnel as if the chamber were a brief enlargement in a subterranean intestine.

Water dripped from the ceiling, but there were no mineralized growths above or below. His stomach knotted, the organic smell even stronger in the chamber. The sweat on his back chilled with the cold draft coming down from the surface. He involuntarily went rigid when another moan, deep and ominous, sounded far below. This time, Corwin shook his head and after lighting a candle and placing it in the lee of a rock, continued into the next passage.

This one was almost level, and he was able to move along quickly in a three-quarters crouch. Within twenty feet he entered a second chamber, and turning the light to the right, he could see bright, iridescent mineralized growths oozing from fissures in the walls. This chamber was at least twelve feet high, and Corwin admired the brilliant colors before moving the light to the left. There, the chamber's ceiling sloped down to a shelf, itself a gleaming, mineralized red that sparkled with bursts of purples and blues. Just above it, as if sitting to await Corwin's arrival, legs and arms crossed patiently, a gallery of skeletons, with tatters of skin and hair still attached, the skulls gazed at Corwin from out of the glare of his light. Minerals had percolated into the sutures of the craniums, causing each junction to reflect light as if every skull were divided into continents and countries bounded by iridescent frontiers.

Corwin cried out and bolted.

He banged his head several times fleeing back to the first chamber. He wasn't able to stop himself until he'd squirmed nearly all the way up the narrow passage to the surface. Out of breath, his heart vibrated rather than beat. Blood ran down his forehead into his eyes.

His hand hurt. When he glanced down, he saw that he'd gripped the flashlight so tightly, the rubberized body had bent slightly. The lens and bulb were smashed.

Corwin rolled over and looked backwards. He swept away an accumulation of blood with the back of his hand and felt ashamed. In forty-four years of field work, including fifteen months in the thick of the Korean War, he'd never panicked. Never. Despite weather, despite group chaos, despite even impending death, Corwin had never panicked. Perhaps because of the blow on the head, he became dizzy, and he pressed both palms against the walls of the cave. For a moment, Corwin's sense of time and place became confused.

"Sometimes, if I didn't know you better, I'd think you hadn't a feeling in your soul. Damnit man, that's your son!"

After weeks of chemotherapy, Alice's voice was almost a whisper. She sat before the fireplace looking sadly at Corwin. It had been several days after Jason's disastrous annulment proceedings. To Corwin's horror, Jason lay his head down and began weeping in a courtroom packed with lawyers, parties to other domestic cases, and, Corwin supposed, curiosity seekers.

"Alice, what did you want me to do?"

"Show compassion. He loved the girl; she was his wife."

"For God's sakes, *love?!* She spoke no Western language, and she cooked a chicken in our fireplace!"

What would Alice have thought to see her husband crying out and fleeing like a beast? Corwin rolled over sufficiently to take out a handkerchief; he raised it and dabbed at the cut on his forehead.

Knowing he would need the other flashlight to explore further, Corwin began to inch his way up the passage towards the surface. Remembering the burning candle, he turned back, picked it up, and climbed upwards.

At the surface, daylight was nearly gone. He tried to console himself by remembering that he certainly wasn't the first person who'd bolted when they'd discovered an aboriginal burial chamber. Oddly, he'd just read about one in a journal. It had been discovered on an island not much more than a hundred miles from Krilof. Yet this coincidence added even further weight to the foolishness of his panic. He had no excuse, and he was glad he was alone.

Δ

Corwin was exhausted. By lantern light he applied a bandage to the cut on his head and boiled water for oatmeal and tea. It was a strangely clear and calm night, unusual for the Aleutians, an area that saw fewer than thirty clear days a year. Above, the heavens glowed, an infinite mural of stars. Though the quietness and clarity of the heavens might have held his interest at another time, it didn't now. Corwin left his half-eaten meal to congeal in the dish, and he crawled into a sleeping bag pre-warmed by the hot springs beneath.

Distracted by a headache and events of the day, he couldn't sleep. Though the significance of his discovery should have yielded a sense of anticipation, Corwin instead felt sullen and actually resented the additional documentation he must now do. He wanted nothing more than his home, his books, his study, and to be rid of this sad, lonely search. When its purpose came to him, Corwin became angry.

Jason. How tragic that the boy had brought troubles between him and Alice, even after her death.

At her funeral, a troubling affair, Corwin had braved it through various program offerings of string quartets and—worse—poetry readings by Alice's sister. Several weeks before, Alice had tried to convince him of the appropriateness of planning her own funeral, and of its tone:

"You know, it'll really be a time to celebrate passing. All this," she looked around the hospital room, "the tubes, bottles, monitors...will be over for me."

"Celebrate? The ancients befouled themselves with soil and tore their hair. And you expect me to listen to poetry and music?"

And he lowered his head to the edge of her bed and wept. She held his head, the thin, weak fingers worked their gentle way up and down his neck.

"Husband, Husband: Who will you talk to when I'm gone? Who will love you? It so troubles me. Will you live the life of a maroon?"

Corwin kicked his way out of his sleeping bag and crawled out into the open air. He was almost in a rage at having Jason for a son. Every day between him and Alice could have been peaceful and loving if it hadn't been for Jason's capriciousness.

Jason here; Jason there. Jason everywhere. Jason was the sole cause for every unpleasant minute between him and Alice.

His temper ebbed as it had flared, replaced immediately by a fatigue so profound that Corwin felt twenty years older. It was all he could do to creep back into the tent. The warmth of the sleeping bag felt like a benevolent hand closing around him.

Δ

In the morning, after checking in by radio with the boat, he gathered the necessary material together, loaded his camera, and descended through the narrow entrance without thought. Corwin resolved to complete a very basic preliminary survey and have done with the cave.

As he passed through the first chamber and set up a candle, it occurred to him he hadn't even noted what the weather was like outside. When an eerie moan sounded, Corwin didn't hesitate. *Let the damned thing moan,* he thought as he lowered himself into the second chamber.

After setting up candles in the second chamber, he paused to study the burial site. The bodies were partially mummified; some skin and hair still remained on a few of the skulls, and when his eyes adjusted Corwin saw a wealth of artifacts: large elaborate oil lanterns; several dozen jars, large and small; and baskets, mostly rotted. Next to each body on the ledge were spear and arrow points as well as various devices Corwin didn't recognize.

A specialist, he knew, would revel in this find. Clearly, Corwin thought, the site was at least five hundred years old, if not more. No matter, it would all have to be photographed. Unfolding his meter stick, and bracing himself against the pervasive stink he began to take photos.

He worked steadily for an hour before putting the camera and meter stick aside. He stretched a kink out of his back, then took the thermos and poured tea. Picking up the flashlight, he sipped and took several steps towards the end of the chamber. Within a dozen feet there were two passages continuing downwards, both narrower than anything he'd want to explore.

Leave these for braver fellows.

Turning, he noticed an alcove that worked its way under the shelf. Stooping to a half crouch, he was about to enter when the light fell across a pair of boots. *His* boots. Corwin recognized them at once.

He stood. Corwin had them custom made by an expert bootmaker in Chile, and he'd worn the boots through a half dozen field seasons. He had relinquished them only after Alice pestered him about Jason having proper foot gear for his adventure north.

"Alice, they're made of pigskin, and they'll never wear out. I'll have them until I retire. I'd almost prefer giving him my thermos."

But, in the end, he'd yielded. Now here they were.

Corwin took a grip on himself, and, lowering himself to a full crouch, shined the light directly into the alcove.

Jason had surely died several years ago. He had made a rudimentary bed, probably out of scavenged canvas; only his skull and boots protruded. To one side was the remains of his pack, the same one he'd traversed Africa with. Corwin stiffened when he saw both of Jason's portable easels and three leather portfolios; two of these had peeled apart because of mildew and moisture. A sheaf of paper had turned to a wad of pulp. Corwin moved towards the third portfolio, and inside several bird drawings were surprisingly discernible. *Probably of charcoal or pencil,* he thought.

There was no rifle.

He withdrew from the alcove and sat, drawing his legs up to his chest and wrapping his arms around his knees. He turned the flashlight off and studied the opposite wall, its reds and purples gently illuminated in candlelight, always Corwin's favorite method of lighting.

It occurred to him that candles were one of his few areas of agreement with Jason. The boy was perhaps nine or ten when Corwin found him reading a comic book by candlelight. He'd looked up at his father, braced for a long and complicated lecture.

"Jason, if your mother saw you with a candle, she'd become very angry."

"Will you tell her, Father?"

Corwin studied the candle, then, sitting on the edge of the bed, quickly and skillfully constructed a shadow from both his hands.

"There. That's a rhino. Candles are good for shadow shows. In fact, for lots of things. Better than other lights."

And he'd taught the boy several different sorts of projections before Jason had fallen asleep. Several nights later the inevitable happened: Alice discovered the candles.

She entered his study quietly, barely managing to maintain a serious tone.

"He said you two were in cahoots."

Corwin rocked back and forth on the floor of the chamber and once again marveled at Alice's instinct: How had she known the official reports were wrong? He lay his head upon his knees and nodded silently, for they were indeed wrong. Jason, typically impractical, had packed his entire storehouse of art supplies from the cove to the hot springs. It must have made a comical sight, thought Corwin, like a medieval peddler descending onto an ancient holy place.

What had happened those five winters ago? Had the captain of his trawler become impatient with Jason's usual tardiness and procrastination and left him? Corwin vowed to photograph everything and force the authorities to get at the truth, but his resolve faded away when he realized the futility of it; he straightened and fell back against the wall. Whatever the reason, Jason was just as dead.

Above him, he could feel the disturbing presence of the numerous Aleut mummies staring out blankly at the candlelit chamber. And also Jason's.

Corwin continued to sway back and forth and his mind went vacant; he could think of no plan of action but to continue his rocking motion. In fact, his mind became confused when he reflected that his son lay dead here, and his wife lay dead three thousand miles distant. And he was now alone.

Corwin began a dull humming. He would refuse to think about how Jason and he were never as father and son should be; and though Alice and Jason had died miles apart, how she had remained faithful to their son's memory and spirit. He would refuse to remember the evening Alice told him she was pregnant, and he'd astonished her by saying, "I want it to be a daughter. I've been in war. In Korea. I don't want to have a son just to see him die."

Alice, uncharacteristically surprised, stammered, "But you're always so silent about Korea."

Corwin would refuse to remember this and all the other nights when they had been a family until so many stupid, annoying issues had crept between them. Corwin would refuse to remember any and all of this, and resolved to sway to and fro in this cave until some truth came to him explaining how he and Jason would someday become father and son forever.

It was Corwin's right to refuse to do anything else but to know fully that at this moment his son Jason lay dead next to him.

Δ

Eighteen hours from Krilof Island Corwin woke, left his stateroom, and walked to the stern of the trawler. His body ached from digging and carrying rocks and soil to conceal the entrance to the cave. He'd taken a day to complete this, making the trawler wait for him at the cove.

"There's another norther coming, Professor," the captain had urged over the radio.

But he hadn't returned to the cove until the job was done. They were being paid to wait. After examining the entrance from every angle, then burning the film and his notes, he hiked back quickly without a rest.

Corwin told them about the geyser, for that explained his delay. But nothing else. Now, looking down at the prop wash of the trawler, Corwin knew his decision to let Jason share eternity with the Aleut dead was right. Corwin embarrassed himself by thinking that perhaps, in back of it all, Alice had this resolution in mind when she'd exacted the promise from him. But this notion was just foolishness.

It was now past midnight. The trawler ran without deck lights; only the port, starboard, and mast lights were on. Corwin enjoyed being entirely cloaked in darkness, enjoyed the privacy it offered. He put his hands on the rail and leaned over. The water, frothed into an iridescent white by the prop, soon lost this glow and slipped away in a wake that was inky and inviting to him.

All he had to do was step over the rail and let go.

Corwin wrapped his coat around himself and knew that if he hadn't committed suicide at the cave, he wouldn't here. However Corwin might eventually die, he knew it would be consistent with the way he lived. His immediate plans were far less romantic.

What he wanted to do was to weep for Jason, something he had never done. Perhaps when he visited Alice's grave that might happen; maybe even sooner. For Corwin this was a simple, unambiguous desire yet the oldest and most tragically fitting song in the litany of all humanity, one sung thousands of years before Homer. It was, he felt sure, the most sacred of homages a parent could offer a lost son or daughter: To stand at the edge of the sea or a lake or a simple field and to sing the dirge for children lost to unseeing strokes by whatever gods or god controlled this fragile planet.

Bingo

*T*hey wouldn't have found Bingo for weeks unless they'd become desperate for an extra hand that morning. Harold and his three men found him dead of a bullet wound to the head, lying naked, half in, half out of his cabin, with a condom still on his shriveled member.

It was Sunday, and the sole trooper on duty was at the other end of the highway system at the scene of an accident.

It didn't seem right to Harold to leave Bingo lying there on the threshold; they should move him either in or out of the cabin. But after discussion, they compromised and covered the body with a sheet of plastic.

Bingo knocked around the docks for twenty-five years, and there wasn't a boat he hadn't crewed on. He liked to party and could do a prodigious amount of blow and weed. And of course, liquor. He'd worked deck during the big Bering Sea crab years when crew shares went around $30-$50 thousand a trip. That's when I first met him, when he was working in the Bering Sea.

And there was Bingo's success with women. He was casual and stupid, and women married or living with fishermen especially favored him when frustrated at their husband's or live-in's long absences. He liked to boogie down at the bars, head out the road to his cabin, then screw himself and his partner silly. Next day, he would have little memory of the previous evening.

So probably this had a part in Bingo's death.

But in the last five years, he did more drinking and partying than working, and he had trouble holding a job on a boat. That alone would have killed Bingo if a bullet hadn't.

The unique fact about Bingo was that he emerged as the only survivor of the 1982 *Miss Marmaduke* disaster off Amlia Island. There were eight crew members lost including a federal fishery observer.

The deceased were young, had families, had graduate degrees, had ambi-

50

tions; one was writing a book. The captain/owner of the Miss Marmaduke *was a strapping fellow who had played pro ball for a San Francisco Forty-Niners' farm team, had a degree in accounting, and owned eight laundromats in Seattle.*

Even then, Bingo had been pretty dissipate, and not one of us missed the irony of all those men buying the farm while someone like Bingo survived.

There is no explanation sometimes, the way the sea claims people. None at all.

Fever

Brad lay on his back in the snow watching the large flakes fall downward into his face. He noticed how the flakes spun like tiny wheels just before they'd strike. The heaviness of the wet snow muffled the sounds around him, and the snowmobile that sputtered ten feet from him sounded like it was a half mile away. He wished it were.

It was the second time today he'd been thrown from it. He sat up on the snow and looked dejectedly at the machine. It sat on the riverbed fouling the surrounding willow thickets with its black oil exhaust. It was a yellow, chunky machine, heavy and powerful; on the back of it was a box where Brad carried his specimens and equipment. He got back to his feet and walked over to the machine and studied it. He had been a field biologist for a dozen years, but of all the various sorts of equipment he'd worked with he hated snowmobiles the most.

He remounted it and accelerated until he was cruising slowly; the machine crawled along with difficulty in the wet snow and Brad had to wipe the slush away from his goggles repeatedly. Finally, approaching a red flag that thrust upwards from the thick river ice, he shut the machine off and went to work at the hole. Slowly he dragged a net out. He carefully attached a marker onto each living fish and dropped the dead ones in a sack. Looking up at the cloudy sky he thought how ironic this land was: Yesterday it had been minus thirty-eight, now it was almost twenty above. As undependable as his snowmobile.

Occasionally as he worked he stuffed his hands inside woolen mittens that had become fouled with fish slime weeks before. The sharp pain in his palms from handling the net forced him to tuck each mittened hand under the opposite arm. He jumped up and down to warm his feet since his snowmobile boots had become soaked with sweat and had lost their insulative value. He wondered what an onlooker would think to see him, hands under arms, jumping up and down on a frozen river. But he didn't have to worry about that: He was sixty-eight miles from the nearest village and seventy-five miles south of the Arctic Circle. At least he had privacy.

It was nearly dark as he drove the machine out of the riverbed onto the main trail and headed for his cabin. He had covered his entire study circuit of fifty miles today and was dead tired, but before going to sleep he had to measure and preserve over seventy-five fish he carried with him. Also he had to treat his dog's sores, a result of a fight with a porcupine. The dog never seemed to learn about those critters, and he hated to be left behind in the mornings. As Brad approached the cabin he stopped the machine several hundreds yards distant. The cabin, covered with a foot of fresh fallen snow, looked an archetypal wilderness sight. Yet Brad had the sensation that something was wrong. He turned the machine off and listened. As the roaring of the engine died away, he could hear the flakes pattering to earth around him; removing his goggles, he listened carefully. The dog wasn't around. At first he thought it might have found another porcupine and was hiding under the cabin with a nose full of quills. Yet that wasn't right, for even Brad's dog allowed himself several weeks of porcupine aversion before forgetting and tackling another one. Starting the motor, Brad drove to the cabin, stopped, removed the fish from the machine, and entered the cabin. He put the fish on the sink but didn't remove his mittens or parka; standing still he looked around. Through the open door of the cabin he could hear the snowmobile's engine crackling away as it cooled. He could hear nothing else.

He left the cabin and closed the door behind him. Behind the cabin he looked in the doghouse. It was empty. Taking his flashlight out, he looked under the cabin, playing the beam from one foundation piling to the other. No dog.

As he backed out of the small entrance, Brad felt his back ache; a day of net pulling hadn't prepared him very well for looking for a dog who was so damned stupid it had never learned to avoid porcupines. To hell with the dog. He pocketed the flashlight and was about to enter the cabin when he remembered he needed wood. He walked back to the woodpile under the eaves and, as he returned with an armload, he looked up to his left. On the roof eight feet above the ground the dog lay frozen with a broken neck.

Δ

He dropped the wood immediately and walked inside. He didn't need to look twice: The sudden painful death was frozen across the dog's features. Brad sat close to the wood stove and poured himself a whisky. What in hell could have happened? He stopped and thought, yet he didn't think. Putting the glass down he realized he was sitting in a dark cabin beside a cold stove, fully clothed, but he remained seated. What in hell could have happened?

A bear?

Yet it was December, and bears were in dens; occasionally a stray would come out during warm spells, but he'd seen the work of marauding bears, and they didn't place dogs they had killed carefully on roof tops with broken necks. Also, a bear would have finished the job by getting into the cabin, or at least by trying to get into the cabin. No. Not bears.

He ran all the other resident mammals through his mind and came up zero: Not wolverines, not wolves; moose was ridiculous; marten were too small. Also, the dog couldn't have jumped to the top of the roof. Eighty-pound mutts made poor second-story artists. He sipped the whisky.

He didn't like what was left, not at all. He stood and lighted two gas lanterns then looked carefully around the cabin. His footprints were all there were on the floor. Everything appeared untouched. And he had heard no planes that day. He had heard nothing. Brad turned to walk back outside but stopped just short of the door; he felt vulnerable walking outdoors now, but knowing that was absurd he swung the door open and walked out. Without looking at the dog, he brought in a dozen loads of wood. Then he unloaded the snowmobile, bringing his cross-country skis into the cabin last, and shoved the door bolt home solidly. Using a bit of diesel fuel as starter, he had the stove going immediately. As the dry spruce crackled, he adjusted the damper and sat down. Slowly he removed his boots and started coffee water. The whisky made him feel more optimistic. Maybe the damned fool dog had managed to get up there somehow.

He made himself two large sandwiches and noted that the fire hadn't been out too long as the bread was still soft. With a hot cup of coffee in front of him and one sandwich already eaten, he re-created the dog's ascent to the roof: Somehow overcoming the soreness from his quill wounds, the crazy mutt had managed to leap to the top of the sauna and to sail across the seven-foot gap to the cabin. Possibly the dog had seen a red squirrel robbing insulation from the cabin. The dog hated squirrels. Squinting into the gas light, Brad tried to remember if he had ever seen the dog jump seven feet. While eating the last bit of sandwich he decided that's what happened: The dog had broken his neck jumping to the roof of the cabin.

Feeling warm from the food and drink, he shook his head sadly. He'd grown very fond of the dog in the four years he'd had him, yet it had never been too bright a dog. He went to the corner of the cabin and hooked up the batteries in preparation for his afternoon call. As he waited for the room to warm before switching on the transceiver, he looked around at the inside of the cabin again, this time proudly. It was the most fully equipped winter cabin he'd ever lived in; it had cost the taxpayers twelve thousand dollars to supply and another eight thousand to fly everything in and construct. Still, these studies would set the project ahead five years. Professional researchers preferred the comfort of the office during the winter; hence, a study like this had never been done.

He turned on the transceiver. Adjusting it, he expected the crackle of static but it was silent. He double-checked everything, yet the set remained quiet. He knew nothing of transceivers. It seemed odd it would pick this time to go haywire. More than any other afternoon, he had wanted to talk to someone. He turned the set around and looked at it helplessly; it appeared normal and intact. His mind returned to the dog. He pulled on a pair of boots and went back to the sauna.

After pacing it off he estimated the distance between the sauna and cabin to be about fourteen feet. It would have been impossible for the dog to reach the roof on its own power. Walking back to the door he hesitated before entering; turning, he reached into the box of the snowmobile and removed a worn, rusty shotgun. He bolted the door behind him, cracked the shotgun open, put a shell in, then propped it up in the corner near the sink.

He sat at the table and measured the fish. He took special care with each specimen for in doing so he could forget that someone or something had killed his dog. Usually he found the tedious job of working specimens the worst aspect of his work, but not tonight. Behind him his short-wave portable radio boomed out Beethoven, courtesy of Voice of America. As he finished the last fish, he put them in a plastic sack, then stored them in back of the snowmobile. He sat back at the table; there was nothing to do now, and he didn't think he could sleep.

He went to the calendar and calculated that he'd gone five and a half weeks without a supply plane, and he especially looked forward to its arrival this coming Saturday. He would fly into town, wrap up a couple of days of laboratory and office work, then head south on the direct flight to New York for a science symposium. Ten days in New York. He let go of the calendar and rubbed his hands together. He had been out here since October, and frankly he was tired of fishing, being cold, and driving the snowmobile. Saturday couldn't come too soon for him.

He allowed his mind to think about the dog again, yet still he couldn't comprehend how it could have come to be on the roof. Catching himself bogging down in the subject, he threw open the stove and stuffed another piece of wood in. He thought of what he'd do in New York.

As usual half of his time would be taken with answering questions about living and working in the far north: Jesus, it must be godawful cold in the Arctic. You mean you actually work outside during the winter? Do they still live in igloos? I hear you can make two thousand bucks a week up there, but a hamburger cost twenty bucks. Brad laughed, for they knew about as much about where he lived as he did of New York. In any case, he'd enjoy himself: concerts, theater, and he hoped very few stuffy seminars. All at government expense. Outside he heard a thud.

He was at the door with the shotgun before his mind informed him of what it was. He threw open the door and forty feet away stood a cow moose and her calf. Seeing Brad in the doorway, they bolted, parting the willows in the thickets with a concert of splintering and crashing. He closed the door, bolted it, and put the gun aside. He was jumpy, there was no doubt about that. Jumpy. Those moose had been in the vicinity for two weeks.

He unsealed a bottle of eight-year-old whisky and poured a hefty half-glass full. Rummaging around in the kitchen drawer, he then removed a cigar. He pulled up a chair at the table and turned the portable radio from station to station and band to band; finally he settled on revolutionary march music from Radio Peking. He listened, sipping the liquor and puffing at the cigar. His gaze took in the transceiver: It was damned queer it chose this day not to work. It was a three-month old set and he had read in three trade journals this was the best brand available; it seemed unlikely it would just go out by itself, a brand new set. He went over to it, removed the rear plate with a screwdriver and peered inside. A wonderland of printed circuits coiled around like silver and gold worms. Nothing seemed missing or broken. He read the notice on the rear plate: "Do Not Remove."

Δ

He awoke the next morning shivering. The fire had died down to almost nothing. Looking at his wristwatch he saw that he'd slept almost eight hours. His head ached from too much whisky. On the table sat the almost empty bottle. He closed his eyes in regret when he noticed the gas lights were still on. Although it was still dark, and would be until almost eleven, he turned one of the lights off and sat down at the table. He thought about a dream he'd had in the night, and this was strange as he usually didn't remember dreams.

Yet this dream seemed unusually powerful.

In it he had been driving the snowmobile much too fast toward the cabin. Coming out from behind the cabin was the dog, bounding along and howling its usual chaotic greeting. Brad hadn't slowed the machine down, but blinked the light on and off at the dog, then stood up on the running boards and yelled, "Get out of the goddamn way, out of the way," at the dog. It bounded heedlessly at the speeding snowmobile. When Brad clamped the brake handle shut, the machine didn't slow at all; rather it sped directly at the dog. In the dream it knocked the dog thirty feet snapping its neck and killing it instantly. In the dream he had tumbled over himself getting to the dog while screaming over and over, "Goddamn it! Why didn't you get out of the way! Why didn't you get out of the damned way!"

He opened the pantry and removed a dozen eggs.

Brad had eaten sandwiches for three days in a row and decided to have something cooked for a change. Going outside he opened the meat box and was removing the bacon when he saw the fish in the rear of the snowmobile. Cutting four thick slices of bacon and throwing them frozen into the skillet, he cursed himself for not doing the fish the night before. Perhaps the sight of the dog on the roof had shaken him more than he thought. Now he would have to do them after breakfast. He brought the fish in to let them thaw, and while eating he listened to the news.

Afterwards he set up the scale and equipment. He sat at the table and measured the fish. He took special care with each specimen, and that helped him forget that someone or something had killed his dog. Usually he found the tedious job of working specimens the worst aspect of his work. It was fortunate that a weasel or marten hadn't pulled them from the machine during the night and scattered them all over. The partially frozen fish chilled his fingers, and he warmed them by holding his hands over the stove. Finishing the last one he took them outside and tossed the sack up on the roof. Up there it would freeze solid and be safe from roaming animals. It was only then that he heard the ravens.

Two hawk-sized birds squatted beside the dog's carcass pecking away frozen chunks of it. Startled, they flew away. Repulsed by the ravens feeding on the dog, Brad walked in and got the shotgun. He put a half dozen shells in his pocket. Walking back outside, he saw both perched in a tree twenty yards away. They didn't fear him, for he was in the regular habit of feeding them leftover food scraps. The ravens clucked, anxious to get back at the carcass. Quickly he shot the first one, and as the other fled vainly in a panic, Brad reloaded and shot it. Now they lay quiet in the snow like glistening chunks of coal. He walked over to them and nudged each one with his foot. They wouldn't feed on the dog anymore.

He put the shotgun away and sat back at the table. He drummed on top of it and shook his head as he recalled his supervisor insisting on the snowmobile. Brad had told him they were no good: noisy, ate gallons of fuel, not dependable. Brad had almost demanded the study to be done on skis. But no, the supervisor wanted his field biologists mechanized: "You can do twice the work and be more efficient, and if you break a leg you can get home with the machine. Try skiing home under those conditions." To his supervisor, it was a simple and obvious decision.

Suddenly Brad felt overwhelmingly sad, but he fought it down and quickly went to the sink and busied himself by putting bacon scraps into the frying pan with some stale bread. He took the pan full of scraps outside, went to a tree stump and left it there for the ravens. Returning, he took out his record books and with his calculator worked on his data for several hours. Occasionally he checked at the window to see if the ravens had come for the scraps, yet by mid-afternoon there was still no sign of them. Putting his data books and calculator away he opened a novel, but before sitting down to read checked again for the ravens. The pan still lay on the tree stump, its contents now frozen solid. He set the book aside thinking that he'd bring the pan inside to let it thaw, then put it outside the next morning.

Brad was returning to the cabin when he saw the dead ravens in the snow. He walked over to them. It was snowing hard now, and the flecks of fresh snow had spotted the birds. He rubbed his hand over his forehead; a fear gripped him as he kicked one of the birds over and saw the blood soaked into the snow. He walked quickly to the cabin.

Sitting at the table he trembled; first it was the dog, now the ravens. He couldn't comprehend who or what would want to kill dumb animals for apparently no reason. He hadn't heard any shots. Brad got up and opened his shotgun to make sure it was loaded. It was now dark outside, yet he feared turning on the lights as he would be quite visible through the windows. Filling the stove with wood he crawled into his sleeping bag and stared at the door. He felt that whatever had killed the dog and the ravens might soon try to kill him. He pulled the sleeping bag up to his chin and wished with all his strength it were Saturday. He didn't want to be alone anymore. He began to cry quietly, and as he fell asleep he hoped he wouldn't have any more horrible dreams like the one he had the night before.

The Sacking of St. Barnabas

After the earthquake and tidal wave, the inhabitants were forced to abandon the tiny native village, moving south to another. Most of the houses were ruined, but the little Russian Orthodox Church still gamely stood.

The stout, dark cannery ship anchored in the bay the first winter after the tidal wave. During a lull in crab deliveries, a dozen of us workers skiffed to the beach and began sifting through the wreckages of the houses.

It was several hours before we became frustrated at finding little more than old clothes and kitchen articles. Our attentions turned to the frail church.

While most willingly ransacked the church, three of us refused, and we sat near the skiff listening to a fourth recount stories of St. Barnabas from Lives of the Saints. *Above us, the mountains loomed, serving as weary witness and audience.*

In the Islands of the Four Mountains

Richard sat on the mound of camping equipment while Gordy stalked up and down the beach glancing out to sea. He looked at Richard often.

"I wonder where the hell the plane is. The weather is liable to close in. You never know about the goddamn Aleutians."

Richard continued writing up notes; he didn't look up at Gordy.

"Why don't you wait until we get back to Dutch Harbor to write up those notes. You can do a neater job back there."

"I thought I'd do it now. There's nothing to do."

"You can do a neater job back at the base. Save it until then."

Richard put the notes away in his pack and took out a pocketbook. He hadn't wanted to break camp before the plane arrived. Out here, you never knew. Yet Gordy was anxious to return to town; he kicked rocks into the surf.

"Dumb son-of-a-bitch probably flew into a mountain. I don't like Fielding; he isn't careful. Amphibious planes are tricky."

Richard turned a page. A small surf broke onto the shore; several gulls sat down the beach with heads tucked into their feathers. It was a quiet day. Gordy walked to his pack and began removing a revolver. Richard closed the paperback.

"If you shoot one of those gulls, I'll report you."

Gordy's fingers stopped in mid-motion as he was putting a shell into a chamber, yet there was not a chance for him to reply. Around the point the plane rumbled into the bay, low to the water.

They watched as the plane wallowed in for a landing, taxied to the beach, then pulled itself onto land with a great roar of its engines. After shutting down the engines, Fielding threw open the rear door. He stared at all the gear with a sour, doubtful look. Gordy had put the revolver away and ran up to the plane.

"How much shit do you have, Gordy? It looks like more than twelve hundred pounds to me."

"Larry flew us in with the same plane; we haven't picked up anything except seventy-five pounds of rock samples."

"I know Larry flew you in here; the son-of-a-bitch takes off for Hawaii and leaves me with the dirty work. It took me thirty minutes to find you two; his directions were lousy. Let's start loading. It isn't going to get any lighter sitting here."

Everyone worked silently; Fielding crawled through the plane and loaded the nose compartment, then carefully filled the main compartment with gear. Finished, he had only a crawlway between the cockpit and the rear door.

"You might as well get in; you have more than two thousand pounds. This is the last goddamn time I'll let any of you guys get by with this."

First Gordy crawled in; he sat in the copilot's seat. Richard squeezed in, closed the door, and sat in the only vacant seat. Fielding started each engine, allowing them to run for a while. He released the brakes, and the plane slowly wallowed into the bay. It plowed water badly. Fielding looked back at Richard.

"You belted in?"

"Yeah."

Pointing the plane into the wind he gunned the engines and immediately the plane dug into the water throwing back spray from its propellers. Slowly the aircraft picked up speed, and, gradually pulling itself from the water, it began to skim over the surface. As it lifted off, one engine stalled and the torque of the remaining engine caused the plane to dip abruptly to one side, bringing the wing float into contact with the surface of the water. The plane smacked against the surface and rebounded into the air; almost remaining airborne, it hung in mid-air for an instant, yet dropped back to the surface where a violent cartwheel broke the fuselage open, sending pieces of cargo and plane flying in all directions. Shuddering from its final impact, the plane settled into the water and sank in less than ten seconds.

Δ

Richard walked slowly up the side of the mountain. He stopped and turned around: beyond where he stood was the bay. He couldn't remember the name of it. Putting his makeshift crutch down, he sat, being careful to keep his leg rigid; it had only stopped bleeding that morning. Below him in the bay he could see the outline of the sunken airplane. He studied it; he could make out the whiteness of the fuselage and the red wingtips. It sat at the bottom of the bay broken crazily in half. A hundred feet below him on the beach he could see the small shelter he had constructed the previous afternoon; in front of it lay Fielding. He studied the figure of Fielding carefully; even from the side of the mountain he could see the badly injured man talking and wagging his head back and forth. Fielding was out of his mind; his smashed skull sickened Richard. He had been amazed when Fielding had pulled himself from the water and collapsed onto the beach. Richard's glance moved slowly from Fielding to the plane.

He had managed to jump from the broken fuselage landing in the cold Aleutian water with a smack; the plane sucked in water and he could hear Gordy screaming and struggling. As he swam from the plane he could hear Gordy cry for help, and then the metallic groan sounded and the plane sank instantly. The final thing Richard heard before the plane went under was Gordy shouting for him, but Richard swam away, not hesitating a second. Although it was late September, the water seemed not to have been affected by the brief Aleutian summer, and Richard's legs were useless before he'd gone one hundred yards. Remembering his lifeguard's training, he removed his trousers and inflated them. He paddled towards the beach, which was about thirty yards distant, yet his arms weakened rapidly and he could get no closer to the beach whose rough kelp-covered rocks he could see in detail. He leaned on the trousers and felt the cold enter his torso. Tiny ripples of water emanated from his body as he shivered convulsively, and he was falling off into unconsciousness when he felt bottom. Opening his eyes, he knew this was his only chance, as somehow he had drifted within ten yards of shore. He floundered in near panic, dragging his trousers behind him. Somehow, after a hectic two minutes, he lay on the beach. The rocks and shorewater around him were red and slick with his blood. Looking down, he saw a long gash from his knee down to his ankle, almost as if someone had unzipped his flesh all the way down his lower leg. He fainted.

Δ

Forcing himself not to look at the plane, Richard hobbled down the mountainside to the shelter. So far he had found nothing to eat, also no fresh water. It seemed odd not to find fresh water in a group of islands that were usually wrapped in gray, misty clouds which tumbled from the ocean in endless lines. Fielding still lay where Richard had dragged him, muttering to the sky. When he'd first seen Fielding's gruesome head wound he'd vomited. No one could have possibly known it was Fielding. Looking away, he had dragged him up the beach, retching often. Since then, Fielding had lain, mumbling incoherencies and rolling his head from side to side. Richard sat down. He was awfully weak and thirsty. As yet he hadn't searched to the south. There had to be water close by. Before the crash he and Gordy had surveyed the island, and they'd seen small streams and ponds by the score. He tried to recall where he'd seen one, but his mind was unclear and stolid. Fielding yelled a name.

Richard moved away from him; it had been a woman's name and he couldn't tell what it was. To avoid looking at Fielding he walked down the beach. Waves slapped gently at the shoreline. Looking from the bay onto the ocean, Richard saw that it was a gentle day with clouds hugging the mountaintops. Richard had enjoyed his stay on the island. He and Gordy had mapped the rock formations during the daytime and in the evenings had sat around the camp writing up preliminary notes. With luck, work would end early and Richard would hike away from camp; Gordy, who when not occupied with rock formations and oil exploration, dribbled on endlessly with mundane stories that bored Richard. He would have been very content with another crew leader, but it had been Gordy all the way since last spring. Until yesterday.

Richard had never known Fielding; he was one of the pilots who flew around the half-dozen geological crews located in the Aleutians as part of a fossil fuel energy program. Fielding would wordlessly load and unload camping equipment and supplies, and Richard always admired him for being obviously bored by Gordy, who felt it necessary to carry on with all pilots as if they were his close friends. He had always wanted to spend some time with Fielding, but not this way.

He sat down on a rock and looked down the beach at Fielding; all during the early morning he'd expected him to die. His head bled almost constantly and Richard could not comprehend how someone could keep living after losing that much blood. With difficulty Richard rose and continued down the beach. He hadn't gone another twenty yards when he found a very small stream running into the bay. At first he almost dropped to his knees before the pain of his injury brought him up straight; almost falling from momentary dizziness, he steadied himself on his crutch, then carefully lowered himself to the streamlet and drank for several minutes. The water felt heavy and cold inside of him, and he sat to one side and enjoyed the heady feeling it brought. Down the beach he heard Fielding. He wondered what he might haul water in. He closed his eyes wishing the voice would go, but it didn't. He supposed that he should try and get him water. Perhaps he'd find a tin can on the beach, but he now felt tired and wanted to sleep, yet his conscience forced him up. He had to go almost a hundred yards down the beach before he found a large rice wine bottle with Japanese markings on it. He hobbled back to the stream, filled the bottle, and slowly approached Fielding.

Actually, Fielding didn't have much of a mouth left. Richard wondered where to give him the water. He stooped down and reconciled himself with the fact that he'd have to look directly at Fielding in order to give him a drink. He opened his eyes and became immediately nauseous. Trying again, he faced Fielding, opened his eyes, and put the bottle in what appeared to have been his mouth. Satisfied that he'd tried, Richard put the bottle aside. He felt certain that Fielding wouldn't last the day out.

Δ

On the morning of the third day, he lay down the beach from Fielding knowing that they both would probably die. The search might take weeks. It was lousy luck that the pilot that had brought them to the island had taken a two-week vacation in Hawaii. That meant only that pilot, Fielding, Gordy, and he knew the exact location of the field camp. All anyone else knew was that they were doing geological exploration in the Islands of the Four Mountains group. That wouldn't be much help. Probably the regional geologist for the company would attempt to locate the other pilot and start from there. That could take days.

Fielding no longer muttered or screamed. He simply moaned and rolled his head from one side to the other. The nights were horrible. Fielding's moaning in the darkness with the winds rolling through the bare volcanic passes kept Richard awake. Shivering, he hugged himself, trying to stay warm. And that was beginning not to be very possible. It was late September and the nights were becoming cold. They had no cover, no food, and no matches. Everything had gone down with the plane. This morning Richard had developed a bad cough, and he felt feverish; also, his leg was throbbing, and he hadn't worked up the courage to look at it. He felt he should be out scrounging the beach, but his head remained hazy and he often felt himself slip off into a sort of sleep.

It must have been around noon when he remembered the garbage pit at their old camp. Vaguely he remembered Gordy spilling an entire box of wooden matches when they had unloaded the plane a week before. Richard rubbed his eyes; hell, it was more like ten days now. He looked at his wristwatch and thought, yet he couldn't remember the day they had arrived on the island. Anyway, he did remember the spilled matches; he had swept them up and thrown them into the garbage. There were dozens of them. They had buried their garbage nearby. If he could hike to their old camp he might be able to dig them up, dry them out next to his body, and start a fire. They needed fire. He couldn't depend on being found very soon.

In the Islands of the Four Mountains

Before he left the shelter he thought hard and figured it was a mile hike around the bay to the other camp spot. He looked at his leg and was shocked at the sight of the swollen redness. The flesh hadn't begun to heal, and the wound looked almost as sickening as Fielding's head. Before he began pegging down the beach, he went over and looked at the pilot who had quieted considerably since the sun had come up. He breathed heavily, emitting a noise similar to snoring. Perhaps his end was very close. As Richard picked his way down the beach he kept a lookout for anything that might be of use; bottles and fishing floats were everywhere, mixed in with pop cans and egg cartons. With no one to comb them, the beaches in the Aleutians were a history of offshore activity. The pain in his leg began to throb badly and he leaned against a rock and rested. He looked back at the camp; he had come about a hundred yards. The throbbing seemed impossibly intense and he became nauseous. His body shuddered and he had difficulty remembering why he had left camp. Then he recalled the matches in the garbage. He needed fire.

In two hours he'd gone half a mile; he looked back the way he'd come and saw specks of blood alongside his trail. He sat. The throbbing surged through him and he retched. While wondering if he would ever reach the old campsite he fell into a coughing spasm, yet afterwards he pushed himself to his feet with the crutch and continued. For the first time since the plane crash he felt afraid of dying. The only other time in his life he had considered death was when he had drawn a very low number in the draft lottery. He'd been plagued for weeks with nightmares about dying in Vietnam. After that danger passed he hadn't thought of dying and never dwelled on the subject again, for petroleum geology wasn't a dangerous occupation. Dying in connection with the job wasn't something he had considered.

He was exhausted again; this time he was close to another small stream. He drank and while resting thought of his wife. He had seen her only twice during the summer. Thinking hard, he couldn't remember what she looked like and he became worried. He should be able to recall what his wife looked like. He remembered his wallet. Digging through it he removed credit cards and old receipts until he finally found a photograph of her. Around her sat two children. He frowned, wondering who the children belonged to. The photograph was soggy and he held it carefully to prevent it from falling apart. As he put the wallet away he remembered two things very clearly: One was that his wife's name was Judith; two, that she never allowed anyone to call her Judy. Rubbing his temples he tried to remember more but couldn't. He felt dead tired, and he leaned back against a rock. He looked up at the sky and saw it had turned cloudy and was raining. The water fell from the sky in slow, gray sheets, drifting obliquely to earth. He felt very cold and knew he had to get to his feet. He reached for his crutch but it fell away from him. Again he leaned back; oddly, the rain falling against his head felt cool, and the sound of the wind coming down from the mountains relaxed him. Finally he could keep awake no longer and he slept.

When he awoke the bay had been whipped into a foamy white frosting by the hard wind which now blew directly from the open ocean. Rain fell hard, and no longer did it fall gently on his face; rather it spattered against him, almost stinging. Although nowhere near freezing, he was severely chilled and he shivered; looking around he located his crutch and got up. He looked for Fielding. He almost panicked when he didn't see him, but he remembered his hike away from camp. Leaning on the crutch he wondered why he had left; suddenly he was hit with a hard gust of wind and nearly sent to the ground. Bracing himself he faced into the wind. What on earth had made him leave the shelter? Cursing, he turned and walked along the beach, taking his bearings several times to assure himself he was heading towards camp.

The wind kept increasing while he walked until finally he could only keep his footing by leaning almost at a twenty degree angle. Rain fell in torrents and he was soaked to his skin. His trousers felt stiff and abrasive, and his leg ached. Finally he saw the temporary shelter and quickened his pace until he stood in front of it. Shielding his eyes against the rain he looked around for Fielding and was frightened and surprised not to see him in front of the shelter. He stooped down and looked in the tiny shelter; standing straight he looked up and down the beach through the onslaught of rain and wind; however, there seemed no doubt about it: Fielding was gone.

Richard lay inside the shelter and listened to the wind rage; gusts shook the shelter and several times he thought it would be blown to pieces. He fell into fits of coughing and felt hot. He thought it peculiar that someone in Fielding's condition could walk away from camp; the only animal on these islands were fox, and fox couldn't drag away someone like Fielding who stood half a head higher than Richard and probably weighed two hundred pounds. Somehow, in spite of the awful injury and lack of sight, Fielding had walked away. Mad of course. Richard felt somewhat ashamed that he was glad Fielding had gone away. He hugged himself, shuddering; the idea of Fielding wandering around muttering and groaning scared him badly. He looked out the door of the shelter but could see nothing. The wind moaned, forcing itself across the island from the ocean; waves from the bay washed into the beach, and Richard covered his ears from the constant confusion of noises. Several times during the night he managed to sleep, yet he'd usually wake right away. Twice he thought he heard someone stumbling around outside the shelter and had cringed in the corner wondering if Fielding had returned. He'd called but there was no answer. It seemed that after he called, whatever was making the noise went away; perhaps it was his imagination.

Δ

In the first light of the fourth day he could see that the rain fell in horizontal torrents, and water flew unimpeded through the cracks in the shelter. He remained soaked; he dragged himself to the entrance of the shelter and saw the bay was chaos. Six-foot waves blasted into the beach sending spray into the air where it was picked up by the wind and swept hundreds of feet inland. He tasted the water that dripped through the roof and it was almost pure sea water. No one could ever find them in a storm like this, even if they knew precisely where they were. Several hundred yards down the beach he saw a fox padding quickly towards him; it too held itself into the wind, and water dripped from its lush silver-blue fur. Soon it saw or sensed Richard and stopped. For a full minute it studied the shelter, then turned and loped inland. Richard fell back down. He was looking down at his feet when he noticed that his injured leg was so badly swollen the cloth was taut as a sausage skin. Startled, he almost jumped to his feet, but he slumped back and closed his eyes.

Jesus! Even if they rescued him he'd lose his leg for sure; yet he laughed as it occurred to him he didn't need to worry about losing his leg: He was going to die. His injury, the lack of food, the dry clothing, the storm—any one of them would be reason enough. He opened his eyes and looked at the leg; it was odd it didn't hurt. There was a vague tightness but that was all. He felt feverish and tired. If it hadn't been for the thirst he would have slept, but with effort he went to the entrance, caught hold of his crutch and ventured out.

Immediately he was knocked down. He sat up and reached his crutch just before it was blown away, but when he was struggling to his feet he heard something odd. It was a slapping, as if someone were bringing their hand down solidly on bare rock; shielding his eyes he looked. Listening carefully, he decided the slapping was more of a thud. Pushing into the wind, he was able to lean against the shelter and steady himself. He looked for several minutes; finally he was about to go inside, but out of curiosity he took one last look. It was then he saw Gordy.

He could tell it was Gordy from the color of the shirt. His body raised and lowered with the surf, smacking onto the rocky beach; his limbs had become very white and wobbled stiffly as the body washed in and out with the surf. Almost falling into the shelter Richard cringed against the wall and began sobbing until he blanked out. When he awoke it was night again.

He was very hot and covered with sweat. He felt like crawling out into the cold wind, but when he tried he was unable to raise himself. Trying to roll over, he couldn't. Then something odd, a very new sort of sensation, made him lie back and rest. He mentally listed all his injuries and considered the hopelessness of his situation. As he did this the wind blew even fiercer against the shelter and everything around him was wet, black, and clammy. There could be no possibility of rescue; hence there was only one conclusion: He was going to die, perhaps today, maybe tomorrow. But no longer.

He wondered if they would ever find his body. Also, he was curious as to whether fox ate human flesh, and he could think of no reason they wouldn't. Richard wondered why he didn't feel afraid, but he felt only tired and glad it was soon going to be over. In spite of the dullness of his mind, he remembered the horrid scene with Gordy's body being pounded and beaten by the surf, then Fielding's terribly maimed head. He was glad he wouldn't go through that. No, he would simply die in the shelter. Quietly.

Δ

They hung over him like ghosts, drifting in and out of vision. Deep warbling sounds emanated from the figures, at times growing closer, then more distant. Richard no longer could hear the wind. Oddly, he felt warm and at ease. He tried to begin thinking but gave it up. He became very heavy and felt his body tip from right to left. The warbling became more distinct and he heard someone repeat, "My God, My God," several times. For a second he thought he recognized Judith's voice, only to have the voice become deeper then slide away.

"Richard, Richard. Do you hear me?"

He felt resentful because he had become warm and comfortable. The voices disturbed him, and again he could hear the surf and wind. Finally he was able to see a man in white overalls wearing an orange life jacket working above him. The voices continued. Sometimes arguing, then sometimes being quiet.

"We're going to lose this one...hold the goddamn I.V. higher, Pete. Get blanket...move him then...going to lose this one...Jesus God, what a stench."

Richard felt confident he was going to die. The fuzziness returned, and the voices dulled out to warbles again. Slowly he became much warmer, and the figures moved above him more rapidly. He watched them until a lightness took hold of him and lifted. Rather than be frightened, he enjoyed the rapid lifting sensation; above him Richard saw an intense blueness. He became incredibly warm and, knowing things would soon be over, closed his eyes and concentrated on the feeling that now took hold of him, kindly, but irrevocably.

The Patton Seamount

On the open sea, land became insignificant, and the only force was the ocean. High on the upper deck of the Silas Bent a look in any direction gave rise to the ceaseless parade of ground swells. The surface of the Gulf rose and fell like the behemoth drawing restful breaths in its sleep, and the ship swayed in time to these. Along the peaks and valleys of these brine-clad legions, shearwaters flew inches above the metallic gray sheen, their delicate wings occasionally skimming the water.

At night the ship ran from one oceanographic station to the other. Behind the stern, the Bent's propeller turned our wake a fierce white; overhead the constellations and stars were not steady as they were on land. Instead they rocked several degrees north then south with the motion of the seas.

Sitting on the stern in the lee of a life boat, I became aware of the peaceful trinity formed by the ship, the heavens, and the seas. For that watchful moment, I knew no constraints except the winds and the remotest edge of the planet.

Weather

The mountains formed the spine of the peninsula which lay between the Bering Sea and Pacific Ocean. Some were actively volcanic yet had summits covered with layers of snow which remained throughout the year. During the long summer days the peaks of the mountains formed perfect silhouettes against the light turquoise sky. In all seasons the winds blew across this peninsula, curling over the mountains, then sweeping downwards onto the tundra flatlands. These ran onwards for several dozen miles until they met the shoreline of the Bering Sea.

The days were dominated by wind. The mountains stood up to these winds, their steep-cliffed shoulders braced like fortresses against the constant storms, and after millennia had been sculpted into cold and foreboding sorts of landmarks that did not inspire beauty. In fact, it was thought that it was the wind's forced passage over the bleak mountains which gave them a cruelty that seemed to be their special trait.

Δ

The air station was constructed in 1944 when the Japanese had invaded this end of the world. After the armies settled their business and left, hundreds of huts and roads remained. And the airfield.

Though the huts and roads were mostly abandoned, the airfield served as a hub from which a dozen Aleut and Eskimo villages were serviced by air taxi operators who flew small planes in and out of the field in the spring and summer. Larger multi-engined aircraft arrived and departed carrying cargo from larger cities and, during summers, carrying iced fish to brokers in the east and west.

At the station there was a kitchen/dining room, an apartment for the manager and his family, a half dozen rooms for pilots and passengers who might be stranded due to weather, and a central reception area with a radio and mail room at one end. Against the back wall of this area was a display counter with cigarettes, a few candy bars, and little else. At one time it had been intended to be the beginnings of a small store.

Δ

The station manager read the weather report then placed it on a clipboard. There was no change. Three pilots sat around a table and looked out the front window. They talked about the poor summer weather: The storm coming on, the winds and rain increasing, the visibility decreasing. The chance for it to get better tomorrow.

At first the youngest of the three had prepared to leave. "To beat the really bad stuff," he'd said. But the manager and the other two pilots knew he didn't want to fly in the growing storm.

"You'd better hang around, see what it'll do, heh?"

The youngest pilot, glad for the advice, sat back down. Outside, the weather grew thicker. Rain fell and raked thick sheets of icy rain across the tundra. Only with difficulty could the pilots see their planes which were tied close to the station. Each craft strained at its tether, as if attempting to depart pilotless.

"I hope those damned tie-downs hold."

All three pilots held coffee cups and studied their planes. It was getting tougher and uglier out and there was simply nothing they could do about it.

The station manager tapped a large finger against the wind gauge. He studied the needle which no longer went beneath the forty-knot mark, then sat at a desk and opened a crossword puzzle book.

Every year he did hundreds of them.

The double door to the kitchen swung open, squeaking loudly. The manager's fifteen-year-old daughter came out into the waiting room. She wore shorts and a tight sweater.

"You guys stayin' for supper?"

Each admitted they would probably be staying for supper as it was ninety-seven miles to the closest restaurant or hotel. They tried not to look at the girl's extraordinarily large breasts which pushed the sweater out almost a half foot. The manager studied his daughter over the top of the crossword book. The beginnings of furrows formed across his brow.

"Go back in the kitchen, Shelly, and fix me a toasted cheese. Maybe a glass of milk."

She'd already moved towards the pilots. Tossing her head back, she looked at her father sourly, then walked back in the kitchen. Each buttock jiggled tautly as she walked. The oldest of the pilots took off his glasses and peered at the manager.

"You gonna have to buy that poor girl a bigger sweater, Epson."

Epson smiled at first, then lowered the crossword book and glanced at the kitchen door, then back at the pilot. He began to say something, then didn't.

Outside the wind continued to build.

Δ

They'd all eaten quietly, listening to the wind as it buffeted the station, first from the east, then the southeast.

"Don't seem to settle on a direction, does it?"

The manager and pilots worried. The manager thought of the various pieces of equipment outside while the pilots worried about their planes. Once during dinner the youngest pilot walked to the front of the station and checked the planes from the window. Returning, he sat down on the bench and resumed eating halfheartedly. There was a general awkwardness at the table resulting from listening to the wind and eating with people who wanted to be somewhere else.

Everyone went to bed early. After the last radio check, the manager observed aloud that the wind had leveled off at sixty knots and perhaps had even dropped somewhat in the past hour. All three pilots looked at the wind meter from where they sat, somewhat grateful to see the blinking indicator light holding steady beneath the sixty-knot mark.

Before going to his room the oldest pilot looked from the window at his plane, rubbing the side of his jaw and shaking his head. The youngest pilot came up behind him.

"You think they'll hold? The tie-downs?"

"Should."

Each went to bed. Despite the wind's unsettling noise, the young pilot could hear music towards the rear of the station. Not long after he got under the blankets, the music stopped.

Δ

The youngest pilot awoke to a loud noise. Sitting up in bed he listened and immediately realized the wind was stronger, and the noise was the rumble caused by gusts blowing across the metal roof. The wind now was steady from the southeast, from the mountains. A gust struck the station violently, the strength of it jostling him on the bed. He leaped out and dressed rapidly.

When he opened the door the hall was dark, and only a single light from the radio room illuminated the reception area. When he entered the main room, he saw the manager stooping before the wind gauge in pajamas and slippers, his hair disheveled. The manager straightened and looked towards the pilot. His eyes were huge and unbelieving, and to talk he raised his voice over the wind.

"It's over eighty-five knots now. It ain't supposed to go that high."

The pilot moved towards the window yet braced himself as another gust, much harder than the previous one, hit the building like a solid object. An ashtray fell from the table; pegs fell from the cribbage board. He was about to turn and wake the others when he saw something which made him go rigid. Outside, like a manic insect or bird pinioned to earth by one wing, the closest plane was flopping to and fro by a single remaining tether. Before he could regain his senses, he saw the plane struck by a sudden gust which forced it to swing even wider, crashing into the adjoining plane, his plane.

Without thought he bolted to the door. After he'd thrown the door open he remembered nothing but suddenly being hurled into the bulldozer which was a dozen feet from the station. The randomness of his entanglement had entwined him around the hydraulic ram between the massive blade and the front of the machine. It had only been a second, or even less, from the time he opened the door until he'd been thrown into the bulldozer.

His head throbbed, but above all this he could hear pieces of the airplanes disintegrating when tumbling downwind. Into the station.

The noise of these fragments striking the station made him grip the bulldozer, clinging to it with all of his strength. It was obvious to him that if any of the objects struck him, they would kill him.

Suddenly something, probably a plane fragment, struck the bulldozer behind him. Metal shrieked momentarily, then ripped and blew beyond the machine. A subsequent crash and sprinkling of glass told the pilot it had smashed into the large front window of the station. Perhaps he heard a scream, or yell. He wasn't certain, and later couldn't remember that well, as the continuing dismemberment of the three planes overwhelmed everything else.

It took several seconds for him to connect the sudden jolt he felt in the ground with the collapse of the building. Yet as the heavy corrugated iron roof plunged through into the floor, a horrifying array of prehistoric groans and rentings emanated, even drowning out the wind briefly. The old building's death came within seconds, much faster than had his plane's demise.

The idea of the entire building collapsing seemed unbelievable, even as he clung to the blade. Pulling himself up he tried to look over the blade but fragments of glass and metal had caught in back eddies and twisted about in dozens of miniature whirlwinds. Terrified he pressed his face into the machine and, despite the fact it was summer, he shivered.

He remained this way until the bulldozer began to vibrate with the wind. He noticed the wind no longer howled; rather it exploded across the landscape making his ears pop. He wondered if it would help if he prayed, and as he considered praying he began weeping from a combination of fear and the realization that anyone who had been in the station was crushed to death. Trying to control himself he repeated, "I lived by not praying, and I'll die like I lived," and it worked. He stopped crying and simply wrapped himself tighter against the metal. The fact he had not prayed was the single thing he looked back on with pride.

Δ

At first light the wind didn't weaken, yet it enabled him to see that debris and piles of volcanic silt had accumulated against the bulldozer, affording him more shelter. He was able to let go of the machine and lie still, staring upwards. His arms and legs ached from the hours of clinging, and he could still hear nothing except the wind sweeping across what was now flat terrain. Occasionally silt would blow into his eyes.

Turning away he pressed his face against his arm and waited. In late morning the wind rapidly died away until it was nothing more than the usual gusts of wet summer wind coming down from the mountains.

Doubting his senses, he remained hidden another hour. When he did emerge, he was amazed at how coolly and methodically he behaved, as if he had been following the precise directions of a script. He knew that radio contact was made three times a day from the station, and he assumed the company who owned the station would send out someone when they couldn't make contact. Until then he was on his own.

He walked about making sure he was all right. Then he found a long piece of iron and began prying about in the wreckage of the station, which as he'd surmised earlier was flat against the ground, pounded into its foundation.

After surprisingly little searching he found the manager. He had died in the middle of the kitchen, apparently with suddenness. With effort he dragged him to a flat area in front of the bulldozer.

It was far more difficult finding the manager's wife. Still, after an hour he located her in what must have been the stall shower in their apartment. As he removed her, he wondered why she'd been in the shower in her nightgown and slippers. She couldn't have anticipated the roof collapsing. No one could have.

He was carefully digging out a package of plastic garbage bags from the wreckage of the kitchen to use as death shrouds when he saw ravens circling about five hundred yards to the north. After covering the bodies he walked in that direction and discovered ravens worrying the corpse of the second pilot. Though not touching it, the large black birds hopped about, clucking and hooting in their peculiar way. Strangely there were no marks on the pilot's unclothed body. His eyes were open and stared in a permanent reverie at the sky. He fashioned a litter and moved the body next to the others.

That left the oldest pilot and the manager's daughter.

It was late afternoon when he located them. Beneath thousands of pounds of corrugated iron roofing he found them in what had been the oldest pilot's room. The daughter's body was stippled with wounds and gouges. She lay less than three feet from the man, who'd died instantly in his bed. The youngest pilot recalled having dinner with the oldest pilot's family the previous Easter. He'd seen slides of him and his wife in Arizona holding their grandchildren. For the first time he hesitated in his labors and put his pry-bar aside; then he stood and wept while looking at the girl and man. Quickly he regained control and resumed his work.

He put the daughter next to her parents and the pilot on the opposite side of his colleague. Not trusting the plastic shrouds, he dug about until he found a sizable portion of tarp. Then he carefully covered all the bodies, placing heavy iron scraps onto each corner to hold it securely.

He rested for the first time and it wasn't long until he realized how thirsty he was. He walked to what had been the pump house, then followed the remains of the waterline to a small lake. He stooped and drank deeply, and since this was the first water he'd had in eighteen hours, he felt its coolness settling into him.

Overhead it was clear. His figure made a long shadow on the tundra, the sun already low on the western horizon.

Δ

He slept that night behind the bulldozer blade, wrapped in a tattered blanket with the bodies so close he felt uneasy and couldn't sleep. Actually, he was somewhat afraid of them. But not long after dawn he was awakened by the sounds of a cargo plane clumsily taxiing down the runway, its huge wheels plowing through drifts of silt. The plane's engines spewed back dirt for over a hundred yards, then it turned and rumbled over to what had been the station. He crawled from behind the blade and felt himself crumple to the ground. Behind the window he could see the pilot and copilot looking out, their eyes fixed on the covered bodies and flattened station. They gestured frantically.

He remembered very little of the remainder of that day.

Δ

During the year following the incident at the station he decided to quit flying. Since he'd spent five years working and saving to buy his plane, then three years building up his small flying service, most of his friends discouraged him from quitting.

Yet he had never fully appreciated the importance of wind in flying. Always there was the sound of air moving past the plane, and he no longer wanted to hear that. His wife convinced him to seek counseling, but it didn't seem to help that much. He just couldn't talk about what happened to someone who spent his work day comfortably in an overstuffed chair drinking tea and nodding almost by habit. Yet he had gone to keep his wife happy.

Despite his efforts, she left him, returning to her parents. But she came back, making him promise to at least try and pull himself out of the frequent depressions and long periods of moodiness which came and went without him willing it. During bad times he would think of the night behind the bulldozer blade and the destruction of the station.

Several months after he'd received the insurance payment for his plane, he bought a small bait and tackle shop out of the city. He'd always liked fishing and slowly became interested in the store and customers. Occasionally one of his former flying associates would stop in, but they would never talk flying. Word had gotten around.

Towards the end of the summer during the following year, his wife escorted a reporter into the backyard where he was splitting wood. She had assumed it was an outdoors writer from one of the newspapers. After she'd gone back into the house, the man took out a small tape recorder and said, "I'd like to ask you a few questions about the disaster at Mountain Station. A One-Year-After story, you know?"

He looked at the reporter, then set the splitting maul aside and shook his head. For a moment he felt dizzy.

"No story. I don't talk about that. Ever."

There must have been something in the way he'd said it which eliminated the possibility of debate. The reporter quickly packed up his recorder and left. The pilot stood and listened as the reporter drove away.

He returned to splitting wood, drawing the maul upwards, then driving it down, the weight of it easily cleaving the log in two. Kicking each piece aside he placed another log on the block, brought the maul back and down, splitting it. He worked slowly, taking pleasure in the steady rhythm of the task. He would look up only occasionally, when the breeze would pass through the crowns of the white spruces, making them groan softly. Waiting for this to pass, he would then resume working.

At the Foot of the Meshiks

In mid-spring, the Meshik Mountain Range was still covered with snow. Its slopes drained directly into Port Heiden Bay where I'd fished since April. I didn't use nets to catch large fish; instead I used those with finer mesh to capture smelt and herring for study.

The commercial fishing season was still weeks away, so I worked alone, day or night, depending on tide, on the east shore, a flat expanse of thick esturine mud.

While picking my nets, I would look up towards the mountains, straining to stand straight, taking a rest from all the bending. The prevailing winds from Bristol Bay swept towards the mountain summits, picking up snow and blowing it upward, creating white ribbons across light blue skies.

The mountains' white slopes contrasted with the dreary yellows of the vegetation that was weeks from greening. The lowlands adjoining the bay rose slowly, steadily upwards until they joined the Meshiks. The waters of Port Heiden Bay were a silty monotone of gray. With the village of Meshik hidden behind the bluffs, there wasn't a single structure visible anywhere. In any direction, the sky and land were linked in a solitary vigil.

The Cape of Saint Gregory

On some days Simpson fished, and on others he didn't. This had little to do with the weather. If his garden or animals needed work, he stayed in. If he felt in the mood to fish and the weather looked all right, he went out. Despite this, he did better than most small-boat fishermen.

When he delivered his fish to the cannery, the workers and other fishermen watched from the dock as he picked up the bulky halibut from his fish box and pushed them into the bucket. His large double-ended dory bobbed around as the heavy bucket was lifted clear, and he realized with satisfaction that everybody wondered how he caught so many fish. After securing his dory in the evening, he would be soaked in fish blood and he liked to heat up two large buckets of water on his oil range and take a long bath. With the second bucket he would soak while smoking a cigar and reading yesterday's newspaper. For Simpson, life was not bad.

The morning after a day of particularly good fishing, he sat on his front porch and worked on a wood carving of a bird. Towards noon a young boy walked through the gate and sat on the front steps. Oddly, Napoleon the gander didn't bother the boy. He glanced tentatively at the wood carving, then shyly at Simpson.

"Is it true that you're an ex-convict?"

Simpson stopped carving and looked closely at the boy; he thought the kid looked somewhat dull-witted, he placed him at around ten or eleven years old. "What in hell makes you ask a stupid question like that!"

"Some of the other kids say they come over here a lot and that you told them you are an ex-convict."

He concentrated, trying to remember which lie he'd told to which kid, but he gave up. He couldn't fight it.

"Well, I was only in prison once."

The boy continued asking him about jail, then everything else. Simpson answered each question then gave the boy a piece of red cedar to carve. The boy sat on the steps carving in silence, then quite suddenly looked up at Simpson.

"Could I go out fishing with you?"

"No. I fish alone.

"Why can't I go just once?"

"Because halibut fishing is very dangerous—big hooks whipping over the side of the boat, dangerous power equipment, and big fish flopping around. I'm afraid a young fellow like you would bust his ass."

The boy left somewhat later, thanking Simpson for letting him carve. Simpson got out what remained of his home brew from under the porch. He had just opened the first bottle when a woman walked up to his gate. He drank as he watched her confront Napoleon; it interested him the way various people reacted to the gander.

She opened the gate quite suddenly and Napoleon went for her at once. She kicked at him when he hissed and charged, cursing the bird. Remembering she was a guest, Simpson called the gander off. She sat on the porch. She was tall, perhaps over six feet, and thin. She wasn't what he'd call pretty, and she wore a pair of glasses which were taped together at the bridge.

"Hello, I'm your new neighbor. I'd like to thank you for entertaining my son today."

It made sense; they had the same eyes. He shrugged and drank. Usually he paid no attention to neighbors. For all Simpson knew, she could have lived in the neighborhood for five years.

"They say you're the most successful fisherman in town."

He laughed.

"Listen, my boat cost nine thousand dollars. There are two-and-a-half-million-dollar boats fishing out of this port which catch more in one day than I do in a month."

"But still, for what you have you do very well."

He didn't listen to what she said; rather he wondered what she wanted. He knew she hadn't come over just to chat about how good a fisherman he was.

"Do you think that one day," here she stopped and looked over towards the ocean, "that maybe my boy could go along with you? Ever since we came to the coast he's wanted to go along with somebody."

He put an empty bottle of home brew aside, got up and went to get a fresh one. He offered her some, but she turned him down. Simpson opened the bottle and drank.

"I'm sorry. But halibut fishing is dangerous. Hooks as big as ham hocks. Dangerous. Wouldn't want to take a chance."

To himself, he wondered what sort of a mother would let her kid go out halibut fishing with a stranger. Stupid. Damn stupid.

"Actually, Roy is quite good around machines. He's got a good head on his shoulders. Very mature for twelve."

"He's twelve? I thought he was younger."

"Oh, he's very mature. Does all the work around the house."

"I still wouldn't take him. You must not be familiar with halibut fishing. It's risky business. I'm afraid that's final."

She made small talk about his geese and chickens, then left. After she was gone he drank silently as he watched the sun sinking into the Pacific. He pulled out another bottle of home brew, and sometime well after sunset he tumbled off the chair and fell asleep among the cedar shavings on the front porch.

The next time he fished he caught almost three quarters of a ton of halibut, a catch worth close to three thousand dollars, At the cannery almost fifty people looked down from the dock as he delivered. That evening he sat in his tub soaking, reading the newspaper, and smoking a cigar. To one side of the tub was the last bottle of home brew, still frosted from the chill of the cellar. He worked his toes against the tub's bottom, read, and felt the cold beer settle into his system.

When Simpson heard the geese begin to honk, he cursed and quickly slipped into an old robe he hadn't worn in six months. If the intruders were Jehovah Witnesses, he vowed silently to kick their carcasses down the stairs. When he pulled open the door, he saw it was the neighbor lady again. Walking back to the table, he plopped down on a stool and picked up his beer from the floor. She looked around nervously.

"I'm sorry. I, well, I didn't mean to disturb you."

"Okay, okay. I was just about ready to get out; water was cold."

Certainly she could see he was lying; straightening up she muttered, "Oh," and Simpson relieved the awkwardness by inviting her to sit. He went into his bedroom and in back of the partially closed door began to dress. She talked loudly so he could hear through the door.

"I was thinking about our conversation last night, Mr. Simpson."

"In regards to what?"

"Well, I don't mean to be pushy, but in regards to my boy going out fishing with you."

He stopped in the midst of pushing his foot into a sock and shook his head.

"Goddamnit, it's just too dangerous out there."

"Actually, as compensation I would pay your fuel and whatever else you might think fair."

He came through the door still shaking his head.

"Lady…"

"My name is Arlene."

He looked at her. In the light of the room she seemed even taller, although not quite as skinny. Her hands were big, and they apeared rough from hard work. There were small but noticeable wrinkles at the corners of her mouth and eyes. Her eyes were gray and quite large, the pupils made even larger by the thick-lensed glasses. To Simpson she looked like she was at least forty.

"Arlene, today I made about three thousand dollars, and I don't really need to be helped on my fuel. It's just, well, a reckless request. The boy would surely get hurt, unless I slowed down, which I don't want to do. I'm sorry, but it's just out of the question."

"Well, I've been here almost three months working in the canneries, and I've yet to get Roy out on a boat. He dreams of the day when he can get out with somebody. He's read every book under the sun on fishing."

"You'll just have to make him understand."

"If you take my son out with you the next time you go fishing, Ill stay with you tonight and any other night you want."

Simpson looked over at her and could see she meant it. She returned his look without blinking. He took his beer and drank. He was forty-five years old and something like this had never happened to him before.

He and the boy left early in the morning. The boy was very sleepy, but when his mother hugged him he was still awake enough to push her away and look self-consciously at Simpson. Once out of the boat harbor, Simpson steered towards some islands in a bay where most small boats fished, but as he drew close to the islands, he brought the dory around and steered into a thick fog bank. The boy asked questions about every two or three minutes. As on land, Simpson would answer each question, surprised that the boy never duplicated them. He explained the compass to the boy, and how he steered the boat. They emerged from the fog bank in a half hour and Simpson gave the dory full throttle. The bow jumped upwards and began to plow through each oncoming roller.

The boy realized something different was happening after they steered a straight course for an hour. He asked how far offshore Simpson fished, for the rising sun had dissolved the mist and fog, and the boy could see that the nearest land was a long way away. He became nervous, but soon settled into the task of steering the boat by compass while Simpson cut bait, loading up hundreds of hooks with cut octopus in preparation for working the gear.

Simpson was surprised at how rapidly the boy caught on to almost everything he was shown to do. Later, while Simpson steered the boat, the boy sharpened hooks with a file. Land was now dozens of miles behind them, and finally the boy turned to Simpson and asked him where they were going to fish, for they had been underway for almost four hours. Simpson laughed and said they had another hour and a half to go, and he added that when they finally got to his gear they would be thirty-nine miles off the Cape of Saint Gregory. The boy thought awhile, then asked how many small boats fished that far offshore. Simpson looked around and shrugged, eventually addmitting, "None."

It was a beautiful clear day and the dory was all by itself on a sea that was brilliantly blue and quiet. All around them wedges of sea birds, sometimes numbering in the thousands, flew by. Also, birds littered the surface of the ocean feeding in rafts, and the boy frequently took his eyes from the horizon to look at the different types of birds. When Simpson spotted his first string of gear, he turned to Roy and took him firmly by the shoulder.

"Roy, you stand clear while I work. You stand clear, understand?"

"Yes."

Roy stood behind the small cabin watching while Simpson hauled the first string of gear. On it were three halibut, all small. By mid-afternoon, the only fish he'd caught were those three. While running to the last string, he and the boy drank coffee and ate sandwiches.

"Do you frequently catch so few?"

Simpson laughed.

"You're suggesting I'm not doing worth beans?"

"Well, Mr. Simpson, we've only caught three fish."

"Yes, but look at them. They are three of the best damned halibut in the Pacific Ocean."

Roy shook his head and smiled. The woman was right: He was a serious young man. Simpson thought of the woman Arlene for the first time since the other night. She was an odd one, he decided. Odd. He was tempted to ask the boy questions about her, but kept himself from doing so. Still, he wondered where Roy's father was.

"Where's your father, Roy?"

"I don't have a father."

Simpson thought about that while swallowing a last bit of sandwich. He felt he'd embarrassed the boy,

"I didn't mean to pry."

"Oh, I don't mind. That's just what she tells me."

Suddenly Simpson resented the woman and felt sorry for the boy. Quickly, Simpson imagined numerous theories concerning her background, and he became uneasy. He resolved to have nothing more to do with her.

When they reached the last string of gear, Simpson looked up at the sky and reckoned they were at least two or three hours ahead of schedule.

"Now this time, you can work the gear with me, but goddamnit don't get a hook in you."

The boy worked with uncanny ability, dodging the hooks as if he'd been doing the work for years. Simpson operated the power lift while Roy worked the gear; suddenly Roy jumped back in alarm.

"A fish. A huge fish!"

Simpson shut down the lift and jumped across coils of line until he looked over the rail; swimming at the surface was a large halibut circling effortlessly with the hook gaping from the corner of its mouth. Roy gripped the boat tightly.

"How big is it?"

"Oh, maybe 250 pounds. Step back."

Simpson reached into a box and got out a pistol. He shot the halibut in the head twice. Then, with the help of the lift, he heaved it on board.

"You don't bring those in alive; they can break your leg with a single swat. Let's hope there's more like him down the line."

Simpson's hunch was correct. By the time they'd finished the last string, they had almost a thousand pounds of halibut for the day. Roy was jubilant, but Simpson hurried as he noticed the sky becoming cloudy; to the southwest a dark, massive front was moving their way. Although not telling the boy why, he began tying everything down while Roy steered.

"There's going to be a storm, isn't there? That's why you're tying everything down. Will it be bad, do you think?"

"It may pass us by, or it might be just one of those typical summer squalls. At sea it is always best to be on the safe side."

The boy stood close to him as he steered directly towards the Cape of Saint Gregory where the closest shelter was available. It would be four hours until they reached it.

The front caught up with them effortlessly, and they were shrouded in dark misty rain before they'd been underway an hour. Soon the light rain turned into a hard downpour, and Simpson gave his raincoat to the boy. He put on the old one which he'd used to cover the bait, but it had holes and soon he could feel the rain seeping into his wool jacket. The wind began to come in gusts, making herringbone designs on the water that were all too familiar. He switched on the pump, watching the mixture of fish blood and slime spew out into the sea. The boy kept looking back and with each gust of wind would glance at Simpson.

"I'm scared."

It was a straightforward declaration. Simpson shrugged.

"Well, that makes two of us in this boat that are scared."

The boy smiled that strange smile of his, and Simpson asked him to warm water on the tiny stove for coffee.

"This is going to be a long goddamn day, Roy. Your initiation will be a bit ragged."

"This dory is awfully well organized. I mean, everything is where you need it."

He liked having the boy say that, for Simpson was meticulous about his dory; but it wasn't long before the sea began to react to the wind and the slow gentle swell was replaced by choppy waves which broke into the bow as the boat plunged down the backsides of the huge sea rollers. Simpson drank coffee and steered, knowing what the dory was going to do three or four seconds before it happened, and rapidly compensating with a turn of the helm. The compass never varied by more than two or three degrees. As he watched the compass and the sea, he regretted going to bed with the woman. He had been to bed with a moderate number of women and she didn't seem different from any of the others, most of whom were without a boy who wanted to go out fishing. Now he knew the sea was becoming ugly, and he didn't like the idea of being responsible for another life besides his own. It was definitely something he shouldn't have become involved in.

The Cape itself wasn't visible any longer, and the seas were now larger than the dory. He was forced to throttle back to avoid burying the dory into the seas, but the dory rode well with the sea on its stern and they made good time in spite of the storm, which now Simpson guessed was mostly bluff. He figured they were in the worst of it, and the seas were no more than six or seven feet on top of the rollers. His confidence was shaken somewhat when he calculated that the tide would change in about thirty minutes. Often the change of tide would calm a sea, but more often it would stir it up until it became chaotic and lethal. Although Simpson had an excellent sense of time, he turned over the wheel to Roy and opened the box to his chronometer and saw that the turn of the tide was, as he'd assumed, thirty minutes away.

"Why did you look at the time? That's the first time you looked at the time today."

"I made a bet with myself that I knew what time it was."

"And did you win?"

"Every time. Every time."

He took the wheel and told Roy a funny story, but he didn't have his heart into it. He felt each minute slip past and he wondered what the tide would do. Finally the waters began to subside momentarily and become somewhat calmer. All around the dory the sea seemed to stir unevenly and the color of the water was lead gray. Almost imperceptibly the giant rollers that had been lumbering from the open ocean began to become less a roller and more a wave, their slopes becoming quite steep. In thirty minutes Simpson closed his eyes in regret, for now the swells had become full-sized waves, and where before gentle rollers sped towards the Cape from the open ocean, large sickle-shaped waves with curling white tops began to tower above the dory, crashing down, curling ominously with white plumes. Simpson saw immediately that the effect of the tide change was creating gigantic seas.

"Roy, I want you to go into the cabin and try to sleep. We'll be a long time getting back, and I want you to get some rest."

"Oh, that's OK. I'm not really tired."

"Do what I say. Lay down and get some shut-eye. Now get in there."

The boy stooped and crawled into the tiny cabin. Simpson took a piece of line and tied himself firmly to the cabin; then he yelled to Roy for his raincoat and, putting this on, braced himself.

The seas were now massive, coming upon the dory's stern in mountains. As each wave crashed down, the dory would lift up just several moments before being inundated by the white wall of foam that tumbled from top of each wave. The dory was pushed along at a terrific rate, and Simpson counted himself lucky for being able to run before it. They'd be at the Cape in two hours at this rate. Then, all of a sudden, just as Simpson was beginning to adjust to the sea's intensity, one of the waves broke much later than the others and crashed into the dory with an explosion of green water.

The coldness of the waters wrapped around Simpson like a dead pair of arms. Immediately he spat out a mouthful of water, and then turned on the pump. As the water level lowered he gunned the engine and brought the dory around with full power so it faced into the seas. There would be no more running with the seas until he bailed out the water completely. Simpson grabbed a bucket and began throwing out gallons while alternately checking the wheel to keep the dory straight.

When he turned to grab the wheel after several minutes of bailing, he saw Roy standing before the wheel steering. Without a word he turned and bailed even faster. The dory pitched violently over the crests of the waves and almost skimmed into the troughs, but somehow most of the water was bailed in less than fifteen minutes.

Taking the wheel again, he saw that Roy was shivering badly and hurriedly pushed him into the cabin.

"Take your clothes off and jump underneath that sleeping bag."

Now Simpson had the choice of either jogging into the seas or quickly turning and going with them again, risking being swamped by another wave. Grimacing he shoved the throttle forward in preparation for bringing it about; the dory would not stand too many of these pounding, destructive waves before it would come apart. He had to make the Cape.

The turn was quick, and this time he watched to the stern for waves that were breaking differently from the others. When he thought a wave would overtake him, he would shove the throttle forward and spin the dory around, facing it bow first. He did this repeatedly until he lost track of everything except the whitewashed blue sea which roiled all around the dory.

Around ten that night they pulled into the anchorage on the northeast end of the Cape. After anchoring, he crammed himself into the small cabin and sat next to the boy. He started the stove, boiled water for coffee, and warmed a can of chili.

"Mr. Simpson, have you ever been in that bad a storm before?"

Simpson had been surprised at the boy during the entire time at sea, and he would have never guessed the boy was scared if he hadn't said something.

"Yes, but I was on board larger boats,…ships, rather."

"You sailed on large ships?"

"I was a merchant marine officer for twenty years before I got sick of it. To be blunt, and just between the two of us, I'm really fishing way the hell out too far."

"That's why you catch more fish than the others, I guess."

"I suppose. But this is the third damn time this has happened."

He reflected that he had never owned up to the foolishness of this summer's fishing to anyone, and he wondered why he had said as much to the boy.

Δ

They arrived in town twenty-seven hours after leaving. Simpson steered the dory over to the cannery and began delivering the fish. While this went on, the boy's mother climbed awkwardly down the ladder. The boy and she hugged almost a full minute before the boy realized that a dozen people were looking down from the dock. He pushed his mother away and turned his attention to the halibut that Simpson put into the bucket.

Simpson told them that he would see them later and finished delivering his fish. He managed to run his boat back to the harbor and walk up to his house. Without bathing or eating, he stripped off all his clothes, fell into bed, and slept.

When he woke she was sitting in a chair facing him. He blinked several times and looked around, noticing right away that she was with-

88

out the boy. From under the blankets he could smell the foulness of his body and cursed himself for not bathing.

"I have water on the stove for your bath."

"Thanks."

She went into the next room and he got out of bed and wrapped his robe around him. She fixed him coffee while he looked at her moving around the front room preparing his bath.

"I'm afraid your son had a rather sorry introduction to the sea."

"He was in good hands. He had an adventure he'll remember for the rest of his life."

Simpson laughed before he could stop himself.

"Hell, I did, too."

She started and looked at him, then poured the water for his bath. Simpson felt uncomfortable. When she turned and saw him standing there she sensed it immediately. Wrapping a coat around her, she said she had something in the oven and left. He got in the tub and washed, then lay back and soaked. He cut his bath short and dried off hurriedly, then sat at the table and began making a peanut butter-and-jelly sandwich, eating the whole thing in two or three bites. He was making his second sandwich when she returned.

She sat across from him and, for the first time, Simpson felt like talking to her.

"You know, all my life I wished that a woman would ask me to go to bed with her. When I was a kid I dreamed of it. I guess every young guy does. I never thought it would happen."

"I realize you must be famished, Mr. Simpson, but all that peanut butter will stop you up like cement, plus that brand is loaded with sugar and additives."

He was a bit irritated at being ignored. He didn't like being ignored.

"I just want to say that I don't plan to collect on the remainder of the deal. I don't think the entire situation does either of us very much credit."

She looked across at him and smiled.

"Roy says you sailed in the merchant marine on big ships?"

He reached out and screwed the cap back on the peanut butter, muttering and shaking his head. She crossed her legs and pushed her broken glasses further back on her nose.

"There is no need to get mad. I mean, there isn't too much point in discussing it. And I want to know more about you. I'm curious about people."

"Well, goddamnit, Lady, there isn't a helluva lot to know."

She got up and shook her head.

"Well, I'm sorry, I seem to be making things worse. Maybe I'll come back later."

He looked at her. "Sit down. Please. Don't come back later. You're not making things worse. You're just damn odd, that's all."

She sat back down. Simpson put the peanut better and jelly away, got out a bottle of store-bought beer and began drinking from it after she declined a bottle. She watched him drink.

"I don't see why you think I'm odd."

He wiped his mouth clear of foam and smiled.

"Well, Jesus Christ."

She reached into her pocket and took out a cigarette.

"You still haven't told me about yourself."

Simpson took a deep breath, sat upright, and began a mock television-announcer monologue: "Well, it's like this Arlene: I was born forty-five years ago in San Anselmo, California, the son of a veterinarian. After public schooling I went to the California Merchant Marine Academy where I graduated..."

When she began laughing he motioned for her to quiet down.

"...finishing about in the middle of my class. After that I shipped as a third mate on various vessels of United States registry until I sat for my second mate's license; then I began shipping as a second mate. After that I shipped for twelve years until I sat for my first mate's ticket. I flunked that, shipped out again for a year on a Panamanian freighter, then sat for my first mate's ticket again; passed. I was married twice and divorced twice by the same woman by the time I was thirty-four. I have a grown son and daughter, but I've lived alone for ten years. Three years ago I took all my savings, moved north, and had the dory custom made in Tacoma from old Norwegian designs. I've been fishing ever since. I do pretty good. My hobbies are making and drinking home brew, raising geese and a few chickens, and carving old sailboats out of cedar."

Her laughter had drowned out most of his monologue, and Simpson joined her. Both of them laughed until he stopped suddenly.

"Well, you are an odd one, Arlene. But your boy is a good boy and he can go out with me again if he wants. And as my friend."

"Thank you. Roy will like that very much."

He motioned towards the door.

"How would you like to go downtown and maybe I'll buy you and Roy dinner?"

She shook her head, smiling.

"No, not really. I would perhaps like half a beer. Anyway, Roy's asleep now. You know, it is three in the morning."

He opened another beer, poured her a glass and sat back down.

"Do you want me to leave, Mr. Simpson."

"Well, actually not."

They both smiled, and as Simpson looked at her he decided that she had a very good smile. In spite of the fact that she was odd.

Reports of Disappearances II: The Congressmen

They were flying south from Anchorage when their plane was reported overdue.

There hadn't been any mayday, or even a transmission concerning anything amiss. Any U.S. Congressman would have stirred up more-than-ordinary concern, but with such a powerful figure as the Majority Leader of the U.S. House of Representatives lost, plus his Alaska colleague, the story went nationwide.

The search was of historical magnitude. Military and civilian personnel used ground parties, ships, and all sizes and varieties of aircraft, including the U.S. Navy's Blackbird spy plane with diverse types of photographic capabilities. Even the use of oceanographic vessels with special echo-locators were employed in areas where a ditching might have been plausible.

We all had theories, most of them focusing on the pilot, a somewhat daring Alaskan known for pushing the limits of weather. We all understood the dangers of too much bravado.

The search went on well into the second month, but eventually it ended. The water and rugged terrain had behaved like a dumb stubborn beast, swallowing whole something about which it hadn't care or knowledge. No amount of effort could make it divulge where or what it had done with the congressmen and their pilot.

In Memory of Hawks

Eskimo Joe watches Austrian television while drinking dark beer.

This is my welcoming sight when I return from another day trip to Vienna, trudging the entire way from the train station. On the television screen dances an Austrian version of the nightly news. The German words pelt Joe's confused brows, confronting him with linguistic mysteries.

"Do you understand what the hell they're talking about?"

I don't, and I say so. We've exchanged the same dialogue a half dozen times since I purchased the television. I realize it's not a question; it's an indictment. He continues.

"I understand some of the pictures. See. That's the President; that's his wife. But look: Who's that?"

"Did you find out what's the matter with the car?"

"Water pump."

I wander into the kitchen and put water on for tea. While waiting for it to boil I look out the side window towards the Danube River: A gentle slope descends towards this landmark. It is a quilted countryside of farmland that has been tilled since the Caesars. The fields are dotted with ricks of hay. Nearby, a pair of apple trees have turned rust ochre with the autumn nights. Midday shadows become longer, and the sun rises and sets to the southwest.

While I dab a tea bag in scalding water, the ancient cottage vibrates slightly as a truck rumbles by on the nearby road.

It is indeed true: Joe and I are securely hidden here.

Cup in hand, I push through the backdoor and into the yard to see the hawks. There is a maze of pens and feeding trays. Some of the pens are large, others smaller. The hawks look towards me with steady eyes. Several flit to their feeding trays, bending down and peering at bare wood with hopes of an early feeding. I whistle lowly and familiarly and several others strut about on their perches, pacing. There are thirty-six hawks, thirty-nine falcons, and six eagles.

We are the guardians of these birds and our days in Austria are centered on the care of them, a task we both hope will soon end.

To the right, hidden from the view of the birds of prey, is the chicken pen, culls that we buy from surrounding farms. Several dozen of them step about high-legged as if wading an invisible creek. They peck at feed troughs, deadly ignorant of their relationship to the hawks.

I walk around the corner and mentally select six culls for the evening feeding. Chickens, be they North American or European, are related through profound stupidity. Slowly I go to the feeding hut and begin the evening rite. The clatter of equipment is unmistakable. Outside a few of the hawks call out; even more fly to their trays to wait.

The chickens flap miserably as they're seized and hoisted by their legs.

ii.

About six miles out of the ancient town of Krems, Austria, seemed the best place to raise the hawks. Joe hadn't arrived yet since I needed no help with eggs and incubator. I'd found the small cottage and adjoining land within four days of arriving in Austria. It was late June.

The cottage belonged to Frau Gertz, a widow. She speaks halting yet clear English. Somewhat stooped at the shoulders she has a face fixed in sadness with clear white, wrinkled skin; above a firmly set mouth is a white downy mustache. Frau Gertz looks out upon the world through sharp, blue eyes.

Removing a key chain from its peg, she walked slowly towards the road, hand pressed into the tiny hollow of her back.

"Please to follow."

During the half-kilometer walk from her house to the cottage she talked about her son and complained about tourist buses creating a nuisance on the narrow lane. Even as we walked, one of the giant vehicles forced us to step off the road and press anxiously against a hedgerow fence. Heads bobbed and weaved, looking down at us from behind tinted glass rectangles. Frau Gertz swept away the road dust with a delicately veined hand and stepped back onto the road.

"My son married a woman who was ambitious, and now they are gone to Salzburg six years ago."

As soon as I saw Frau Gertz's cottage I knew it was right: Secluded and far enough off the road to be quiet, but close enough for moving materials and feed. Finally the questions:

"Where in the States is the American gentleman from?"

"Anchorage, Alaska."

"Alaska! Ach! Very cold in Alaska."

I hoped that would conclude the questions. But no.

"'Herr Peale': It is pronounced right, *ja?*"

"Correct. John Peale."

"What will you do here, Herr Peale?"

"Raise birds. I'm a visiting professor studying at the University in Vienna. Hawks. I study *falke.*"

"Ach so! Falke."

She nodded and then looked beyond the cottage towards an utterly clear sky, repeating *falke* once more.

"My husband loved hawks. Very much. My husband died in the war but loved hawks when he was alive on the farm."

On the return walk to her house, she hardly spoke. During the following weeks she has referred to me as Herr Professor Peale and I don't correct her. On the drive back in to Vienna after securing the farm, I was amazed how easily I lied to the elderly Frau Gertz.

iii.

It is May.

A motel in Tulakana, Alaska, is a night's respite from camping.

Joe applies a salve to hands chaffed badly from the climbing ropes. We had visited nine nests in an eighteen-hour period. It was our best day. Thirty-seven eggs.

While I make adjustments on the portable incubator, Joe leans back and, delicately using thumb and forefinger, lifts a beer to his lips. A VCR plays a movie neither of us watches.

"Do you feel bad about what you're doing?"

My hands stop their work. I feel a visceral roll, as if suddenly reminded of a sadness.

"Bad?"

"Guilty, I guess."

In the next room an oil exploration crew laughs above the sound of a tape player. A beer bottle slams into a trash can followed by a whoop. Joe looks steadily at me as I muster a reply.

"I spent twenty-five years taking care of hawks and hawk country; now they're going to take care of me."

My voice nearly squeezes off the words.

Joe rests a careful eye on me while holding the beer between two calloused fingers. Lifting the bottle, he drinks, nodding and swallowing in the same action.

"I can understand that."

The next morning Joe falls. At the end of the safety line he swings as a clock pendulum would swing. Flat on my buttocks, I dig my heels into the rock while the female gyrfalcon menaces, banging my helmet and screeching against this outrage, the male whirled above, talons down, angry.

Through the tautness of the line, I feel Joe strike the face of the cliff; he struggles grimly to regain footing and does. Just.

An hour later we sit on a level plateau while I apply antiseptic to scrapes and gouges. Joe trembles, a face frozen in wonder.

"I'm fifty-three, you're forty-nine. This is stupid. We are no longer young men."

Beyond us the Sitkin Mountain range flexes upwards into a gray sky that still maintains the dangerous winds of winter. Thick layers of snow weigh heavily upon the steep shoulders of the mountains. Great schooners of clouds tumble from the north, pregnant with icy squalls.

Below us in the river valley, a pair of golden eagles circle patiently.

We are indeed no longer young men.

iv.

It is twilight. The fledgling hawks and myself observe Joe exit the cottage, beer in hand. Recently fed, the young birds watch as Joe slowly drags an old chair into the center of the pens, gives me a disapproving look, and observes, "We have responsibilities Herr Professor Peale." Something he's come to call me in the manner of Frau Gertz.

He mounts the chair; the hawks fidget. In the feeding shack, an old radio plays music from a string quartet. Joe steadies himself by gripping the back of the chair. Then he stands straight. During the afternoon and evening, over a dozen liters of heavy Austrian beers have rendered his face long and solemn. Again he looks at me. "We have responsibilities Herr Professor Peale."

Taking a sip of beer, he stoops and puts the bottle down. Joe begins a transformation: His legs bend slightly, his back assumes a gentle arc, and slowly his arms come out to full length. He holds this pose.

Now his wrists turn, and his hands angle upwards. Then, gradually, he begins flapping, as if flying underwater. The arms work in unison, the wrists constantly adjusting. Joe's voice is heavy with the beer. "We must teach these hawks to fly."

One leg is lifted free of the chair, arms and hands still sweeping up and down. The hawks study this; several fly from one end of their pen to the other and cock their heads in wonder. A large female gyrfalcon lifts her wings. Unlike Joe she flaps them rapidly, calling out shrill notes.

I look on remembering Frau Gertz's words from three days before. She'd taken me aside when I paid the rent. Holding me by the elbow she tapped her chin with a cautious finger. "Herr Professor Peale, your assistant is a very eccentric man. He must be an artist."

Several other birds join in, and the force of the driven air causes tufts of their drunken tutor's hair to flutter against a sweaty forehead. The shadows against the cottage reflect the beating of the gyrfalcons' long, narrow wings. They are superimposed in silhouetted counterpoint over Joe's arms that rise and descend evenly. I hear the music in the background despite the beating of wings.

v.

Midsummer in Vienna.

Ludolf takes the corner of his napkin and dabs at his eyes.

"*Ach!* Such a pass things have come to, John."

We have lunch at an outdoor cafe in the *volksgarten*. We are shielded by awnings from a strong July sun. Trees and carefully sculpted flower beds create a calm; beyond this streetcars and autos rumble by. Close to a nearby fountain, children throw a large ball for a dog.

Ludolf had greeted me by saying this was his favorite outdoor cafe. He hadn't known about my sudden and unfortunate retirement and certainly not about the hawks. It had been difficult for him.

I consider Ludolf and not my fall from scientific grace. Two decades ago he had been a robust Austrian taxidermist in search of hawks, clothed in dirndl mountaineering garb despite the Sitkin Mountain range being nine thousand miles away from Austria. Now he's an elderly gentleman of seventy-six with a cane and part of his intestines removed as deftly as he removed many a specimen's viscera. The skin of his hands is thin, nearly translucent; he still wears the dirndl dress, but he is old and no longer goes into the mountains. It occurs to me that soon I too will no longer go into the mountains.

A waiter slides two cups of coffee and a plate holding cheese and evenly sliced bread with deeply browned crusts. I push the coffee closer to Ludolf who stuffs his handkerchief back in a too-small vest pocket. Words seem necessary.

"Ludolf, old friend, I thought about this for months." There is a sudden catch in my throat and I hesitate. A short-lived breeze causes the awning to flutter. I force a smile without knowing its purpose. "These birds, my friend, will eventually live in the courts of Omar Khayyam. They and their offspring will be the lords of their kind after we're long dead."

Ludolf takes a slice of bread, sighs, places cheese on it and bites. As an afterthought, he removes the handkerchief again and dabs at his cheek. His large head bobs upward, and I notice that his eyes are as sharp and knowing as Frau Gertz's.

"And Joe? My good friend Eskimo Joe? He is with you in this dismal business?"

But he knows Joe is with me in Austria and nods his own answer. His eyes leave me, looking towards the children playing. His big chest heaves a sigh.

"There have been good times, no?"

"Yes."

He smiles for only a moment, then suddenly remembers the occasion. "I will help you but not for money."

As we stroll from the park I remember our only pair of kestrels. From his past visits to Alaska I recall his endless praise of the tiny falcons.

"OK. But I want you to have a pair of kestrels." He attempts to interrupt. "No, no, Ludolf. You'll keep them well and I want to do something. I'll bring them in next time."

We exit the *volksgarten* and walk along the wide boulevard where Ludolf will climb aboard a streetcar and return home. He nods, then tips his hat to passing nuns; hooking me by the arm, he leads me to a bench. The great expanse of overhanging trees affords plentiful shade, yet Ludolf removes a handkerchief and dries his brow.

"John, these Arabs will soon come to Vienna for a conference. They will need to know a price."

"They go as a single lot. There are seventy-nine birds, all wild North American stock. So, $750,000."

I reach down and retrieve Ludolf's walking stick that he's let fall.

"Gottinhimmel!"

When I help him onto his streetcar, Ludolf still is muttering. The economics of this situation have finally taken on clearer proportions.

vi.

The previous year in Anchorage.

Dr. Harlan Pierce is a tall, bony man who keeps dozens of potted plants in his office. Between two mammoth ferns is a cage with two Panamanian golden finches which hop about peeping through thick red beaks. Since he is the Regional Director, his prize is a corner tenth-floor suite.

With sleeves rolled up and watering can held above his head, he tended several massive hanging plants.

Without turning around he announced, "My ferns have mites." Then he put the watering can down. To his credit, there was no attempt to conceal the issue at hand.

"John, I'm sorry to say your Predator Bird project has been eliminated. I suppose you suspected. Surely you know the situation with Department funding."

His hands are large and smooth except for bulbous knuckles. He grasps a clear glass paperweight with a gaudily armored beetle embedded in it, a memento from his days researching bats in tropical Puerto Rico.

"Why me? There are over thirty projects in this office?"

He formulated an answer as I studied the mountains beyond Cook Inlet. The grayish waters were choked with ice floes that drifted in and out with the tides. On the shoreline two dogs pursued early arriving gulls which soared upwards in a cold vernal wind.

Why me? Those are the words from memories.

It seemed the hawks, Eskimo Joe, and I were esoterica. Ducks and geese, you can shoot; caribou, you can hunt; environmental assessment was work politically justifiable; enforcement work, necessary.

"Then there are the falls, John."

I struggled from the grip of memories and looked up. It occurred to me that Dr. Harlan Pierce was nearly fifteen years younger than I. People talked of his ambitions. The paperweight had been pushed aside and his hands had locked together atop his desk.

"Falls?"

Over the twenty-five years I was guilty of falls: into crevices, from the faces of cliffs, down through the branches of tall cottonwoods. Months of convalescence. Why continue to face the infirmities of mended bones and aching rheumatic joints?

There followed words about honorable service and arrangements to consume the eight months before my coming twenty-fifth year, a warehouse needing inventory work, schools needing educational slide presentations. Dr. Harlan Pierce looked at me sympathetically and held his hands palms upwards. His voice cradled words.

"John, I'm not about to see you lose your retirement. Eight months is a small budgetary sacrifice. We can do that much for you."

A week later I was in Bethel, Alaska, placing soiled ten dollar bills into the palm of a city clerk. Bail was met. In this way a meeting between Joe and me was effected.

We sat in a small cafe. Joe struggled to contain trembling hands as he hoisted a coffee cup to his lips. The sounds and smells of breakfast resulted in a momentary quiver, then finally he sipped, held his breath, and sighed.

"When do we start?"

"There is no start. Project is over."

The coffee cup moved lower. Reddish eyes peered at me over the rim. A small bead of coffee worked its way down his chin.

"Just like that?"

"Just like that."

Outside a truck wallowed by in the slop of spring thaw, grinding the road to a mushy pulp. The strains of a country western ballad struggled through the electronic maladies of a battered jukebox. Carefully Joe brought the cup to his lips, sipped deeply, and swallowed. There was a nearly inaudible groan but little more.

I tried to think of something else to add, but there was nothing more to say.

vii.

I take the streetcar to the end of the line. Walking past a soccer field and huge warehouses, I reach the banks of the Danube.

This river is *Donau* as written in German, and it is not blue.

I consider forty-nine years. Digging into a yellow envelope with an impatient finger, I remove my retirement check: $475.32. This will possibly pay for repairs to the ancient Mercedes if Joe cannot repair it.

Today I left the cottage and walked to the railway station in Krems with hopes of cheering up, but this didn't happen.

In Vienna a small package of mail arrived at the Cook's Travel Office. The little English lady bade me good day and gently handed the parcel through the slot in the door. "Oh, Mr. Peale, you have good fortune today."

I retreat to a nearby coffeehouse, order a hot pastry and pot of tea, then begin sorting. It is all for me, and none for Joe. In addition to my retirement check, the inventory of letters and packages is brief:

-A birthday card from my daughter including a note which reads, in part, "We should write more."

-A letter from a former brother-in-law from Texas wanting to hunt bear in Alaska: "I need a really trophy-sized bear rug."

-A package of fall/winter catalogs tied neatly in a bundle.

-A tiny envelope which had been trapped in the mass of catalogs. When it drops out, I see it's addressed in a familiar hand: Ludolf's.

I open this quickly.

"Fahir bin Sharif will arrive with the Oil Ministers in one week. But I urge caution. Customs Officers have asked after you. Ludolf."

I sense a coldness stabbing downward.

As I review hundreds of carefully made plans, my tea cools and I pay my bill, the pastry left half eaten. Late morning wandering leads me to the banks of the Danube and considerations of possible failure.

My fingers remove the birthday card and on the cover are two large numbers: *Five-Zero*. For reasons I don't understand, this reminds me I've lived alone for the last twenty-two years and that I've never wanted to. I re-read the message on the birthday card and it occurs to me I barely know my own daughter, and in fact vaguely recall her mother.

"I always sent them money."

This is testimony delivered to an impassive Danube River. I see people walking down a promenade paralleling the wide river. A woman pushes a spacious baby carriage, the type popular in the states years ago. She stops, reaches down, and tucks a blanket around the infant. There is a bit of cooing.

A jogger runs by, twists momentarily at the waist, and calls something over to the woman who waves. The jogger dodges two children who drive wide wooden hoops with sticks; it has been years since I've seen this game played by children. They stop and peer into the baby carriage.

Slowly I again open Ludolf's note:

"Fahir bin Sharif will arrive with the Oil Ministers in one week. But I urge caution. Customs Officers have asked after you. Ludolf."

Quickly I look behind me in the direction of the empty soccer stadium and see a lone car parked near streetcar tracks which had fallen into disuse. Squinting, I think I see someone in the car, but shading my eyes I decide it's empty.

I rise and walk down to the promenade, past the children who still admire the baby carriage and woman, and I stroll downriver. I'm tempted to call Ludolf, but this would be foolish. He has told me all I need to know right now.

I recall several recent conversations with Ludolf: Caution is a word I'd used to console him about not telling him the location of Frau Gertz's cottage. He had been hurt. I explained there would never be a need for him to conceal what he didn't know. He nodded judiciously and approved.

Boarding another streetcar, I get off and reboard others until I reach the *Sudbahnhof*. Waiting the thirty minutes for the train, I buy a *Herald Tribune* and, while settling into reading, see a woman sitting at a nearby table. I'm fascinated by her and try to think why until she gives me a hostile stare. It's this hostility that gives me the necessary clue. She reminds me of Laurie twenty-eight years ago: Tall with auburn hair and large green eyes that always disapproved. "You have a lack of ambition, John. A lack of ambition."

Feeling the heat of these old words, I get up and walk towards the train, slapping the folded newspaper against my leg in rhythm to my stride.

While I'm on the train to Krems, I decide to purchase an Austrian suit since I'm still wearing American clothing.

It is time to think of blending in.

viii.

In the village of Old Spruce spring winds descend from the Sitkin Mountains rendering the words of Eskimo Joe and his ex-wife Lena nearly inaudible. In the next room I lie on a hot water bottle trying to make the pain vanish. Soon there is a promise of relief: The pills begin to take hold, and the heat seeps through my aching hip into my groin.

Lena narrates past wrongs to Joe.

"You never loved me or took care of me. You don't know how to treat a woman. You are a bad man."

The wind yields a few seconds of quiet and I hear a cap unscrewed from a bottle of bourbon. Joe allows her indictment to unroll without defense. Once again, the old house yields to the wind by fractions of inches, complaining of old age with words formed from creaking boards and rattling windows. In a drugged oasis I afford myself the luxury of recalling local folklore.

There are three Joe's in this area: Dancing Joe, Anchorage Joe, and Eskimo Joe. The first two are Eskimos, whereas the last is not, having earned that sobriquet after five hard-fought marriages, each to Eskimo women. Someone chuckles out loud.

Is that me?

My brain fuzzes as pain crawls into my middle. My hold on the bed frame recalls the harsh grip of talons.

Then slowly a soft drugged hand reaches out and caresses me while I sink into confused dreams. Either in a dream or from the other room I hear voices. They draw away from me, and I sleep.

A gust of wind causes the bed to shiver. I open my eyes. The other room is dark and the wind increased, assailing the house with the edge of a cold, sharp sword. A small light reflects oily globes that are Joe's eyes. Sitting on the floor, legs crossed and cradling a bottle, he stares. He thrusts two fingers before me.

"Two more days of egging. Hold up for just two more days then." He lowers the fingers to the neck of the bottle, and runs the pad of an index finger around the capless rim. "And it's Austria and big money, John. So, hold on. Lena said it's this wind that has brought pain."

He nods at his own words, turns over, and, tucking his bony legs into his chest, sleeps. The bottle rolls in a semicircle while disgorging its contents, the freed vapors burning my nostrils.

I feel the wind and remember a childhood fear of its sound and force. This was on the flat country, away from these mountains that have beaten me, where steam-driven locomotives opened their throats and cried with a wanderer's song.

I think of these days and recall the beauty of painless sleep.

ix.

Fahir bin Sharif greets me in the garden of the Embassy of the Royal Sultanate of Qatar. Servants have set a massive glass-topped table near a fountain; strong coffee is served in tiny cups. Fahir bin Sharif is in Western dress except for a burnoose. He holds the diminutive cup between his thumb and forefinger and says the Sultan's business secretary will soon join them.

I can't decide whether there is a semblance of a smile as he repeats the business secretary's name. Fahir bin Sharif gestures towards a vast fountain where water tumbles down from smaller to successively larger tiers. Thick vines with wide marbled leaves grow on each tier which finally spills water into a pool carefully wrought with ornate tile. An underwater mosaic depicts massive Arabian steeds, riders with hooded peregrine falcons poised on outstretched arms.

"All this water, it is beautiful, no?"

Only after taking in the wonder of the whole do I see that the steeds' eyes are large green emeralds and those of the falcons yellow topaz. Goldfish with vast membranous fins swim lazily across this mosaic. Fahir bin Sharif hasn't yet mentioned the reason for our appointment, but he picks up a plate of confections and gently offers.

"These are prepared by the finest bakers from my country. Please."

In a lunch the day previous, Ludolf had prepared me for bargaining with so much advice that I forget all except one thing: "Fahir bin Sharif can be trusted explicitly. He is above chicanery. But trust no one else."

Noiselessly, the business secretary strides around the fountain and, following Fahir bin Sharif's lead, I rise for introductions. Leaving us standing, the business secretary picks up a sweet cake from a platter and breaks it into pieces, spreading the crumbs with sweeps of his arm, feeding the fish. Their golden bodies twist with excitement, breaking the surface to get the crumbs.

The business secretary is severe, a man used to the suddenness of power. He wears full Arab dress and has small, dark eyes that lock immediately on mine.

We all sit.

"This price you ask for has been dismissed by His Royal Eminence as unreasonable."

There follows somewhat over a half hour of intense bargaining, with Fahir bin Sharif saying nothing. Finally the business secretary stops, saying something in Arabic to His Royal Eminence's Keeper of Hawks, who nods quickly.

"Then I agree to your price, after suitable inspection of the hawks, naturally. This will be arranged at once."

We all stand as the business secretary stands, and without another word he leaves us. I loath him, angered by this bargaining. Fahir bin Sharif clears his throat gently.

"He is a direct man, as is the nature with men of business. Let us have some American bourbon to celebrate this arrangement, a toast to his Royal Eminence's noteworthy acquisition and to the conclusion of what must have been arduous work for you and your assistant."

"How did you know I had an assistant?"

"Ludolf, of course. He and I are friends of long standing, as you know."

We retire to a small library; most of the volumes are in English, though a few are in Arabic. A servant brings the bourbon and, while drinking, we sit in overstuffed chairs and I listen to Fahir bin Sharif discuss falconry. After a genial atmosphere has been established and the bourbon has caught hold, we negotiate the potentially complicated business of payment and simultaneous delivery of the hawks.

Before we part we shake hands. His grip is firm and steady, though clearly he is unused to this western custom.

It isn't until I'm upon the streets of Vienna and boarding a streetcar for the *Sudbahnhof* that it occurs to me that my time in Austria is at an end. Though a chilled autumn rain brushes the street, I walk into the train station feeling a heady optimism. This is an unusual sensation for me.

Suddenly I recall the need for caution.

After all, there is Ludolf's message to consider. Yet a week afterwards I had received a letter downplaying its importance. When we met for lunch Ludolf was apologetic about it.

"I was hasty, John. It was during the monthly inspections of my shop and store. The officials only asked because friends from Alaska are worried about you, your long absence without contact. And they know of our long association."

Despite a sense of reassurance I remain cautious. I take different routes to and from Vienna each time I go. With Joe's repair of the ancient Mercedes, I've taken to parking at various railway stations then commuting into Vienna.

An urge to visit Ludolf and tell him the news overwhelms me, and though not subject to whim, I succumb. In my life I've been too regular, a creature attached and sheltered in regular habits. Walking from the station, I hail a taxi. My first since arriving.

I arrive at Ludolf's just prior to dinner time.

He works carefully over a giant European brown trout. His grandson Horst shows me through the store and display room, then into the large workroom where all the finely wrought equipment of his profession is situated with the perfection of years. Through binocular magnifying glasses, Ludolf's eyes are saucer shaped and liquid, enhancing his surprise.

"Why, John, this is a surprise."

When Horst leaves, I quickly tell him of my success at the Embassy of Qatar. Carefully he covers his work and nods.

"Good. I am not surprised."

And it's true, he doesn't look surprised.

In the late afternoon I walk alongside Ludolf towards a park. I suggest an early dinner and he agrees. "But first, I walk, John. The oldness in my limbs, stooped over and working all day. First a walk."

We enter the park. The hardwood trees begin to suggest the yellow and gold of autumn, and a few leaves sprinkle the immaculate lawns. Ponds and fountains are being drained for winter and workmen scrub them with long-bristled brushes. One of the workmen knows Ludolf and they chat, then we resume.

Pigeons strut about at the feet of an elderly lady who painfully reaches into a bag and removes bread crumbs. They coo, flutter, and hop impatiently upon her lap and feet struggling for food.

We come upon a hill where a path of finely crushed rock descends towards a small creek which has been landscaped carefully. Brick paths parallel both banks; benches constructed of heavy wood with ornate, wrought-iron frames are adjacent to the paths. Ludolf stops and looks down.

"Sadly these are all the signs of winter, John."

As I draw alongside him a mysterious sorrow is clear, almost tactile. He hooks the handle of his cane over the handrail, grips it with both hands, and shakes his head.

"Ludolf, is something wrong?"

He looks at me. His eyes are moist. His lids close and open as if hoping for sleep.

"John, you have been betrayed. Doubly betrayed. In Alaska, now here. You must leave Austria at once."

Ludolf's feet suddenly fail him, and he leans forward, putting nearly all his weight on the rail. I grab his arm, and quickly we manage to sit down on a nearby bench. Gripping his cane with one knobby hand atop the other, he stares at the ground, then looks up at me. A large but old hand reaches out and takes my shoulder and shakes it gently. "At once, John." He looks sadly at me, begins to say something but stops. After a moment he adds, "I will say nothing of this meeting to them. I hope to God they didn't follow you here."

I study the old man and he looks away, actually down. There is a barely discernible groan, and all I can feel is a whirl of confusion.

"Why, Ludolf? For God's sakes, why?"

"The kestrels, John. They found them, threatened to suspend my license, impound my shop and store unless I cooperate. I could lose decades of specimens. My daughter and grandson Horst, this is their heritage. *Gottenhimmel,* John, I am so old and weak. These American officials are intense, righteous men. Austrian officials do their bidding. They wish to make an example of you. For God's sake, leave while there is time."

He left me sitting on the bench. I still feel the weight of his hand on my shoulder. Turning from the waist I see him hunched, shuffling down the path, the cane probing the ground ahead of him. Leaves drift down from the trees, turning, spinning, and coming to rest.

Soon, I see Ludolf no more.

x.

The Sitkin Mountains in late spring.

The storm catches us at high elevations. Winds that blow down from the summits have their own vocabulary. Joe and I listen while pressed futilely against the rock wall of a narrow mountain sheep path.

Soon the rains come, bending sideways with the winds; I think it the coldest rain I've experienced, but when I wipe my face my hand brings away slush. Joe's eyes tell me what I know: We must find a temporary shelter.

Though familiar with this area, I realize this path is unfamiliar. Yet soon we stumble around a sharp bend and find a small alcove. I watch Joe climb over stubble into the alcove while I carefully follow, crying out several times from the pain in my pelvis. The alcove affords us a leeward vantage point from which to watch the storm unfold.

Taking off the pack which contains the eggs, I dig out pain pills and swallow a double dose. Soon the codeine eases into my system and I enjoy the feeling of the storm.

These mountains are gray and seem to invite spring squalls to wash their ancient faces. The winds cause a continual background roar which I listen to with respect. At this altitude no vegetation interrupts the rocky sculpting which rises on all sides forming a narrow pass.

The sleet turns to snow.

Because the day is warm, the flakes melt immediately. Yet each flake is the size of an infant's hand; they plummet from out of the low clouds. Looking up I try to follow just one on its path downward, but they fall too fast, and I get dizzy. Closing my eyes I listen intently to the sounds of the winds build to a full storm.

I'm surprised to feel warm; I realize Joe has put a double layer of plastic blankets over me from our emergency kits. When I open my eyes, he sits above me in the alcove. He too looks out at the storm while chewing a piece of dried venison.

Closing my eyes, I fall asleep at once.

xi.

It is late evening. I realize, oddly for the first time, that I share something with these hawks: All of us were born without parents in attendance.

As I prepare the feed I am surrounded by the hawks which worry their feed troughs, jostling for a favorable position. The fully barred adult plumages are apparent on most, and their wildness is obvious. Or is it?

In the cottage Joe sits chatting lugubriously at the television in a mixture of English, Yupik, and what few words of German he'd learned in four months.

In the autumn chill of the Austrian air, I sense the memories of the Sitkin Mountains and look up before recalling where I am. Quietly I work from feed station to feed station, and the hawks struggle for their share. While I wash my hands I hear their curious feeding vocalizations, high-pitched and rapid.

"It was Lena. That's how they got onto us."

Thinking of other matters, I'm startled by Joe. Supporting himself by hands thrust against each door jamb, he stares at me from the back door of the cottage. Hair hangs down over his eyes; the yard lights cast strange shadows on his face, and all I can see are his eyes blinking slowly.

His feet shuffling in the dirt, he turns carefully and goes inside. If he were sober he'd realize it doesn't make any difference now. I hear Joe's weight fall violently upon the couch; then I hear the snoring.

Their feeding now finished, the birds quiet down.

If these hawks were like me they would try to imagine their parents. In dreams they would picture them strong and free in the winds of the Sitkin Mountains, eyes ready for prey.

I dream, but of the Reverend William S. Peale and his wife Ella May. He was the Doctor and she the Mistress of Divinity. At night I would peek into their bedroom and see them asleep, two somnolent bodies lying precisely parallel. Even now I can see the Reverend Peale's lips forming the word "adopted," and the squeak of his rocker as he twisted at the waist to look through lace curtains at the world outside.

After their death I have only their name. But I dreamed the truth of my real parents, and at night I knew them. Perhaps I imagined them to be like the parents of these hawks.

There is now the matter of the birds.

As I turn out the yard lights and enter the cottage, I feel the constancy of their eyes. This makes me uncomfortable. Slowly I pick up empty bottles of beer, relocate Joe's left leg from the floor onto the sofa, and enter my own bedroom. I am not comfortable reading and cannot sleep. Into the night I listen to radio and somehow doze off. In my sleep I hear, "We have responsibilities, Herr Professor Peale," and I wake to find the radio playing and Joe snoring in a muted rattle. Almost at once I'm asleep again.

xii.

At the Krems railway station, Joe and I sit looking upon a light sprinkling of snow which whitens nearby mountains. Joe wears a billed hat emblazoned with an American baseball club's logo, new running shoes with lithographed wings on each heel, and a shirt stenciled with, "Where the Hell is Togiak, Alaska?" Somehow he interprets this as a disguise and I say nothing, anxious for him to make the train west to Munich. That morning we had argued, and we're not over it. Falling back on nearly a quarter century of being the biologist and him the field assistant, I had resorted to an order and we had exchanged foul words. The elderly and frail Mercedes was kicked, a suitcase was thrown into the back too hard. And there was silence.

It is an hour to train time and the minutes pass awkwardly. A woman comes by selling hot rolls; trains arrive from Vienna and depart in a whirl of dust. There is the smell of stale air with each passing train and the wind bites uncomfortably. Finally Joe sits up and imperceptibly looks my way.

"What are you going to do alone?"

"I'm going to release all the birds, clean up every possible remnant of their presence, turn the key over to Frau Gertz, and do like Ludolf suggested: Get out. Probably to Portugal. Portugal is cheap."

Joe nods and lifts his head suddenly as a vagrant wisp of air brings scents from the station's bar. Then he frowns.

"They'd all die. Every one of them. You won't do that. But you won't tell me what you're going to do, will you?"

Since he's calmed, I communicate the travel arrangements instead of answering him.

"Stay in London three or four days before flying over to Anchorage. If they ask why you were in Austria so long, tell them you were in Salzburg for the music."

I hand him a packet of tickets and money and, because of the late morning cold, we both rise and walk into the bar. I buy a *Herald Tribune* and we share the paper. We have several hot brandies without saying anything. I glance up to see Joe looking over the top of the paper.

"When Elmer drowned, I didn't have money for a casket. Not even enough to pay the priest for the funeral mass."

I remember Elmer's funeral ten years before: Joe's only son, Elmer had remained in the village with his mother and had died in a fishing accident. The newspaper seems sticky in my hand; Joe's eyes are specks, intent on something unfathomable.

"Do you think Lena held that against you."

"Probably. Probably. You know, if you ever come back to Alaska, they'll put you away from a long time."

"Yes. Alaska is not good for me right now. I'm not so sure about you."

When the train for Munich pulls in I find it impossible to say good-bye to Joe. We are nine thousand miles from home and both of us are uncertain if we will see each other again. I repeat the travel plans, then feel stupid. Pulling open a door, he drags up his suitcase behind him. After a silent shake of hands, we nod silently at one another. I push the door closed and watch the train pull away.

The slow click of the wheels over tracks becomes faster. Then the train to Munich is gone.

xiii.

Across the street from the Embassy of the Royal Sultanate of Qatar, I wait in an uncomfortably small tea shop for evidence of a decision. Though anything but an expert on the Arab mind, I rely on the human characteristic of gaining much for nothing as being international.

The hard work of completing the construction of suitable carrying containers during the preceding two days has irritated my hip, and the ebony walking stick I effected with my new dirndl clothing now serves a real purpose. After parking the rented van in front of the Embassy, I hobble across the wide flagstone street to the cafe.

Ridding myself of the hawks has been anticlimactic since I'm confident of my plan. Because of the hard work at Frau Gertz's cottage, I'm able to deliver the hawks before the Embassy of Qatar a day early. I carefully deliver a note to the receptionist that explains my conditions to Fahir bin Sharif: He can have all the hawks for nothing simply by not informing my government of our arrangement. On the day of the arranged delivery (hence my apprehension), I simply won't show. His government's end of the bargain would be satisfied. My non-appearance would simply remain unexplained.

Within forty-five minutes Fahir bin Sharif and two men exit the Embassy. With Fahir bin Sharif standing at a distance the two men, obviously expert in their craft, inspect the vehicle without touching it. Finally they open the hood, then the door; then they slide up the rear door. At that point Fahir bin Sharif enters and inspects the birds. While one remains on guard, the other two return to the Embassy.

I read the entire newspaper, plus do the crossword puzzle. With difficulty, I force myself to remain calm. I know the critical decision is being made within the Embassy walls. Then an intriguing event happens: A side entrance opens in the Embassy and a half dozen men, keen-eyed and nervous, exit and deploy at strategic intervals. Then Fahir bin Sharif precedes his Eminence's business secretary onto the street, followed by two giants in traditional Arab dress flanking a much smaller man, who, except for a burnoose, wears a standard business suit. They walk to the truck, and while everyone, save Fahir bin Sharif, waits outside, His Eminence inspects the van's contents.

After they exit, Fahir bin Sharif nods to the guards, and within a minute everyone, along with the van, has disappeared through a rear gate. The Embassy resumes its stolid calm to Vienna's busy weekday streets.

Despite watching a fortune disappear, I feel a victory. Within a day the hawks will be secure within the palace walls in Qatar. They will not become zoo or museum specimens, which past experience has shown is inevitable in situations involving international confiscation. They will live long and well in the shadowed halls of sultans.

As I leave the cafe my initial feeling of victory leaves me. Leaning heavily on my walking stick, I enter the subway before I'm able to recognize the return of a pervasive melancholy which of late is my steady companion.

xiv.

From the kitchen window of Frau Gertz's cottage I watch the onset of an Austrian winter. In the mornings fine frescoes of ice decorate the corners of the window. Having sold the Mercedes, I walk to market in the increasingly crisp afternoon sun. With irony I think of my trunk of winter clothing in Anchorage.

Frau Gertz clucks in concern and loans me her son's old winter great-coat. During the afternoons I clean up the yard, bundling garbage and hauling it away in a wheelbarrow. This work reminds me of days helping Mrs. Reverend Peale clean one parsonage before moving to another. "Always leave something cleaner than you found it, John. It's the Godly way."

At fifty years of age I bend and clean and carry, continuing this heritage.

Several days before I leave, Frau Gertz has me over for dinner. It is a formal affair with her complete finery, and it includes a young grandniece who first serves the dinner, then clears and washes the dishes before quietly leaving. Over brandy I look at Frau Gertz's photograph album: I slowly leaf by sons, daughters, and their offspring who look moodily at the camera. The lens records the family of Frau Gertz with dispassionate clarity.

Another album of far older photographs is brought out. At first there are photos of Frau Gertz's father, mother, and siblings. These were taken in studios: Wife and children seated, the husband standing behind. Frau Gertz's finger moves from person to person, reciting a different name. Then there is a single picture: a young man and woman. It is Frau Gertz as a *fraulein*, standing beside her husband-to-be. Before them is a collie. Herr Gertz holds a walking staff and wears a rucksack.

"This is 1934. We were very happy then."

The photographs are now paged by without comment, ending with Frau Gertz and several children seated before Herr Gertz in uniform. We both look at this portrait silently, then she puts the albums away. She brings out a phonograph.

We sit and listen to music, sipping brandy. There are deep shadows in Frau Gertz's house, and it is several minutes before I see that the photos of her husband have brought tears. Though normally embarrassed by tears, I am not now. She sits steadily in a wooden, hardback chair allowing the tears to build in the deep lines around her eyes; overfilling, the tears fall downward slowly. Rising to turn the record over, I move my chair beside her and put an arm around her slight, frail shoulders. Slowly, she allows her head to rest on my shoulder and I feel an occasional shudder.

When Frau Gertz shows me to the door it is late and we're both taken aback by the presence of a light sprinkling of immaculate snow. This newly fallen layer gleams in the soft glow of a quarter moon which has risen over the Krems valley. Frau Gertz bunches a shawl in front of her and her eyes brighten.

"*Schon.*"

My feet press clean-edged prints into the snow as I return to the cottage. An instinct causes me to turn quickly and I see an owl gliding between two fruit trees whose naked branches reach into the night sky. Once in the cottage, I sit awhile in the overstuffed chair. After some scrounging, I find a quarter-filled bottle of bourbon. I toast the cottage several times before crawling beneath blankets and submerging into a brief winter sleep.

xv.

In nearly all of the northern hemisphere it would be called early spring, but it is winter in Old Spruce. In the tiny St. Basil Russian Orthodox Church, tiers of votive candles are lit in memory of Eskimo Joe. This is the only light in the Church as the village's light plant had broken down the week before. The half dozen mourners are stooped and unmoving in the soft, amber light.

At the front of the church a Reader recites ancient Slavonic mysteries for the departed. Close by, Lena sits, clutching a handkerchief which she lifts occasionally and dabs at each eye. I'm surprised she's here, the only one of Joe's five wives.

A former brother-in-law of Joe's named Karl had greeted me at the airstrip that morning, a shoulder hunched into the cold.

"He was alive one minute, then dead the next. Painless. Nurse said it was his heart."

I sit next to Karl who stares dully at the floor while the words are read. The church is constructed of ancient planks and beams: floors worn to a glossy finish by a century of the devoted. The Reader, nearly eighty years old, is stooped and holds the books with small, arthritic hands. He reads in a halting, nearly inaudible voice. The frayed hem of his black robe trails behind him as he shuffles around the end of the coffin, made of freshly stained pine that fills the small interior of St. Basil's with the strong odor of solvent.

Except for the Reader, the ceremony is silent. Five of us, for there are only five men present, lift the coffin and carry it into late afternoon twilight. Slowly, we place it into the bed of a small, badly dented pickup. The driver, a young man, waits impatiently, slapping his mittened hands together. Karl helps the Reader, now wearing a thick parka, down the steps and into the truck.

One man squeezes in beside the Reader and two sit on the tailgate while Karl and I walk behind.

As the truck pulls away, I look behind to see Lena walking slowly towards Old Spruce; her body and legs are thick and she walks unsteadily along the side of the road, wisps of breath vapor brushing over her shoulder.

Though I'd hurriedly dug out winter clothes while passing through

Anchorage, I feel intimidated by the sharp cold, though experience tells me I'm fortunate it's a still day. My nostrils pinch together, and my breath curls out in ribbons of frosted air. Soon the little truck is far ahead, and by the time Karl and I reach the small cemetery, they are waiting for us.

"Come on, I'm freezing."

The driver is obviously rendering a service he'd prefer not to. The coffin is lowered too fast into a grave which, I know, was dug at the end of the previous summer. Joe's words come to mind from a previous winter I cannot remember.

"Just in case, John. If not used, they make good cold storage." I recall they contained no irony or meaning aside from what was said.

The Reader drops the prayer book, and it skids downhill a half dozen feet. It is retrieved by the driver who wipes the snow from it with an exaggerated motion, then extends it while wearing a smile decorated by a cigarette. The older men frown but say nothing, helping the Reader back to the truck.

Karl stays while the truck rumbles away towards the village. Though behind me, I feel him at my elbow.

"Joe told me about last summer. You guys in that foreign place." I look at Karl who stares at the ground where a remaining unused grave is covered with a sheet of plywood and large rocks to hold it against the wind. He shrugs himself into his parka even further and expertly places a pinch of snoose under his lip. "Anyway, what I mean is that my cabin up Sawmill Creek is good and solid. All you'd need is groceries. Nobody goes there anymore."

We both nod and Karl turns and walks down the curving road. He steps aside to avoid the village's loader that struggles up the hill with a load of thawed soil that has been kept under the school.

I watch as two young Eskimo men begin to shovel the warm soil atop Joe's coffin. Both work quickly, but one puts his shovel down and says, "I'm sorry. Joe was a good guy." Then he resumes work.

Beyond the cemetery, below us, is the village of Old Spruce, now almost dark. Windows show small, insignificant lights. Between it and the cemetery, on a smaller hill, is St. Basil's, where the most subtle of glows can be seen through small stained glass windows. The blue cupola is outlined perfectly against the slopes of the distant Sitkin Mountains.

How can I stop the flood of memories that now overpower me? What is a quarter century of friendship compared to the mountains, the village, and the church? We were once two young men who climbed these mountains discovering the places of hawks. And the fact is, our flesh aged despite us. But we did have time to know the wind and its creatures, feeling the glitter of warmth, as do hawks in the long midsummer sun.

Alma

*T*hey found her dead behind the crab pots near Point Chehalis Cannery. The paper said she was thirty-four years old, but during the previous year, everyone who saw her agreed she looked twenty years older.

It was thought she was from the village of Unalaska on the Aleutian Island of the same name. Somehow, she'd come to Old Harbor on Kodiak Island, and eventually she'd ended up a street drunk in Kodiak City. Alma was a mean and sloppy drunk: She swore at passersby, and she was seen having sex in public on several occasions with one of various drunks she associated with. Also, she would urinate anywhere, leaning forward, the flats of her hands on the ground, a contemptuous smile on her face.

"This is what I think of Kodiak."

She had been curled up behind the crab pots dead for several days, and since it was winter, her body was rigid and had to be strapped flat onto the gurney. She had been strangled with a tattered piece of her underclothing. "It could be any one of a dozen street drunks," the police clerk told the reporter. "They all hung out behind those pots, passing a bottle if they had it."

Alma was dark and short like most Aleuts, but even making generous allowance for time and abuse, probably had never been very pretty. I wrote her obituary, and it took up very little space. Despite half a dozen calls, I could find no one who knew much about Alma. In fact, people really weren't sure she was from Old Harbor. It could have been Nikolski, or even Atka. The only decent information sources were her booking sheets, and they were contradictory. On a Friday night, she might declare herself from Old Harbor, only to state when being booked on the following Tuesday that she was from Unalaska.

When you lived like Alma, your place of death was far easier to determine than that of birth.

Mysteries

The plateau was divided in two by a straight and solitary road. It curved where the plateau narrowed, then followed the rocky shoreline of a deep lake held in a bowl formed by steep mountains with gray slopes. These were scarred by rock slides nearly reaching to the edge of the quiet, blue water. Where the road met the lake was a campground.

A late September sun was sinking behind the mountains and shadows spread quietly throughout the bowl. In the campground was a single, peculiar vehicle; it appeared to be an ungainly hybrid between a factory-made motor home and a moving van. On both sides was printed "Martin B. Prevo, Doctor of Gravity and other Earth Sciences," and under that, in smaller lettering, "Mineral and Earth Compound Location my Specialty. Low hourly rates."

Three people sat by the huge vehicle: Martin Prevo balanced on a stool near an open door where his wife Mary sat, back against one jamb, feet against the other. Martin wore a large cowboy hat, but removed it and curled its brim even more than it had been, then put it back on. When he looked at Mary she glanced away, but she found herself looking at Shooter, their young assistant. She quickly shifted her eyes again.

Shooter sighed and ran a nervous finger over a large welt that swelled handsomely under his left eye, emphasizing its Asiatic appearance. Martin stood up, and Shooter's body jerked such that he nearly quit the table; but when the older man looked towards the mountains the youth stayed put, remaining poised on the edge. Martin began to say something, but hesitated and shook his head. His stance took on the resigned slant of an abandoned warrior, hips cocked to one side, head held up, and eyes gray and searching. Big wicket-shaped hands rested on his hips.

"Damn it all."

The breath left him in an easy sigh, and he lowered his head momentarily, allowing a shock of gray hair to work its way down his forehead. Not taking her eyes from Martin, Mary reached inside the van and retrieved a half-full coffee cup. Stopping in mid-sip she held it steady and looked intently over its rim at her husband: Before, he'd studied the mountains and lake as objects of a skyline, but now his brows wrinkled as he squinted.

From under the brim of his hat, gray eyes moved first to Shooter, then to his wife.

"Someone's coming."

Martin's gaze returned to Shooter until the youth squirmed, then he turned and looked towards the mountains.

All three fixed their attentions on what appeared to be a giant tortoise edging its way down from the mountains. Its carapace was green and wobbled left to right; occasionally it would stop, regain its bearing, and continue, moving slowly downhill towards the campground.

Shooter shaded his eyes to see better, but this was a habit, because there was no bright sunlight now; the campground was cloaked in shade. Mary stood in the doorway and ran a callused hand through dense black hair marbled with narrow ribbons of speckled gray. She did this twice, then she announced abstractly, "It's a backpacker."

Within minutes the tortoise changed into a man carrying a huge pack that in turn was covered by a poncho. A flock of ptarmigan spooked as he passed through a hollow, and for a moment he went out of view. Martin ran a hand over a week's growth of beard, then scratched vigorously, starting at an ear and working towards his chin.

The ptarmigan clucked a tardy alarm, flew fifty yards and settled into a willow thicket. Martin's lips curled.

"Stupid birds. Stupider than anything."

The backpacker now left the slope of the mountain; what seemed a crawl at a distance, was actually a brisk walk. He passed over what little flatlands remained, entered the campground, and eased the pack onto an empty picnic table across from the van. Slipping his arms from the straps, he leaned forward and sighed.

"There's too much weight in it, all right."

Straightening, he looked first at Martin, then at Shooter, who appraised the pack. When his large eyes moved to Mary, she smiled and stepped from the van.

"Hello. You've got quite a load."

The backpacker smiled and then read the sign on the van, immediately returning his gaze to Martin Prevo.

"You're a water witch?"

Martin looked at the sign and nodded.

"Well, that's how I started, but after we came to Alaska I've sort of branched out, last few years. Minerals, gold, platinum, cinnabar, even molybdenum. Good market for that now."

Without asking, Mary poured the backpacker a cup of coffee. He took it with a long, frail hand; squatting, he sipped tentatively, then gave a barely discernible shake of his head. Martin rested a hip against the table.

"Looks like you came a distance. You a prospector?"

The backpacker held the cup before him, eyes closed; keeping them shut, he took a deep draught and sighed. Slowly his lids opened, and his tongue dabbed at a stray droplet of coffee.

"No, I'm a visionary."

His reply hung there. Shooter dug a small crater into the dirt with the toe of his boot then looked at the backpacker. Mary backed up and without looking sat directly on the stool. Martin dropped both hands to his belt, hooking the thumbs over the wide, cowhide band. He looked steadily down at the ground.

"If you're a visionary, then maybe you can tell me why a good wife of nine years would screw my assistant, a boy I took from the reservation and taught a trade, while I'm down-road trying to get a part for this rig."

For the first time, the visionary saw that the rear-end of the van was on blocks; tools and a flat pail of oil surrounded a ground cloth. Slowly he put the coffee down on the seat of the table and fell to thinking.

Mary's black hair framed a face that was a quiet, resigned mask. The hair contrasted with skin white as a plume of new cloud. Slowly, she took a thick lock of her hair, lifted it to a corner of her mouth and chewed. The backpacker shook his head.

"I'm not a wise man, just a visionary. But I've come to think that men and women were born to outrage each other."

Martin Prevo considered this, then picked up the visionary's cup and walked towards the van and poured him another cup of coffee. Over-filling it, he returned head down, and as he offered the cup to his guest, Martin saw that he and Mary looked placidly at Shooter, who held a shot-gun. They all stared as he loaded it with fat red shells.

"I'm going to get some of those little chickens. We'll all be needing dinner."

He walked towards the hollow, balancing the gun on a narrow shoulder. The shadows took him, and soon he was almost invisible. An evening wind came up, sweeping gently over Shooter; then it etched tiny wrinkles across the surface of the lake. Those in the campground shrugged into their coats against the wind. Along the shore of the lake two whimbrels flew, landing deftly at the edge of a tiny rivulet. Their cries became tactile and described a portrait of the coming night.

Δ

No one else came to the campground that evening.

After dinner the four sat around the fire, yet the glow given off offered none of them comfort. The cold of the evening crept forward and subdued the fire; its flames lapped tamely at a pile of crisscrossed logs. The breeze swept the smoke away after it rose less than a dozen feet. In the southwest the setting sun was soothed by a soft unguent of orange.

An old seat had been removed from somewhere in the van and Shooter sat on this with his back to a pile of wood. Martin had inverted a thick chunk of wood and sat; he mouthed a pipe that had either gone out or hadn't been lit. The brim of his hat was his shelter, hooding his forehead and eyes and nearly hiding the rest of his face in shadows.

Between Shooter and Martin, Mary squatted, feeding paper plates into the fire; each plate hissed, smoked, and caught, quickly curling into a half-moon of flames. At the edge of the shadows the visionary sat leaning against his pack; he whittled quickly at a piece of wood, took a sliver, and began picking at his teeth.

Behind them a tape player muttered away at the remnants of a country-and-western song, but the tape was defective. Intermittently the vocalist would be plagued with eerie, liquid spasms. Martin would frown at the machine until it continued normally. Finally the malfunction became permanent, and the song melted into an unsettling whine. Martin reached behind him, removed the tape and tossed it into the fire.

Mary studied the tape as it perished in a tiny version of hell. Shooter almost smiled, but instead stuffed his hands into coat pockets, digging his chin into his chest. Martin looked into the bowl of the pipe and held his eyes there.

"What kind of visions do you have?" He looked up from the pipe and took it between the palm of his hands, rolling it slightly. "Like, of the future?"

The visionary held his toothpick in his mouth while he thought. Then he plucked it from his lips and tapped out a rhythm to his words.

"Rarely. Usually my visions are of details. When I worked in the city I began to study spider webs in the parks. I'd study these and other things like that. Details. Small details that people walked over, around, and by every day. Yes, every day. So, I began to fit these details into, well, larger pieces until they made a whole. It took more and more time, and eventually I moved north." He looked back at the mountains, then returned his gaze to the fire. "And I've been happy. I'm an old man now."

Martin squinted, and leaned forward to peer at the visionary. Indeed he was old. His hair was almost white; a long neck was wrinkled and ropey; his eyes were surrounded by webs of creases but the pupils were clear and steady. Martin wondered why he had not noticed the man's great age earlier.

"I admire both age and someone who uses their head," Martin told him. "I use my head in my work. People rely on me; when they see me they know I can find what they want. Wherever I've been there are happy people; many have become wealthy and soon forget about me. But that's people's nature—to forget who has done good by them; to forget who made them what they are."

Martin stood, stuffed his pipe in a front pocket, then took the chunk of wood and put it carefully on the fire.

"The van won't fix itself."

After Martin left, Shooter stood. He looked towards the van, then down at Mary. She rocked slightly on her hams, speaking without glancing up.

"He'll need help."

The visionary placed two palms flat against the ground, readying himself to rise, but Mary's eyes stopped him.

"No. Shooter knows the van." Her eyes moved upwards and both she and the visionary realized that the youth was enduring a sort of pain. He squirmed, then lifted an arm; his fingers extended and the limb straightened. Mary looked away.

The smoke curled and drifted across the space vacated by Shooter. She pushed the last of the paper plates into the fire and the sudden light illuminated a sad profile before it died away.

"I'm forty-five years old and this is my fourth marriage."

She sat down on the old seat, pulled a blanket around her and shrank into it. After a few preliminary coughs, a small generator started, and the visionary could see the van's undersides swathed in a flood of yellowish light. Martin lay on the groundcloth with Shooter nearby, Shooter's body throwing a long shadow onto the campground.

Arm and hand movements by either man created grotesque puppets that danced, leaped, and swooned across the campground. The visionary tried to watch this unruly ballet but his body was tired from his day's hike. In his sleep he joined the shadows and together they performed a slow, gentle dance.

Δ

When the visionary woke he wasn't sure: On the half of Mary's body facing the fire, the reflected light from her naked torso and thighs shone like that from a full winter moon. The half facing away from the fire was

119

enveloped in various degrees of halftones; the hollow in each buttock was dark, the outline of her back gray, the tiny hairs and goosebumps on her shoulders stood out in relief. She removed a shoe, repeated this once more, then put them on the pile of clothes. Looking down into the fire, Mary folded her arms tightly across her breasts; the visionary couldn't be certain if she spoke to the flames or him.

"I'm so tired of men. They want me and I've never known what to do. I've always wanted to do right, but that changes all the time. You say no and there's trouble; you say yes and there's even more." The visionary thought he heard a groan, very soft, rising from deep inside her. She began to tremble. "It's just that I'm so goddamned tired of men." She turned and walked away, head down, arms still clasped across her breasts. He rose and turned in time to see her walk towards the mountains. There was a light frost on the tundra, and the outlines of her feet melted through it, stamping out a straight trail, one print before the other, until they were lost in the night.

When he gathered his thoughts, the older man found his mouth open and arm raised, finger pointed at the heavens. Walking to the van, he saw that all lights were out. Under the vehicle, Shooter had thrown a sleeping bag on the ground cloth. A trace of black hair protruded from a small airhole and he could hear a gentle snore.

When he roused Martin, it was a full minute before Martin was able to absorb what had happened. Ruffled gray hair surrounded a bare pate, and without his hat, Martin looked like a distant relative of the man who'd been speaking earlier. When he returned to the door, he'd put the hat back in place. Martin stepped out and handed the visionary a pint-bottle of whisky almost a third full.

"Here, there's some of this left. Which way?"

"That way. Directly north."

Shooter had listened from under the van. They watched Martin follow Mary's trail until only his hat was visible, then it too was gone.

The visionary returned to the fire, sat down, and took a swallow of whisky. He had gotten cold, and the chill and sudden burn of the whisky resulted in a shudder. He passed the bottle to Shooter, and he drank.

"Lucky you saw her."

When he returned the bottle, the visionary waved it away.

"Earlier I was thinking I should have pushed on to the roadhouse. It's only another eight miles. Now it seems...." He craned his neck back and marveled at the clarity of the heavens. "Well, I guess it's good I stayed."

Looking up caused a slight vertigo, but the visionary knew it was just the headiness of the whisky. The planets and stars passed over him; he knew them all as if they were close neighbors. Raising a finger he traced

Orion, stopping at the hunter's belt. With difficulty, he took his attentions from the sky. He removed a groundcloth and unrolled a frazzled bedroll then crawled in.

Shooter fed the fire a large dry log, and the flames grew larger, healthier. Slivers of heat ate through logs put on earlier; yellow light glistened from the bottle Shooter held. He offered the visionary what little was left, then looked on while the older man finished it and passed back the bottle. The visionary's bag warmed; this on top of the whisky made his eyes struggle to remain open. A few feet away, Shooter cradled the empty bottle in his arms and glared into the fire.

When the visionary heard the door of the van close, he wasn't sure how much time had elapsed since he'd bedded down. He heard voices and intended to listen closer, yet he fell back to sleep.

Δ

When the visionary woke it was daylight. The lake was covered with a low, thick mist. Frost blanketed the picnic table, and he traced a line through it with his finger. He was working out morning stiffness and pondering the question of an early winter when he noticed the van was gone.

Behind him he heard a quiet hissing sound, followed by a metallic click. Walking a dozen yards to the lake he saw Shooter sitting on a large suitcase reeling in a fishing line. Next to the suitcase was a shotgun in a buckskin case, and a metallic carrying tube for the pole. On the suitcase large letters proclaimed, "St. Bartholomew's Navaho Boys' School." Shooter lifted his lure from the water; it spun slowly, empty.

"Nothing biting."

The visionary nodded.

"It's getting cold. The fish are heading towards deep water for the winter to live on their fat."

While Shooter broke down the rod and reel, the visionary washed his face in the cold lake water. In places, patches of skim-ice floated, reflecting a glint of morning light.

After the older man put away his bedroll, he looked doubtfully at the huge pack. It was an unforgiving burden. Shooter winced as the visionary slid into the straps, then painfully hefted up the pack.

"There's seventy pounds of smoked fish in this pack. I make about six trips out each fall. It seems seventy pounds gets heavier and heavier each year."

As they walked towards the highway, a truck passed slowly. The vehicle's driver looked wearily at the pair.

They stood on the shoulder and looked at the vehicle grow smaller in the distance as it crossed the plateau. Shooter put down his potables and nodded. After they shook hands, the youth allowed a hand to rise and point down the road.

"I could have stayed, but I didn't," His tongue stumbled over itself and the visionary could see that the pain had returned. Shooter dropped his arm and scuffed absently at the dirt. "She didn't ask me to stay, but he did. She...." His voice left him momentarily and he shook his head. "Well, I'm going home to the desert. It's three thousand miles but that doesn't mean anything to me. This land is strange to me. My grandparents are old and they have a few sheep."

He picked up his belongings and walked away across the plateau, the weight of the suitcase rendering his right side lower than his left. His boots slapped out a regular rhythm against the asphalt.

The visionary hiked in the opposite direction. He strode along easily, looking out upon the lake. Slowly, the mist was broken into patches by the sun; two loons warbled deeply in the distance.

While he walked, he saw that many small patches of moss had been disturbed near clumps of dwarf willows, as if leprechauns had disturbed them during a great nocturnal reveling. Yet he knew it was the work of small rodents that harvested the moss to insulate their dens for winter. This discreet labor was a sign of an early winter, a sign that had never failed him. Never.

Suddenly he thought about the Indian youth's solitary trek across the plateau. Couldn't he have helped? The visionary knew the roadhouse owners and they might have arranged for a ride. He stopped and half-turned, but he realized that Shooter would be at least a mile distant. After a pause, he continued, tucking his chin into his chest and straining against the pack. Concerns about his forgetfulness evaporated as an image came gradually into focus. As it did, he wondered if it were a memory or some-thing more ethereal. Soon it was sight, sound, and smell. He stopped: He perceived a warm wind and the setting of a red, southerly sun. Buttes squatted like ancient fortresses in an arid valley; an elderly Navaho woman prepared corn-cakes and looked out upon this panorama, her dark eyes steady and clear. One by one she put the cakes on a stone griddle and pushed mesquite into the fire where it crackled noisily. The cakes browned at the edges and curled, their aroma tantalizing a small dog who crouched nearby.

The sun melted away into a deep ochre and disappeared behind a butte; on a ridge, tired sheep bleated, their bells clanging as they filed down from high pasture. Following behind was Shooter; his long black hair gleamed in the departing sun and he carried a shepherd's crook across his shoulder. When he hesitated to look at the sunset his eyes blinked placidly. Mourning doves began to call from their evening roost. He continued down the ridge. As she watched the youth descend towards camp, the old woman began singing a strange song that imitated the doves. She reached out with a leathery hand and turned the cakes, smiling while she sang.

The visionary heard her song and he too smiled. Lifting his head he looked out upon the lake that was now clear of mist. Morning stiffness had now left him, and shrugging the pack up higher, he walked on briskly.

Flying Ax

No one knew how Flying Ax arrived in Fairbanks dressed up as a Cherokee Indian and telling everyone he was searching for the Great Medicine Spirit. His costume design was part flannel blanket and part military surplus footwear, topped off by a roughly re-tailored overcoat. His hat was a Stetson with a ring of feathers in a wide band made of terrycloth. According to Flying Ax himself, he'd cobbled it all together in the lower-48 from the St. Vincent de Paul for just under a buck-seventy.

He spoke with a Brooklyn accent and was unfamiliar with anything remotely Native American. He smoked dope in a peace pipe, passing it around between any and all, but wouldn't drink because it represented non-Indian ways. Flying Ax was popular with First Avenue hangabouts from the villages, mostly Athabascans in for the winter from Fort Yukon or Minto. He even enrolled in an anthropology class at the university, but he only attended a few classes after hostile students challenged his authenticity. Once I picked him up hitchhiking, and I said, "Boy, that is quite a getup you have on." And he admitted it was, plus very warm.

By late winter Flying Ax was gone, leaving theories and rumors behind: His parents had come north, more or less captured him, and brought him home to their mansion on Long Island; or he'd gone out to Circle Hot Springs and would be back when the locals got tired of him; or he'd frozen to death; or he'd been drafted.

Of all rumors, the least believable was being drafted. Uncle needed men for Vietnam but certainly not Flying Ax. It was early spring when I picked up two Indian men hitching in from Nenana. When the conversation turned to Flying Ax's authenticity, both thought a minute and shrugged the matter off. They'd never really thought much about it, and besides he was always good company.

In Search of Corporal Zolkoff

The pilot landed the single-engined aircraft upon the wide, hard beach during a falling tide. It took two trips, the first carrying Paul and gear, the second carrying equipment. The pilot helped haul supplies to the foot of the bluffs.

"They say you'll be here three months."

He had pushed sunglasses to the top of his head and looked at the equipment with doubt. Paul put down a box of groceries.

"Yeah. Three months. Until the salmon stop running and we take the weir out."

They returned to the plane. Its wide, sturdy tires rested easily upon the coal-black volcanic sands. The pilot looked to the west: The mouth of the river spilled into the ocean, creating small standing waves in the shallows.

"Who is going to help you put the weir in? That's a big river over there."

"Two guys will fly in tomorrow. They say it'll take two days. I don't know. I've never done this before."

Paul shrugged to reaffirm a general ignorance about the task before him. While swinging the door closed, the pilot sighed and said "You'll be up in the bushes chattering with the squirrels before three months are out. Two years ago, they packed out the weir watchman in a wet blanket. Here. Watch that prop. I'm outta here."

Handing Paul a bottle of vodka, he snapped the door closed and in less than a minute the plane was banking steeply to the south where it was swallowed by a dense layer of clouds slipping northward over mountains still covered with glossy, wind-polished snow. For the first time, Paul felt heavy raindrops.

Δ

The two men who had helped install the weir kidded him about being a first-timer, narrating increasingly bizarre and worrisome brown bear stories. On the second night the two men had become drunk on the pilot's vodka. Despite the liquor, one of them managed a statement Paul took as a hybrid between a question and an accusation:

"If I were a school teacher, I'd slip over to Copenhagen or Rome and spend the summer kicked back and fucked up instead of wrestling with a bunch of stupid fish."

"I was recently divorced."

"Who wasn't?"

The next morning they left. The pilot more or less stuffed the two men in the back of an extraordinarily small plane. Peeking among duffle bags, knees, and arms, one of the men gave Paul final instructions: "If you have more questions about procedures, it'll be in the SOP book. Good luck."

This plane labored to become airborne. One wheel would free itself from the sand, only to settle back down and have the other lift free. The wings and struts shuddered as they caught the wind, and the engine buzzed in anger, but finally the entire craft lifted upwards, wobbled equivocally, then climbed. Paul found himself biting a knuckle, but feeling somewhat stupid he rubbed reddened tooth marks while climbing the steep path up the bluff.

He returned to the cabin, a small weathered plywood affair with a ragged top-notch of tar paper. It was about twelve-by-twelve feet with an enclosed entryway. He unrolled the crisp, new map upon the table and pinned it flat with the salt and pepper shaker, a mustard server, and a pocket knife. He studied it for the first time.

The closest village was fifty-nine miles southwest. Though a cannery was nineteen miles directly west, Paul had been told it wouldn't be operating this year. "This is a poor year," one of the men had said. "You won't count many fish through the weir." He had been told it might be several weeks before the first salmon arrived.

After checking the weir for bottom erosion, he returned to the cabin and turned in. Sometime in the night he awoke to a sound. A shuffling. Throwing on his coat, he took the rifle from its rack and stepped outside. The beam of the flashlight fell upon a fat porcupine chewing on a scrap of lumber. It waddled away stolidly, looking back into the light with fear.

Δ

Before the fish arrived, Paul decided to survey his surroundings.

Along the river the tundra and tall grasses were somewhat yellow, not close to the intense greens they would assume during the brief, sub-arctic summer. Evergreen trees were absent, but dwarfed willow and alder grew in abundance; larger cottonwoods lay in small groves around the lake and river. Without forests of trees, Paul could see miles in any direction.

There were no bugs yet since a cold wind still blew in from the sea. Having resided in the north for many years, he knew that in several weeks insects would be everywhere. Paul developed a facial tic at the memory of this.

The tundra was spongy from melt-off, but despite its inhospitable appearance, small colorful birds were everywhere. Bird identification had been a skill he'd wanted to develop this summer, and during lunch he consulted his new bird book and decided they were, for the most part, Lapland Longspurs.

"Lapland Longspurs. Lapland. Laplanders."

After trying to visualize Lapland, he unwrapped a large hardbound book with several hundred empty lined pages. This would be the journal where he'd enter everything. Paul turned pages and flattened them until the book lay open on the table, easy to write upon.

Paul had resolved to note all basic events in the journal: Birds and animals seen; daily meteorological observations; facts and observations about the weir. Lastly, his therapist had urged him to write about personal events and reflections. "It'll be good for you, Paul. I don't want to make myself obsolete, but often a journal is better than any shrink."

So, he now made his first entry in the book, but he wouldn't write about personal thoughts. He couldn't enjoy writing about himself or what had been. After all, Paul's problems weren't unique. Throughout time, human beings had encountered catastrophes and crises. Like other people, he'd be better served with mental discipline than self-pity or maudlin recollections. That was the whole idea of coming out here.

Paul walked the riverbank both above and below the weir. The water was dark with late spring runoff and carried all sorts of small and large debris. As predicted, he had to clean such debris from the screens of the weir three or four times a day. Putting on chest-high waders and taking a long-handled brush, he launched himself unsteadily into the river current above the weir.

He worked along the V-shaped weir, carefully scrubbing the screen with long, even brush strokes. Turning, he waded back towards the cabin side of the river, struggling up the muddy bank. Looking down river at the mouth, he saw hundreds of gulls and terns. The wind came in directly from the north and the immaculate white birds were able to hover in this by holding their wings steady; occasionally they would veer left or right, dropping to the surface of the river to feed on small fish.

Δ

Lieutenant Zolkoff had explored this area for the Russian-American company in 1825. At night, in the light of a quietly purring air lantern, Paul translated Zolkoff's journal that he'd received from the University of Leningrad six months before. His Russian, rusty from teaching only its rudiments to half-interested high school students, made it slow going. He had to consult a soiled, finger-worn dictionary with distracting frequency.

While working, he listened to the radio: Initially to the other weir watchmen reporting their day's activities, then he'd switch to the short-wave bands and tune to Radio Japan or Moscow. When it was his turn to report the day's activities, he'd key the microphone awkwardly and give weather and his fish count. Thus far it had been easy; no salmon had passed through his weir.

Paul read that Lieutenant Zolkoff had named this river the Alexander River, the lake that fed it Alexander Lake, and the range of mountains the Anadyr Mountains. The loyal Zolkoff had named the river and lake after Czar Alexander II, and the mountains for Princess Anadyr, Alexander's youngest daughter.

After first exploring the area then building a small church and trading post, Zolkoff came to write disparagingly about the river, lake and mountains: *"This is a desperate, inhospitable area, and God tests us severely. The bugs are the worst we've encountered, stinging us unmercifully. It isn't until we build fires with green wood and grasses then sit in the smoke do we get any peace. Then we suffocate. Worst yet, Corporal Vassily Zolkoff, my beloved youngest brother, died of a hopeless catarrh on this date. We buried him one verst to the west of the mouth of Alexander River on a prominent small mount overlooking the sea he loved so well. He died bravely for Russia.*

"May God grant eternal rest upon his soul."

It had taken Paul four consecutive evenings to translate the passage to his satisfaction.

During the first few days, Paul had hiked east of the river to the site of the church which had become the centerpiece of the settlement until its abandonment in 1930. Though the original church Zolkoff had constructed burned, plus several of its successors, it had been rebuilt repeatedly.

When he approached the church, a fox had popped out from a favored rest spot beneath its broken front steps. The present structure, thoroughly dilapidated, stood prominently on a high bluff overlooking the sea. A cupola topped what had been a bell tower, and though still prominent, was weathered to a coarse-grained nakedness. Scattered flakes of blue paint clung to the cupola in only a few places. Carefully, Paul picked his way up the stairs. Affixed to the remaining half of a double door was a sign reading, "This is consecrated property of the Alaska Russian Orthodox Diocese and a Historical Monument: Please enter with respect. Removal of any materials is forbidden by law." Under it were several hand-scrawled obscenities. The front of the frail, windblown structure was riddled with bullet holes of various vintages and diameters.

Entering, Paul used caution, the plank floor being rotten and fallen away in many places. The east wall had partially collapsed inwards, resting on the floor. The interior of the church was simply a large, musty-smelling room lacking any suggestion of its former use. Against the south wall, where the altar might have been, was carved, "Big John Williamson shot himself a brown bear near Alexander Lake on October 2, 1938."

This declaration had drawn a colonnade of carved or written rejoinders, some dated, some undated.

He carefully cleared away a spot on the floor and knelt, holding his hands together. He had never prayed for Maureen and Kathy and now resolved to do so. Despite being quite alone, Paul felt stupid; a reflex made him look hastily towards the door. He wondered why he had lied to the two men who helped him put in the weir. Was he reverting to earlier, bad habits?

The admonishing voice of his counselor came back to him: "Paul, being widowed is quite different from being divorced. Since anyone who needs to ask is a stranger anyway, and if you do feel uncomfortable with what you feel are lip-service condolences, tell them you're single. That's the truth. The other is an unhealthy lie, and makes no progress towards accepting the fact of this tragedy."

He rubbed his face, then clasped his hands together again. He talked down at the floor. "One minute I was a husband and father, the next...."

Paul didn't finish; rather he tried to recall the long-ago words of countless Hail Mary's. But his mind offered a blank and he dropped his hands to his sides. He stood, then reached down and rubbed his knee caps.

Exiting the church, he felt ridiculous.

Paul walked along the trail that led away from the church and along the top of the massive bluff that overlooked the sea. Hundreds of swallows with buff-white bellies darted around him, and he stopped, realizing they'd arrived only within the last two days. To the east and west of him, the ocean beat ceaselessly against the miles of straight beaches: Offshore, lazy combers entered the shallows and built to a dull blue, then curled, broke and tumbled, sweeping up the beach. At their uppermost edge, they stranded white spumes of foam where shore birds skittered on stilted legs. Thus far they'd defied Paul's awkward attempts at identification.

The pattern of breakers and beach was fractured only at the mouth of the Alexander River where the water had created a network of shoals. Studying this, Paul felt better than he had in the church and proceeded towards the cabin. He decided on a cup of hot tea before doing chores.

Δ

After cleaning the weir that evening, Paul sat on the river bank in his hip-waders leaning on the brush handle and considering the death of Corporal Zolkoff: In 1827, like now, all wood had to be boated or hauled in, yet they would have undoubtedly made Zolkoff a roughly milled wooden coffin. On the top of it, one of the soldiers might have carved a cross, and Corporal Zolkoff would have been interred in formal dress uniform, including regimental colors, sword, and insignia.

The brass buttons on the uniform would certainly have survived over intervening years; the coffin would be dust, or with luck, small slivers of petrified material; the sword would survive, as would particles of the uniform. Lastly, the bones, if the ground were at all dry, would be preserved.

While peeling off the chest-waders, Paul wondered if he should search for the remains of Corporal Zolkoff. The recently translated journal gave him the location, and historically the grave would be significant. Or would it? Certainly the State or University Museum would treasure the find.

Back at the cabin he put aside considerations concerning Corporal Zolkoff and confronted his radio: He listened to other weir watchmen give their fish counts and, like the days previous, he felt guilty. For some reason, no fish had arrived at his weir. When he broadcast this information there was a pause, and numerous questions were asked concerning the weir. Finally the schedule was concluded for the evening.

He felt somehow responsible.

Clearly, they thought something was wrong. When he'd cleaned the screens, Paul had carefully checked under the panels of blockading screens for scouring, where salmon could slither under the barrier without being counted. Yet the weir remained in excellent condition. He walked down to the structure and studied it: The water flowed through the screens and swept past the stout wooden buttresses which supported the screens and their wooden frames. From buttress to buttress a plank walkway spanned the top of the weir.

He walked out on the weir and looked into the water.

Though it was close to 10:00 p.m., there was still quite enough light to see the bottom of the river clearly. Occasionally Paul could see smaller fish: minnows or young fry; sensing his movement, they fled, leaving tiny clouds of mud. In the middle of the weir was a center post, and on this sat a kingfisher poised for hunting. It eyed him, undecided whether to fly or remain.

Paul formed his right hand into a fist and slowly tapped it against an open palm: There simply weren't any salmon, and that was that. Paul could do nothing more.

That evening Paul dreamt about the funeral of Corporal Zolkoff:

The Russians, along with their native hunters, formed a circle around the coffin of Zolkoff. A bearded priest in long black robes intoned the liturgy of the dead; a young acolyte swung an incense burner which billowed acrid smoke into the quiet summer air. In the dream he had been surprised it was so still, so absolutely still.

The wind always blew along the Alexander River.

Standing quite tall in the garish dress uniform of His Majesty Tsar Alexander was Lieutenant Zolkoff. He had the high forehead and prominent aquiline nose of European Russians. Zolkoff's large eyes gazed steadily down upon the closed coffin.

The prayers stopped. A Russian and a regimental flag were unfurled and two soldiers, at the command of a squat, swarthy sergeant, fired a salute. Four native hunters waited nearby while a workman stooped and began nailing the coffin shut, but an outstretched hand from Lieutenant Zolkoff stopped them.

The priest and his acolyte looked with unconcealed alarm at the officer. The priest said something, but Paul couldn't hear.

Zolkoff bent over and slid the lid away revealing Maureen holding Kathy against naked breasts, as Paul had seen them a thousand times when his daughter was an infant. Zolkoff bent down slowly and kissed Maureen on her mouth.

Gradually, Maureen's eyes opened.

Paul awoke punching and kicking inside his sleeping bag. He had fallen to the floor from the lower bunk, knocking the camp stove and several dishes off a stand. The ensuing clatter caused him to sit bolt upright. His entire sleeping bag was steeped in sweat.

"It was a dream!"

He declared this aloud and it helped. He leaned against the frame of the bunk beds and rubbed his face until it stung.

Getting up, he felt the fear pass away quickly. He dressed and straightened up, then boiled tea water. Paul listened to the wind outside the cabin, and he knew from the sound it was well over thirty knots and directly from the north. Occasional higher gusts kicked in over the bluffs and shook the cabin. While drinking tea, Paul considered the dream and resolved to begin a search for the remains of Corporal Zolkoff.

In Memory of Hawks

Δ

Measuring one hundred meters of heavy twine, Paul staked off ten twine-lengths west of the river. While doing so, he reflected that Lieutenant Zolkoff's "one verst" was certainly an estimate. In any event, recalling an anthropology dig he'd worked on as a student, he would maintain strict procedures.

One verst west of Alexander River indeed put him in the locale of three small mounds, one of which was more prominent than the others and looked out directly over the sea. Paul's heart beat harder: Would it be this easy?

Inspecting the entire perimeter, then the apex, of the promontory, Paul decided it was at least twelve feet higher than the others; also, it was far wider at the base. He wondered how a century and a half could alter a topographical feature like this one. Beach grass grew in numerous tufts, and among these Paul found varied debris blown up from the beach, plastic six-pack holders, aluminum beer cans, and a wad of plastic sheeting. He made a small pile of this debris; then, using his twine, he carefully constructed grid work around and upon the entire mound.

He began digging with a narrow shovel, carefully scraping away the topmost layer of sandy soil. In several hours he'd carved away two feet of the mound and found no sign. Remembering his duties, he straightened; he knew the weir would be heavy with debris and waiting for him to clean. Paul dug his fists into the small of his back, stretched, and looked out to sea. He wondered why there were never any boats either near shore or on the horizon, but eventually he shrugged this question off and walked heavily back to the weir.

Δ

He poured dirt he'd removed from his digging over a makeshift sieve. Paul thought of the frozen chicken that had been in the three boxes of provisions, including a large packet of mail; the supplies had arrived on the plane that morning. It had been nearly twenty days since he arrived and this had been his first supply plane.

A biologist had been in the plane and had told him the salmon had never been this late arriving at Alexander River, but he'd concluded by saying, "But they'll be here sooner or later. I hope."

Paul put away groceries and sorted through mail, glad for the magazines and newspapers. The letters he left unopened; they would be, on the main, from his mother and two sisters. He would save them until much later. They had been alarmed when he'd informed them he was going out into the bush for three months. His mother had said, "This will be your first summer without...well, to be alone, Paul. I think traveling would be a better healing process."

As he opened a large storage can and poured in rice, he wondered why people, even his mother, couldn't say Maureen and Kathy's names anymore. In letters people did anything to prevent writing their names; in conversations it was the same thing.

"Maureen": it was a beautiful name. "Kathleen" was also beautiful. He repeated them several times aloud, felt better, and, taking up the shovel and broom outside the doorway, headed back towards the promontory and his digging.

With the broom he meticulously swept away the loose sand and volcanic ash; he was down nearly four feet now. Often he'd speculated how deep Zolkoff would have buried his brother, but in the end, assumed six feet or two meters. Scrambling up the sides to the surface he poured a bucket of the loose soil over his sieve and began shaking it. The wind picked up the dirt as it flowed through the screen, swirling it about. Paul closed his eyes, and with his nose and mouth twisted, looked away from the sieve; when he lifted the last bucket of soil he noticed a metal fragment on the screen.

Turning it between thumb and forefinger, he saw it was a musket ball from an old muzzle-loader. He stood up and paced back and forth holding the artifact. Since it was in perfect shape, apparently not ever fired, it could have been dropped by a member of the burial party. Paul was eagerly lowering himself into the hole when he remembered the weir.

His thoughts were upon Corporal Zolkoff's gravesite as he slid into the cold water, brush in hand. When dozens of swirls erupted in front of the weir, he nearly stumbled and fell headlong. The swirling was followed by rapidly retreating wavelets of water heading downriver from the weir.

He scrambled from the water and walked to the middle of the weir: In the deep water along the bank, a column of salmon held steady in the current. He tried to count them, but they were packed together tightly and he couldn't. Paul estimated several hundred. At least that many, perhaps more.

He rushed to the cabin and grabbed a hand-counter. Returning, he sat upon the plank walkway and slowly opened a narrow gate. On the riverbed, a small square of aluminum siding had been placed such that he could easily spot any fish passing over it. He waited, counter in hand.

The salmon stayed against the bank, their bodies swaying with the current. In two hours, not one made a move towards the gate. He began to think of the salmon as phantoms. They were shy and secretive this close to the weir. Closing the gate, he hiked to the top of the bluff and just beyond the shoals more salmon could be seen jumping. Water-slicked heads popped out of the sea, and Paul knew harbor seals hunted the fish. In the river the salmon hugged the bank cautiously, and despite many hours of waiting, none approached the gate.

That evening he announced the salmon's arrival over the radio and felt better, more useful.

Undoubtedly, his first responsibility was to the weir now the salmon had arrived; hence, after dinner Paul hurried to the promontory, retrieved his equipment, and returned to the cabin.

Despite the enthusiasm he'd generated over his recent find, exhuming Corporal Zolkoff would have to wait. Several more days, or even weeks, wouldn't make any difference after a century and a half.

Counting the salmon through the weir was easier than sampling them. This was done from a trap on the upstream side of the gate. Paul would simply drop the trap and weir gate closed simultaneously after a dozen salmon entered. He would then dip-net them from the trap, measure each fish, remove a scale, and release them so they could continue upriver. Each salmon fought him mightily during this process; since he sampled five or six times a day, he became soaked with water and slime.

Hundreds of salmon passed through the weir at all hours. With their increased numbers, they became less timid, and with counting, sampling, and cleaning, the job took all available time. Corporal Zolkoff's gravesite remained unworked a week and a half.

Δ

Finally, after a morning count, Paul was grateful to see that no more fish remained below the weir. Hiking to the bluff top, he saw salmon jumping just beyond the river mouth; either tide or some strange whim prevented them from ascending the river. This would give him an afternoon to work on the gravesite. He approached it with anticipation, even relish. He hiked along quickly, carrying shovel, broom, and sieve; in a small rucksack was a thermos of coffee. He would make a day of it.

Walking up to the site, he nearly soiled himself when he saw a giant head emerge from the grave site and mean eyes glare at him from over a stout, furred muzzle. A huge bear bolted from the hole and bounded towards him a dozen paces before stopping. Paul threw down his equipment and made a headlong retreat. Tumbling down the riverbank, he collapsed; tearing off his rucksack, he dug his fingers into the thick mud. His chest rose and fell rapidly and his ears rang.

Though provided with a rifle, he had never packed it. Looking back to make sure the animal hadn't followed, Paul collected his pack and crossed the weir to the cabin, the plank walkway bouncing as he passed over it.

Somehow the giant creature had become curious about Zolkoff's grave site and had begun digging; Paul hoped the animal had done no damage, and he felt guilty for having started the search.

After steadying his hands, he found a box of cartridges and put spares in his pocket. Seeing that each missile was two thirds the length of his hand Paul felt reassured. Putting his rucksack back on, he slung the rifle over his shoulder, crossed the weir, and hiked towards the promontory. Before closing the last two hundred yards, Paul unslung his rifle and loaded a cartridge into the chamber. Despite a prevailing onshore wind, the area had the distinct stench of a barnyard, perhaps stronger.

He approached the rim of what was now a crater: The beast had excavated the area with abandon, widening the hole by a dozen feet, though not deepening it. Paul was relieved to see the animal was gone. He inspected the damage more carefully.

Piles of loose dirt were everywhere, and the orderliness of his digging was destroyed. The grid work he'd constructed from twine was gone; the neat stacks of sieved dirt had been mixed back with everything else.

Angry, he hiked quickly to the edge of the bluff and looked down the beach: A half mile away, plodding away from the river mouth was the bear, its tracks melting into dark blotches with the rising tide. Paul sat and cradled the rifle between his legs. Resting his head against the cold steel barrel, he recognized that for several minutes living meant everything to him. Nothing had been more important.

Δ

One morning in early July, the wind switched direction. No longer did it blow in from the sea, but instead came downriver from the mountains. It began to rain heavily every day. Initially, the river didn't rise, yet after two days it did. Though ordinarily the water level reached halfway up the screens, three feet beneath the walkway, within twenty-four more hours it had risen two feet.

The salmon run slowed to nearly nothing, but Paul was informed this was an interim period between upstream migrations of two different types of salmon. "If the weir washes out," he was told over the radio, "this is a good time for it to happen."

And indeed it did. He had barely prevented the plank walkway from floating away with the current. Unable to wade in the powerful current, he knelt on the submerged planking to pull the screens free from the weir. Released of this strain, the thick buttresses held solidly in the bed of the river. On the fifth evening the entire weir was under water and the Alexander River was on the brink of overflowing its high muddy banks.

With the screens piled on high ground, the weir was no longer a functional barrier to fish.

The weather became fouler: In addition to heavy rains, the wind increased, blowing the falling deluge sideways. In his cabin, Paul worked on translating Zolkoff's journal. When this task became too dreary, Paul would enter necessary information in his own journal. Even during the day he worked by lantern light; overhead, the clouds tumbled down from the mountains, black and pregnant with cold, harsh rain.

Paul subsisted mainly on sweetened tea and thick slices of toast. While dipping the toast into the tea, he would look up at the cabin ceiling, gauging the strength of the rain and wind.

On the radio, he heard watchmen at other weir sites complain about the weather. Some of them attempted to involve him in after-hours radio talk, but Paul felt removed from his fellow watchmen. They were mostly in their early twenties and talked of future job opportunities, girlfriends and consumer goods. His last entry in his journal recorded the failure of Paul's first excavation for Corporal Zolkoff. After the debacle with the bear, it had taken six days of intermittent work to straighten things out; it had taken an additional three days to dig another four feet, and he still had found nothing except the musket ball. The description in Lieutenant's Zolkoff's journal had either been incorrect, or time had shifted terrestrial features around, compounding the puzzle.

After jamming an old shirt between the bottom of the door and the floor to keep the rain out, he re-read his journal entry about the failure of his first dig for Corporal Zolkoff. It seemed concise enough, though it didn't reflect his frustration.

Then again, a good journal should be like Zolkoff's: to the point, with no extraneous verbiage. Of late, Zolkoff's journal had become bogged down in mercantile records and notations about the comings and goings of fur traders and hunters. It was all difficult, even agonizing, to translate.

Reflecting on widening his search, Paul decided that the next highest promontory would be the most logical place. It was another fifty meters to the west, but it lacked the height of his first site. Then again, he reasoned, what might 150 years have done?

That night Paul again dreamt of Corporal Zolkoff's funeral. *The priest, Russians, and native hunters formed a circle around the coffin of Zolkoff, with the Lieutenant standing somewhat apart. In full dress uniform he gazed down wearily at his brother's rough wooden coffin.*

The flag of Imperial Russia was unfurled, followed by the regimental banner. Two soldiers raised their rifles and fired a salute after a sergeant raised and suddenly dropped his sword. A carpenter, his leather apron tied snugly to his chest and waist, knelt. Holding wooden pegs in his teeth, he took one out and put it between his thumb and forefinger and raised a mallet to seal the coffin shut.

An outstretched hand from Lieutenant Zolkoff stopped him. The priest and his young native acolyte looked with alarm at the officer, and now Paul could make out the Russian word the priest said again and again, "Shame! Shame!" Zolkoff bit his lip in determination, then bent over and slid the lid away.

Paul awoke trembling.

He was grateful for consciousness, despite the scare. Oddly, he wished for a cigarette though he hadn't smoked in eighteen years.

Paul's hand moved nervously across his face and he remained uneasy. Outside was silence. Moving to one of two small windows, he saw in the first light of day that the storm had abated. In the stillness of the morning glow he saw a pair of evening grosbeaks feeding in an alder bush; they clung precariously to a frail limb.

Δ

After the southerly winds with their heavy rains, Paul's excavation activities were hampered by a heavy hatch-out of bugs. They swirled in thick clouds everywhere. For the first two days following the rains, the river was too high for re-installing the screens. Yet in order to work at the second promontory, he was quickly forced to wear a beekeeper's head net, and despite this the thick clouds of bugs covered the netting, preventing him from seeing. He had to sweep the netting clear frequently.

When the northerly winds returned, it blew away the hordes of stinging insects, but they proved increasingly resourceful. They lurked in the contours of the grasslands, even behind individual clumps of grass,. Yet with equal determination Paul worked on.

Feeling liberated after the storm, he dug and sieved dirt for nearly twenty hours straight.

He struck Zolkoff's tombstone within three hours. Russian workmen had used considerable skill chiseling away the letters on the three-by-three-foot slab of black stone. Paul guessed that the tombstone had been above ground for a number of years, as the edges of each letter were quite weather-worn. He read the inscription aloud: "Corporal Vassily Zolkoff: Born 3 December 1801, Died 2 August 1827. Rest in Eternal Peace."

Paul knew he should be more enthused than he was, but oddly finding the musket ball had excited him more. Resting momentarily against a mound of dirt, he studied the darkish stone, wondering how significant it was as an artifact. He poured tea from his thermos and, lifting his head net, sipped quickly; within seconds, a dozen bugs kicked wildly in the tea. Discouraged, Paul put the cup aside and resumed work.

That evening he left a pair of flashing construction lights in case a bear happened by. The lights supposedly repelled marauding bruins from the weir. "But often they have little effect," it had explained in the operations manual.

The long hours of digging and sieving had fatigued him badly. He hobbled across the weir and noted the river had receded; he guessed it would be low enough to re-install the screens in the morning. Stumbling through the cabin door, Paul barely managed to pull his boots off before collapsing upon his bunk and sinking into heavy sleep.

The next morning he was able to reinstall the weir. Though the water flowed quickly just beneath the walkway, the screens held. The water was murky from excessive runoff and the screens collected debris rapidly.

Paul monitored the weir until noon, making sure the structure would withstand the rigors of the high water. After cleaning screens, he hiked to the grave site. He removed boards from the hole and looked at the tombstone before he began digging.

Unlike the day before, he worked rapidly in anticipation of the find; he was becoming excited. Several times he checked himself, remembering the necessity of caution. Using boards, he dug in a temporary platform to prevent standing directly upon what he guessed would be the remains of the coffin.

The bugs found him in the hole and, out of the wind, plagued Paul viciously despite layers of hastily applied insect repellent. Deep in the stuffy hole, he gave up on his head net. Within several hours he swept aside a layer of loose soil and exposed a sheet of metal, tarnished black. Taking a breath, he proceeded slowly, knowing that he'd finally located Corporal Zolkoff's coffin.

He had never expected the cover of the coffin to be shielded with a sheet of copper. Slowly he broomed aside the dirt, experiencing a scare when a supporting board cracked and he nearly fell on the remains. One hundred and fifty years had, aside from tarnishing, done little to the copper sheet, though the wooden lid had turned to the consistency of hard-caked sugar.

He worked breathlessly, and Paul cursed knowing the weir would have collected much debris by this time, but he continued. Most of the decayed wood adhered to the copper, which was thicker than he'd anticipated. He was able to pull it away in three separate sections, exposing the skeletal remains of Zolkoff. Quite unlike a laboratory skeleton, the bones were deeply yellowed, the ends of some being nearly as black as the tarnished copper. Corporal Zolkoff's body had been buried face down.

Though there were no remains of a uniform, large brass buttons with a squared Cyrillic "A" lay equidistant from each other along the

Corporal's naked spinal column. Two larger cuff buttons were nestled inside the curled finger bones of each hand. Moving his face closer, Paul looked in vain for any remains of a sword. He straightened fast when he was hit with a powerful mustiness emanating from the interior of the coffin.

Paul was to never know what instinct caused him to turn the skull over, and he felt an initial wave of uneasiness when its bony grimace glowered upwards. But this uneasiness turned to alarm when he saw tiny aged cracks radiating from a neat hole over Corporal Zolkoff's right eye orbit.

Δ

In the next three weeks Paul generated many theories about the death of Corporal Zolkoff, so many he could no longer differentiate between plausible accounts or their wilder counterparts.

He had decided to continue the myth or lie of Lieutenant Zolkoff's journal by covering up the remains, leaving them as much like he'd found them as possible. He'd taken nothing except the bullet he'd found resting inside Corporal Zolkoff's skull. Though he considered erecting the gravestone on the surface, common sense told him what the result of that might be. Instead, he laid it beside the coffin.

Carefully, he covered up the gravesite, even planting clumps of grass over it. He felt like a conspirator with whatever forces had, 150 years before, led to the corporal's demise. Also, he no longer translated Lieutenant Zolkoff's journal; somehow, he'd lost enthusiasm for the officer's written words. Paul knew that was bad scholarship, but he didn't care. He concentrated on the weir as much as his contemplations concerning Corporal Zolkoff would allow. The salmon migration had resumed with even more intensity and there was much to do.

Δ

It was a beautiful day with rare unclouded skies when a plane landed on the beach. In it were a biologist and a Russian Orthodox priest. Initially, Paul was taken aback, wondering if they'd somehow discovered his activities; then the biologist told him it was Diocese policy that a priest offer mass annually at the old church. "After all, it's still a church," he explained.

Saying he'd be back in three hours and giving Paul a mysterious wink over the priest's shoulder, he departed. Puzzled, Paul followed the priest as he labored up the bluff. At the cabin he opened a large case, put on a pair of rubber boots and looked steadily at Paul.

"I will serve the Divine Liturgy. If you wish to attend, you are welcome."

"I'm not Russian Orthodox. I wouldn't know what to do."

"That isn't important. Do what seems appropriate."

He followed the priest down the trail towards the church. The storm had blown debris across the path in several areas, and Paul observed with pleasure that the swallows' young now joined them, young and adult alike whirring hungrily through clouds of insects. He and the cleric stopped. Paul put on his head net and apologized for not having a spare. Instead he offered the priest a worn plastic container of insect repellent. Putting down his case, the priest flapped frantically while intermittently applying the viscous liquid. They continued. As they carefully entered the church, the priest clucked his tongue as he looked at the bullet holes and graffiti; then, being careful, he picked his way across the floor, set upright two discarded boxes against the south wall, placed a board between them and removed a chalice, and a cloth icon; then he donned vestments. Paul found the same bare spot on the floor where he'd knelt weeks before. He wondered if he should kneel at once, or later. As the priest began, he knelt. Fewer bugs surrounded him now, and he removed the head net slowly, reminding him of years before when his mother and aunt lifted their veils to receive Holy Communion.

He resolved to pray for Maureen and Kathy: He clasped his hands together, kneading the knuckles until they hurt. He looked at the priest, now busy with the service. Occasionally he would mutter necessary words, elevate the cloth icon, turn towards Paul, then face the makeshift altar.

Paul's resolution to pray for his dead wife and daughter weakened: Instead he became frustrated and angry. Wasn't this weakness? People prayed for deceased loved ones all the time. Why couldn't he? Had he loved Maureen and Kathy any less? Suddenly a strange compromise struck him: Why not pray for the slain Corporal Zolkoff? He took fresh hold upon himself, yet his chest and throat tightened with silence and stubbornness.

He shook his head and looked at the coarse-grained floor, squeezing his eyes together until his brow hurt. Sweat beaded and oozed down his forehead. Paul put his hand to his throat and squeezed off an involuntary curse.

Beneath the south wall the priest poured wine and water into the chalice and elevated it, imparting the devotion of a mysterious and timeless faith.

Δ

During a silent and awkward lunch, Paul received the pilot's radio instructions telling him to have the priest ready on the beach.

"They're in a hurry. The weather is worsening."

As a sort of apology for cutting lunch short, Paul carried the priest's case. When they reached the crest of the bluff the cleric turned towards Paul.

"You are married?"

Paul wondered why he should guess that a solitary weir watchman was married, then he remembered his gold wedding band.

"I lost a wife and daughter last winter in a car accident."

The priest nodded sadly.

"God's will is often mysterious and painful."

Paul took one step down the bluff, but then turned towards the priest.

"I respect that. But I don't believe any God would take an innocent woman and child. Rather it was part of a cruel and random fate that perhaps no one will ever understand, especially me. I'm sorry."

They walked down the bluff, and he thought the priest was about to answer when the plane made its initial pass, the engine noise obliterating any words. Reaching the bottom of the bluff the two walked onto the sands; the plane landed very hard, rebounded six feet into the air, came back down upon the beach, and braked to a halt. The priest looked on dubiously. The biologist unloaded a box of supplies while the pilot guided the priest into the back seat.

"We'll move you out of here in about a week. Run is about through."

Paul nodded, then quickly backed away from the plane as the pilot hurriedly jumped into the left hand seat and the biologist followed suit.

Through the window the priest waved good-bye as the engine started and the plane scudded down the beach; it turned and took off into the wind. Veering sharply it quickly leveled off and followed the wide beach westward.

True to the pilot's word, a weather front closed rapidly from the northeast. At sea, under the brows of low-lying clouds, rain squalls created sheets of mist. When he reached the top of the bluff, Paul turned and studied the front. It moved quickly, approaching the mouth of Alexander River at an angle. Since it was low tide, several hundred gulls sat upon an exposed sand shoal at the river mouth; they shifted as they too perceived the thickening of the weather with its accompanying winds.

Several dozen of them lifted their wings and took to the air, slowly flying upriver towards the lake. Paul tucked the box of supplies against his chest and walked up the path. Around him, the willow and alder patches began to sway in an oncoming wind that was rich with the smell of late summer.

Reports of Disappearances III: The Commando

*I*t was a massive wooden slab of a fishing boat, built before the war with hemlock timbers, hence stouter than other vessels of its size and type. Yet somewhere between Cape Chiniak and Cape Spencer, taking a straight-line course across the Gulf of Alaska, it vanished.

There was a storm, but The Commando had been through countless storms in the fifty years since its construction, and its crew was experienced and respectful of the sea.

It had a capacious wooden belly that had carried thousands of tons of fish to all Pacific ports since World War II. Portions of its catches had been served on dinner platters, both rich and humble, on every continent of the planet.

The captain and engineer were brothers and could tell stories that doubled up listeners with laughter. I was in the boat less than a month, but I listened to a year's worth of ironic sagas and quirky, farcical accounts filled with Dickensian characters. The son of the captain, my school friend, had been with them on the boat; but, late for college, he had flown south from Kodiak and was no longer aboard. That was luck.

The Coast Guard looked for pieces of the boat from the Cape south and north. Nothing was found. The Commando just vanished with no explanations. Death is impossible to accept when there are no explanations.

One Wing Falling

Teel's nostrils pinched in repugnance when he saw that the crew had stabbed out cigarettes in the leftover grease and bones scattered over their plates. Great black smudges were slashed in the leavings of the midday meal. Babs sat across from him, looking sullenly into her plate. The others had pointedly left Teel alone with her.

He shoved a plate aside and drew up a coffee mug to his lips, sipping and shaking his head.

"I wanted to tell you I don't like any of my people arguing with me when there's a job to do. Questions, that's fine. But no arguments. I don't like that."

She couldn't look directly at Teel because she knew he was in the right, for in a fish camp he was boss and that was that. An old academic tradition.

He looked again at the scattering of dishes and reminded himself that it was his turn. That much was a democracy.

She finally looked up at him; her blue eyes were unblinking and it humiliated Teel that he'd wanted her for the past month but didn't like or even respect her. Suddenly he recalled the words of a colleague about her: "Babs will be all right. She's dumb and pliable."

That is what Stroder had said. But Stroder was wrong. He also added something Teel had picked up in the gossip from other faculty that winter: "There's good sport in that one, too. A screamer. I like screamers. Try her, Teel. Drop your Mr. Professor airs and enjoy yourself for a change. What in hell else is the great out-of-doors for?"

But one could hardly respect Stroder.

Babs looked directly at him, then began nodding. She reminded Teel of a busty owl with shirt and pants on.

"Dr. Teel, I didn't mean to give you the impression I was arguing."

"Good. Leave the dishes. I'll get them later."

He left her sitting on the camp stool nodding and Teel felt good about that. She had expected some transactional dialogue full of *me*'s and *I*'s and lord knows what other garbage. But Teel wasn't one to get involved in such an exchange with a field assistant.

It was enough to agonize through that with Jean during the divorce, he thought, and he walked from the cook tent uphill to his private wall tent where he had a small laboratory and his cot.

He lay down. Outside he heard the plywood door of the kitchen tent come open, and he listened as Babs walked away towards the crew tent where Teel knew the others would be waiting for her. Good. She could weep and lament to them.

"Well, I hope she falls and breaks her goddamned leg; then I can ship her out of here and get on with work the way it should be." He spoke to the canvassed ceiling. He'd never been a believer in bringing women into the bush to do research work. He rolled over in his cot. Against the far wall next to the door was a wooden table with a German microscope he'd owned since graduate school. The metal body was deep black, and the ocular housings were brass. It settled him to look at it. An old, trustworthy companion.

Another plane passed over. Then another.

He turned onto his stomach and buried his head in the bedroll. A third plane came over then began circling. Over the past four weeks during the commercial fishing season the constant umbrella of aerial fish spotters had driven Teel crazy by circling and circling the shoreline near the camp. With nearly twenty-four hours of light, the fish spotters were aloft almost to midnight.

Yet the plane was soon joined by another, and he knew it was hopeless to catch a nap and forget about the difficulty in managing a research project and six field assistants.

He opened the door of the tent and looked up with annoyance. Teel thought back on that particular moment many times after that: How he'd just opened the door of his tent and, by sheer chance, while being annoyed, he'd simply looked up as he had a thousand times previously.

"It all seemed so routine, glancing up like that. Just looking up."

"If you go on and on about it, you'll never forget it. Don't you see Teel, you can't keep churning it over, stirring it up."

Often he would recall everything beginning with the scene before the kitchen table with the dull-witted Babs. Then, much like rolling a videotape slowly forwards, he would arrive at the exact point where he looked up after opening the door.

He'd seen the fuselage of an airplane with only one wing, spinning slowly and desperately to the ground.

"What I can't shake, what I can't forget is the men inside the plane. I could see them. It was a single engine plane that had been on pontoons. It spun. It spun like those strange seeds that tumbled from the trees during the fall, when I was a kid back east. You know, the ones with a large green seed on one end, and a single propeller made of fiber which spun. Or twirled. Anyway, the plane fell like those; not straight to earth, but fluttering downward at a slight angle."

"You've told me this. You keep going over it, Teel. You've got to forget it."

Soon he didn't talk about it anymore. At least not to his wife or colleagues. He went to counseling once a week during the thick hard frost of winter, watching with irony the graceful maneuverings of the tropical fish in the large tank which occupied the entire wall in the psychologist's waiting room.

He'd gotten to know the fish well. One time he told the psychologist, an attractive German woman who wore tight blouses.

"It's forty degrees below zero outside, and these fish of yours in here are thriving at seventy-eight degrees. It's a wonder."

"Do you think the fact that you wanted to have sex with your field assistant has anything to do with the persistence of your recollections about this accident last summer? When the two planes collided? Anything to do with the problems you are having in coping with it?"

After the crash, Teel remembered, he'd been horrified when he suddenly realized there were two planes and not one. The plane he'd first seen tumbled to earth and burst into flames, as if the planet were spilling fire from an angry wound.

"After the crash, since our camp has several radios, I was mission control, so to speak. It took over twenty-nine hours to get rid of the bodies. Our camp is sixty miles from the closest village. We had to wait for a law enforcement officer because you can't move dead people with legal authority. Moving dead bodies turned into a complex business."

"You didn't answer me."

"I know. Why would wanting to have sex with that useless Babs have anything to do with my utter horror in seeing five people die? I can't see the connection."

"But Babs was actually up there. At the wreckage. She managed things up there while you were on the radios."

"Someone of responsibility had to direct things. Two planes and five bodies scattered over a quarter of a mile is quite a task."

As spring approached he stopped going to the psychologist. A friend had recommended a male psychiatrist, but Teel hadn't gone. His classes were going badly and he was facing the reality of another field season. Thankfully, Babs had flunked her preliminary examinations again and withdrawn.

In the night outside his house he would sometimes be about ready to look skyward, then stop. Instead he would do something else. He missed looking at the night sky. In the high northern latitudes the midnight sky was stark, with planets and stars brilliant against it. On some nights the perennial strangeness of the *aurora borealis* sprayed plumes of magnetic colors over the entire horizon, but even on these nights he hesitated before looking up.

Back in the bush that spring one of the first things he did was hike up to where one of the planes had crashed and examine the vegetation. The scorched patch was easily visible between the large drifts of melting snow that clung to the slope. Willow buds were forcing their way out and the alders were growing green and supple.

He paced off the area that was burned. Over forty meters wide. Unlike his previous dozen field seasons, he wasn't intense with his work; he didn't feel the urgency to complete every item before it was time to close up camp and return home. Teel allowed his senior field assistant to take charge of daily routine.

He went on hikes alone. Several miles away the rocky coast straightened suddenly into a long curving beach with black, coarse volcanic sand. On it breakers swept in from the western Bering Sea creating bizarre museums of driftwood that lay in countless poses and still-lifes. He would walk above the tongues of the breakers and ignore the fact he was without a firearm, despite the numerous bear tracks on the long, evenly sculpted sands.

Sometimes he met fishermen camped out and other times not. He made no attempt to meet or avoid them. He found a favorite location at the fifteen-hundred-foot level of a steep mountainside; looking out over the ocean he could see far out to the edge of the sea and sky. Close to shore dozens of fishing boats seined shoals of fish.

"You're overdue for a sabbatical."

A colleague had told him this one day. His detachment from his work was becoming obvious and he began neglecting his classes, leaving more to his graduate assistants. This was unlike him. He knew that his colleagues realized he was changed, and it was interesting to see what each did in response to that. Some made an effort to cheer him up; others avoided him.

Just prior to Christmas break his wife told him she was going to England with a friend.

"There's a workshop in York, and frankly a Christmas season with you isn't attractive. I don't want to be cruel, but that's what I feel."

He had seen her off at the airport without much regret, and he was settling into being alone when the phone rang and his first wife offered him the children for two weeks in January.

"No. I'm going off and can't. Sorry."

He'd lied, but then wondered if he had. Next morning he broke out his sleeping bag and wondered about the label guaranteeing it down to minus fifty. He'd always been amused by such claims. They never really worked out.

Since it was midwinter and no one went into the bush camping, he felt strange at the airport with his backpack. He took a branch airline to the coastal village where he usually staged his field operations during the summer. In the village, whose population swelled to several thousand during the fishing season, it was quiet. In the lee of the old and shutdown canneries were thick drifts of snow. He hiked through the streets ignoring the looks of several people who stared out of the smallish windows of their houses. Dogs barked at him, and several children bundled up against the winter temperatures followed him on beaten-up three-wheeled motorcycles or on snowmobiles. When he reached the small poorly heated office of the air taxi service, his pilot looked up at him with surprise, glasses resting upon the end of his nose.

"Professor! What are you doing here? You're a summer bird around here."

Teel explained he had to take a series of water chemistries.

The pilot stomped about warming his feet, and warned him that his camp was a far different situation in winter than in spring or summer.

"Jesus, Professor. It was thirty below zero here for the last three days and blew forty knots straight northwest. Are you sure? I mean, there isn't any liquid water left out there, is there?"

Teel had smiled and reminded him about the year-round springs that fed the river near camp. Despite his repeated warnings, including an offer of his eldest son to stay with him the first two days, the pilot admitted to the present calm weather and said he'd fly him out there in the afternoon. Teel took lunch with the pilot and his Eskimo wife; when she heard what Teel was going to do, she shook her head while serving tea and Christmas cookies.

They landed on a long snow-covered slope within a quarter mile of camp. After unloading his gear the pilot removed his aviator's mitten and rubbed his cheeks with his warm hand.

"I don't like this a damned bit. Alone and all. But, it's your life. I'll be back in seven days. You absolutely sure you don't want me to come sooner."

As a concession, Teel agreed to being picked up in five days rather than seven.

Watching the plane ski off down slope then quickly lift into the air, Teel was both surprised and flattered as it circled twice, finally dipping its wings and flying off towards town.

Despite winter, it was a beautiful day with temperatures somewhat over fifteen degrees. He put up his small mountaineer's tent, then put on snowshoes and hiked up the frozen river to the first spring. Carefully, he took the necessary samples.

That night the wind came up and, reaching one arm outside the tent, he took the thermometer inside and saw it registered minus twenty-six degrees. He crawled inside his sleeping bag, and by candlelight he read from a paperback.

"I hate lanterns. Hissing pulsing bastards. Candles are fine. The finest literature in the world was read and written by candlelight."

Teel put the book down as the memory of his major professor's voice echoed clearly over two decades. He had been a cantankerous old gentleman, unbelievably pigheaded on most subjects but science. Yet a fine man.

Smiling, he pinched out the delicate flame of the candle and wriggled deeper into his sleeping bag.

The next morning was both clear and calm, though it was not light enough to hike until nearly ten. It remained a respectable minus eight, and dressing as warmly as possible he filled a thermos with coffeeand struggled over the mountainous terrain until he looked down over the long, curved beach where he had walked so often. Now there were no fish camps or fishing boats. The ocean was hostile and covered with intermittent floes of dirty gray ice.

Along the shore a crust of frost had been fragmented and scattered by the daily tides.

The change in appearance of the driftwood astounded Teel. Below the snow-covered tundra, the massive relics had been coated with intricate and fantastical sculptures of rime. Teel hiked down and studied the largest of these, a huge log that long ago had been forced above the high tide level by winds and surf. Its bare surface was covered evenly with fine icy armor. Carefully he reached out to touch it, but slowly withdrew his hand and stared. The surf and tide had swept the beach clear and the black volcanic sands were in such contrast to the snow and ice that his eyes strained into squint. He took his snowshoes off and walked easily along the beach.

At nightfall the wind came up powerfully. He reached his tent just as it was being pulled from the ground. After digging in and reinforcing it,

Teel crawled into his sleeping bag and watched the red nylon fabric pop and flutter in the wind. Below him he could hear the surf building with the onshore wind. The following day was so foul he spent it almost entirely in his tent, and it was only late into the third night that it calmed. The quiet had awakened him, and he saw that he'd fallen asleep while reading, wasting a candle. He was about to go outside when a sudden notion made him take out his wallet and look at a calendar. It was Christmas night.

When he did stop outside he looked up and saw that the entire sky was illuminated with amazing clarity. Every planet and star had distinct edges. He felt like reaching up and sweeping them down from the sky, as if they were jewels on a black cloth placed there especially for him. For a long time he watched, and after a spectacular shooting star slashed an iridescent streak from east to west, Teel crawled back inside and went to sleep. There would be few Christmases like this one.

On the day after Christmas a strange plane flew over, dipped its wings, then came in for a landing. Teel's pilot's two planes each had an orange thunderbolt painted on its tail, his trademark in the region. But this plane was smaller and had no special markings, and it taxied over to his gear. Cutting the engine, his pilot jumped out and explained that his regular plane had developed problems.

Even considering the situation, Teel found himself relieved to see the pilot, and it occurred to him that he'd been alarmed that his pilot might have been hurt in the intervening five days. Both quickly took down the tent.

"How did everything go?"

"Uneventfully. Actually, very nicely."

In town he spent the night with the pilot and his family. He was astounded to find they'd delayed Christmas dinner to share it with him. The wife said grace in Inipuit and their oldest son wanted to know if Teel had seen any fox. Then he asked about marten, and then wolverine, until finally his father told him to leave their guest to eat in peace.

No one was on campus over Christmas break. He took the time to attend several museum collections of marine specimens and found that many of them were improperly catalogued and, worse yet, misidentified.

He became angry. There was no reason for such slipshod methods in a collection of specimens. Because his wife was gone, he took lunch daily in the Student Union Building, and one day Stroder joined him. He looked tentatively at Teel and was about to ask something, but before he could Teel pointed a fork at him.

"Say, your student Aswani, the Tunisian fellow, he's supposed to be in charge of the marine fish collections. I've been working on it this past week and things are really screwed up. Misidentifications, and miscatalogings. Not good."

Taken completely by surprise, Stroder tried to defend his student, but it did no good. Poor work was poor work and, after informing Stroder that he was personally investing hours of labor to put everything right, Teel returned to the Life Science building. Actually, he'd purposely kept matters to business with Stroder, for with the travel vouchers coming through the department secretaries, word was getting out of his winter trip to the coast. Most of his colleagues would consider it eccentric, but he did not intend to discuss it. There was no point. None at all.

The next day he was in the museum working when he discovered that several dozen rare specimens had been preserved in an incorrect fixative. *They'll dissolve within a month,* Teel thought, and he immediately began the process of transferring them. He particularly enjoyed working alone in the marine museum. It was very old and all the cabinets and work benches were handmade of oak and worn glossy from constant use. The grain of the oak stood out in seemingly bold relief. He especially enjoyed the peculiar smell of the museum's workroom. The building was also thankfully quiet. In the distance a radio played, but it was low and indistinct.

Carefully he transferred each specimen. He was nearly done when he looked up and saw Babs. She stood at the entrance to the workroom. Her right hand held a folder and her left rested against the door she'd just pushed open.

"Hello, Dr. Teel. Did Dr. Stroder call you?"

"No. I haven't heard from him."

"Oh."

She then let the door close and stood there looking. Teel recognized the folder to be her admissions packet from the graduate school, and his stomach sank. She wanted back in. Finally she took several steps closer, and Teel saw that she'd lost a considerable amount of weight and looked older. That seemed strange. It had only been ten months since she'd washed out.

"I'm trying to get back in. The chairman approved, but he said he'd prefer that it be unanimous with the committee. Dr. Stroder, well, I saw him at lunch and he's in support of the idea."

Teel barely managed to suppress a smile and thought, *I bet he is,* and he guessed that Stroder would be eager to take Babs over to his project.

"Dr. Teel, I know I had problems out there. After the crash. With everything. I had problems. I didn't study for my prelims and flunked. I've been back in New York with my parents. My father knew a good psychiatrist. After the crash of those two planes it was difficult, Dr. Teel. I would do better now."

Immediately Teel was surprised. During the day of the crash and after, Babs had never seemed bothered or in any way contemplative about what had happened. She became uneasy with his silence.

"I am better. I had a nervous breakdown. I guess you heard. After my prelims."

"No, I hadn't heard."

She raised her folder, began to saying something in explanation, but stopped. Instead she looked around at the museum workroom and, dropping the folder to her side, looked hopefully at Teel.

"I want to continue with your project, Dr. Teel. I invested almost two years in it. I'm sure I can turn out a dissertation I'll be proud of. You, too."

The last part seemed excessive, for Teel never thought Babs capable of turning out a dissertation. Still, he was surprised she didn't want to transfer to Stroder, and he'd never thought her the type to have serious psychological problems over the crash. That still surprised him to silence. In the hall someone pushed something by on a cart with a squeaky wheel.

"Dr. Teel, I just want a chance."

Slowly he screwed the cap onto a jar and washed his hands clean of fixative. His back was to her. The water spattered into the porcelain sink.

"I didn't know of your nervous problems. Considering them, wouldn't it be better to move over to Stroder's activity. Different site and all that?" She was about to answer, too quickly, he thought, so he continued. "Actually, I would prefer that."

She fell silent. He knew she would have to take many more extra classes to make this change. This alone would hinder her badly. He turned and, while taking out several paper towels, finally worked up nerve enough to look at her. As he expected, she was near tears. His stomach tightened.

"Do you know why I respect you so much Dr. Teel, why I want to return to your project. Can I be frank?"

Teel felt a rising of panic. Slowly he took off his lab smock and began to put on his coat. He hadn't planned on leaving, but he was now. Babs stammered, but she continued despite his obvious discomfort with the direction the conversation was taking.

"I respect you because to the others, well, during my first summer working in the field, I wasn't a potential scientist; I was just a, a cunt. I'm sorry Dr. Teel, but it's the truth. But you expected professionalism and had no price except quality. I can do it, Dr. Teel. The crash, well, the crash caused awful problems, but maybe overall it helped me too."

Thankfully, she stopped. Holding the folder against her side, she managed to fight back tears. Teel shrugged his coat on, reached down, and took the folder from her hand. He opened it, noted with the usual annoyance that the chairman's signature had taken two lines, looked for any open space, and rapidly signed. Giving the folder back to Babs, he wrinkled his brow and stepped towards the door.

"I've done that on the condition you pass your prelims prior to the field season, and you inform me if camp summons up intolerable memories for you. Your position in my program isn't contingent on your presence in camp; I have things you can do on campus. For instance, this museum is in shambles."

Babs looked at him, surprised and grateful. But he stepped by her and just barely acknowledged her thanks. After picking up several books from his office, as he exited through the stairwell door, he saw both department secretaries standing around Babs, one hugging her while the other patted her back.

That afternoon he walked home despite the extreme cold. It pleased him to be independent from a car. As he was about to take a shortcut through a thick wood of white birch, the chairman stopped and offered a ride.

The chairman was a small New Zealander who, encased cocoon-style in his thick goose-down coat, peered out the windshield of his car through a meek aperture in the hood of his coat. Forcing the hood back somewhat, he peeked at Teel.

"Awfully good of you to re-admit Babs to your program."

It didn't seem to require a response. When he dropped Teel off before his house, Teel noticed the lights were on and that his wife had evidently returned several days early. The chairman, instead of waving his usual subdued farewell, leaned across to close the door and said, "When I was young and far more adventurous I worked in Antarctica. The military chaps failed to supply us and several of my mates died. Cold, malnutrition. But yet I still remember the winters. The vividness of the skies. The deprivation was terrible, of course; I shall never forget that. But I do remember the skies. See you tomorrow, Teel."

He closed the door and drove away very slowly. Teel looked after him, and in the ten years he'd known him this was the most astounding thing he'd said. Teel had never known that the shy, retiring scientist had worked in Antarctica. He turned while still thinking of what the chairman had said and slowly walked up the driveway. Glancing at the chimney, he could see that his wife had started the woodstove and hadn't adjusted the draught correctly. She never could. He decided not to grouse about that; it probably wasn't important.

Before he opened the front door he looked across the road where an open field was bordered by a dwarfed wood of black spruce. Just below the tips of them the moon struggled to rise, spreading a silverish cast across the silhouette of the trees. A metallic haze surrounded it. Tonight, Teel knew, would be exceptionally cold and clear.

Reports of Disappearances IV: Robert Strom

*H*e was tending a fish weir on the south end of Kodiak Island. When he hadn't reported in by radio as scheduled, his boss flew from town to Strom's remote station. But he couldn't find him.

The alarm was raised, and additional personnel were called in for the search. They found his skiff overturned near chunks of firewood along a beach a few miles from the cabin. They did not find his body. I'd been listening to the progress report of the search nightly on my short-wave radio.

He was a strong young man with a ready smile and plans to finish college and follow a career as a fish and game biologist in Alaska. He loved fishing and hunting, which back in those days was the prime mover in attracting people into the field. He tied beautifully hand-crafted dry flies and carved delicate decoys from wood, giving the finished products to friends as gifts.

It was spring, and it wasn't implausible that a bear came along, picked up his body and moved inland with its find. In spring, bear are notorious scavengers since the vegetation hasn't greened up and the fish aren't in. The search went on for almost a week, then was discontinued. The area around Red Lake was vast, and there were thousands of thickets and diverse niches where a wandering bear might have dragged him, if, indeed, a bear had taken him off.

Just as likely, his body could have sunk in the cold water after a capsizing, and it would be found later that summer.

All summer Strom's replacements tended the weir nervously, always expecting to come across his body. It was a mild summer, but despite this, they stayed close to the cabin. Strom's fate hung about the station, almost as corporeal as if it were a third party.

No one ever found any part of Robert Strom.

Highway of the Moon

After they discharged Earl from the Air Force, he went home and visited his mother. The lumber mill had left her the old ranch house, and she lived in that. In back of the old place she had a small garden, but nothing like she'd had when his dad was alive. During the afternoons Earl would sit in the drawing room watching her sew while outside they could hear the mill going full blast, and the sound of the mill annoyed Earl. After dinner he would go to town and take in a movie or something, but it seemed no matter where he went Earl could smell the burning wood scraps from the new mill. After being at home a week he bought an old truck and began fixing it up. His mother would take him out coffee, and when she looked at him he could tell from her eyes that she knew he was going to leave. One weekend his sister visited, and he got in an argument with her and her husband about Dad's selling the ranch when he was so sick. Earl had stormed outside and wandered in between the stacks of lumber.

Slowly he began to scrape together stuff for the trip north. He used a magazine article as a guide and tried to hide the paraphernalia from his mother, but she found out. One evening she asked where he was headed, and he had just said, "North," without elaborating. She asked him what he would do up north, and he stumbled around suggesting what he might do, but soon it became obvious that he didn't have the foggiest idea.

After a couple of weeks, he packed everything in the pickup and looked it over several times, making sure he hadn't overlooked something. His mother packed him a box of fried chicken and biscuits, and he left Sunday morning when the mill wasn't operating. The morning fog hugged the ground like a cotton duff, and as he drove away the truck's motor disturbed the silence of the fog and the calm of his mother standing alone on the porch with one hand holding the oak wood banister.

He and Grandpa used to hunt valley quail early in the morning. Every-thing would be so silent that Earl was afraid to talk or even breathe aloud. The rolling hills would be wet with "night air" as his grandpa would call it, and their pants would get soaked before they reached the spot by the spring where there were always quail scrambling around the gravel like funny figures in old silent movies. Earl would get a few shots off, and Grandpa would bend over painfully and pick up the little birds. They would sit down and pluck them, and Grandpa would tell him how years before the quail had been so thick they would wake you in the morning.

He drove for two days without stopping to sleep. He knew it was stupid, but he wanted to be rid of the armies of drive-ins, motels, and stores. He wanted north now, and wanted it badly. At each stop he would take out his map and estimate how much longer it would take him, and he figured that in another few days he would be far enough north that he would see the wilderness country he had so often dreamed of. Finally he overnighted in a town where there were lots of spruce trees spread out from the town center and up the steep mountains. Even in the night he could see this town was in a valley surrounded by dog-toothed mountains capped with fresh winter snow. He tried hard to see more of the mountains through the dark, but the glow of the city lights made it impossible; he reckoned that in another few days there would be no more city lights.

In his motel room there was a fireplace with a fresh hopper of wood and immediately he was glad he had stayed at this motel rather than the one that advertised electric blankets. He started a fire, then slowly and carefully fed the wood into the hearth, taking pleasure in smelling the rich scents of the burning wood and watching the pitch ooze in hot boiling globules from the spruce logs.

He, Grandpa, and his dad had gone on a deer hunt up on the mountain, and they had searched all day for any sign of deer, but found none. They camped overnight in Phantom Pass, and Grandpa and Dad made a great fire; way into the night he sat and listened to them swap stories about the fantastic hunting trips they had gone on years before. They had fallen asleep under their blankets near the fire. Earl had watched the fire go from yellow to a deep aquatic blue. Just before he dozed off, the fire was subdued to a brilliant, quiet red glow.

The next morning he was up early and on his way. He could clearly see the mountains that surrounded the town, and he noticed how far the trees went up, almost clinging to the summits and leaning wearily away from the prevailing winds. He wondered what he might be able to see from the summits of those mountains; judging from his map, he guessed it might be the ocean. He wondered if the ocean would look any different from there than it had from the jet airliner that flew him to Germany.

From the airliner it looked flat and pale, like a weak broth. Perhaps from the mountain it would look like it always seemed to look in advertisements and travel movies: Vast, blue, and lonely.

Earl jumped in his truck and began driving; the road took him into a great canyon, at the base of which ran a river. The road clung to the side of the gorge, yet in places it seemed ready to plunge down into the river. The road was dangerous and Earl nearly ran off it while looking up and down the steep sides of the canyon. Yet even with the glimpses he got from the truck, Earl could feel the untouched ferocity in the mountains. This feeling was new to him, for back home he never felt it. Often he'd stop the truck, get out, and look up into the summits and passes for signs of animals; and finally that afternoon he saw a large herd of wild sheep slowly grazing in a meadow blown clear of snow by powerful winter winds. His fingers and ears began to freeze, and he was forced back into his truck. Bouncing up and down on the seat and rubbing his hands together, he waited for the truck heater to take effect.

It was nearly winter, and Dad decided that since the snow was fresh it would be good for deer hunting. All afternoon they looked, but the wind blew gusts of snow into the air, and rarely could they see fifty feet. Just before getting to the truck they had come across a big mule deer bedded down behind a boulder. When it bounded off right by him, Dad had yelled, "Shoot, Earl!" and as he raised the rifle he was amazed at how damned large the animal was.

When the sun went down, he judged it to be around 4:30, but when he stopped for gas he was surprised to find it was only 3:15. This was the first time he felt he was getting north. Driving on, Earl thought if he drove far enough north, there would be no sun at all; he didn't know if he would like that or not.

The highway began to get worse, and snow drifted across the road like gusts of steam. Miles of uninterrupted wilderness passed by; he wondered if the magazine had been correct in saying winter was the best time to drive north. If gas or food stops weren't available, Earl thought, it would seem a poor time to go north. Finally, just when he thought he'd have to use one of his emergency fuel cans, he came across a big glittery service station that looked like it had been airlifted there from a big city. In the restroom, his nose wrinkled as he inhaled the sweet deodorant; he thought how strange it was that only a few minutes before he had been driving through open country. When the attendant saw him squint at the price of gas, he laughed and told Earl there was a real shock in store for him farther north.

While buckling himself into the pickup, Earl looked around and felt odd when he realized that the only connection between him and the old ranch was this truck and his personal belongings. To the forest, mountains, and road, he was another anonymous face that passed by like a phase of the moon. He felt eerie thinking that way, perhaps even morbid, so he turned on his truck radio and searched for a station, but there weren't any. He kept trying. None. He had never been in an area where he couldn't get a radio station; he banged his hand against the dash. Still no stations. He felt excited: If he was this far north, he was nearly at his destination.

The night was overcast, and the lights of the truck sliced clean yellow-white cones into the dark. He wanted to sleep, for the sound of the truck motor began to undulate as if he were listening from a long distance away. He felt very drowsy. On the horizon was a clear white glare. Earl thought it might be the rising moon, yet soon the glare got much brighter and he was relieved to round a corner of a hill and see a town below him. He stopped at the first motel he came to and dropped to sleep instantly.

The best hunting trip was the last he took with Grandpa. He knew his dad worried about the old man. Before they left, his dad took Earl aside and said, "You're twelve now, Son. So listen to your grandpa. But look after him, too. He's getting on." They went into the high plateau country to hunt elk, country where as a young man his grandpa had worked tending cattle. Almost every inch of the country reminded Grandpa of something or someone, and onthe second morning the sky cleared and Earl was amazed to see another mountain range looming in the east. As they saddled up the horses, Earl was eager to ride towards them. Maybe they would see mountain sheep, an animal he'd never seen. Grandpa smiled and said those mountains were two day's ride distant. "In open country, Earl, things that you see aren't always what they seem. Many a man died depending only on his eyes." Though they hadn't gotten an elk, they saw several herds; but they were always too far off. Grandpa admitted, "I'm not up to the hunt like I once was. Not even close." But Earl didn't care. He'd seen country he would never forget.

By 7:30 the next morning, the sun hadn't even begun to come up. He made his way to a cafe where a number of truckers were sitting around kidding the young waitresses and drinking coffee while scooping in hash browns and eggs. Spreading out a map, Earl added the mileages between various points, then totaled them. There were fifteen hundred to go. Could that be right? He recalculated.

The waitress slid the coffee in front of him and had to shout to get his attention. As she trotted away with his order, he thought of the five hard days he'd spent traveling in the truck. It seemed that in another fifteen hundred miles he'd be at the north pole. He was beginning to realize how long and lonely a trip he'd started out on.

He had to make better time than this.

Earl pulled out three hours before the first glow of dawn. He was disappointed to see that the land this highway now threaded through was without mountains; rather, it was wide and open with rolling hills covered by small, sparsely limbed spruces. To the west, the east, north and south, all Earl could see were the long series of rolling hills that ran off endlessly like ocean swells. The truck seemed to have changed tempos somewhat, and Earl noticed the pavement had ended; a road sign told him it would be gravel and dirt road for 965 more miles. He wondered if the pickup could take it. Taking a fresh hold on the wheel, he pressed down on the accelerator; he was anxious to get past this section as quickly and uneventfully as possible. The snow and gravel had become hard packed since it was midwinter and the surface of the highway was such that a fast cruising speed was possible.

He had driven uneventfully for two hours when he saw the moose. It stood directly in his way, and Earl brought the pickup to a sudden stop just twenty or so feet short of the huge beast. With awe he looked at it; at the shoulders it stood nearly as high as the truck, and it was a good nine feet long. It breathed slowly; the vapor rolled out of its nostrils, rose steadily, then dissipated with the wind. The moose swung his head around and stared at the truck, yet it didn't move. Frost covered its muzzle, and some saliva had frozen in lumpy white crusts to the outer surfaces of its lips. Although this was the first moose Earl had ever seen, it seemed hardly genuine.

He had expected to see a moose belly deep in a mountain pond eating water plants, its giant antlers luxurious in velvet. But this dumb antlerless thing blocking his way disappointed him. He honked his horn, and the moose looked away from the truck, took a half step, then stopped. Again he honked, again the moose ignored him. He was considering racing his motor to scare it, when a flat bed truck came from the opposite direction. The plank bed of the flat bed was half rotten and clattered loudly. Coming to an unsteady stop, a man jumped from it, reached back onto the bed and grabbed a board, hurling it at the moose. It struck the beast just below the shoulders. The moose bolted. Earl saw its hind end vanish behind a clump of spruce. Both trucks moved on.

Towards the last, Grandpa couldn't move around much but just sat on the front porch smoking cigarettes and working on leather belts. As he carved the figure of an animal into a belt, he would explain to Earl about the life history of that animal to Earl; about where to find it, how to hunt it, and what its best parts were to fry, stew, or roast. Once when Grandpa had carved a great bull elk, he pointed all around him and said that there once were thousands of elk right near the ranch. Now there were none. When Earl asked why they were gone, Grandpa stubbed out his cigarette and said he sure as hell wished he knew.

It wasn't long after midday when the sun set. Earl figured there was now about three and a half hours of useful light, getting less the farther north he drove. He began to experience a sense of weirdness from this bizarre lack of sunlight.

And it was dark. Really dark. And quiet.

Earl tried the radio again, anything to break the silence, but he got nothing. He suddenly swore for leaving his sister the portable tape cassette player. The country seemed changeless, and it bored Earl. This made him much more anxious to leave it behind, and he pressed the accelerator down further and the truck flew harder over the highway.

When Earl came up to the sharp turn, he knew it wasn't a question of making it, rather a matter of going off the road in such a way as to do the least amount of damage to the truck and himself. On the inside pocket of the curve the truck slid off cleanly into a snow bank. Earl's body jerked against the seatbelt, and some of the gear in the bed tore loose and flew out into the snow.

He felt embarrassed even though he was quite alone. Pushing the door open, he looked at what he'd done. The truck appeared awkward and unnatural buried in the snow bank, but it didn't look like anything was damaged. He felt estranged from the vehicle, as if he hadn't been in it but had just seen it dive into the snow of its own volition. Getting back he tried the motor, and it started right up. He walked out onto the road and looked down at the truck; on second look it hadn't piled in as badly as he thought. Getting out his shovel he dug briskly, clearing first the wheels, then a neat path out to the road. As Earl worked, his breath vapor came out in short bursts, and the blade of the shovel slid almost noiselessly against the snow. He stopped and looked up, and the sky was filled with swaths of stars extending to all points.

He walked out into the middle of the road and, with the shovel hanging at his side, he craned his neck, looking at the heavens. He picked out familiar constellations quickly, especially Orion, the Hunter, recalling the unfortunate hunter's story. Then he picked out several of the planets that glowed steadily on the horizon. Everything in the sky seemed closer now.

He walked back to his truck, inspected his excavation job, got in and drove it out in one try. The truck seemed more powerful now, and Earl looked at it proudly while picking the lost articles out of the snow and stowing them away, this time tying them down more securely. Getting back in, he enjoyed the cab's warmth and resolved not to make another stupid error. He would take it steady the rest of the way. No sense in rushing matters. He had a long drive ahead of him.

After he adjusted to the routine of driving again, Earl noted that he hadn't spoken to a soul in nearly six days, not counting service station attendants and bleary-eyed motel managers. He thought of how that might be a first for him, and firsts interested Earl. In the Air Force one could hardly go six hours, or even six minutes, without talking to someone; at home his mother was always making with small talk, or a friend or relative would call. He thought that perhaps it would be better never to talk.

Talking, even the little he did, had always led to trouble: It had got him into the service, into difficulties with girls. He couldn't recall when it had ever got him out of trouble. Yes, it was better not to talk much. There was once a movie star he admired who didn't talk but very little; Earl modeled himself after him when he was a teenager. He wore his hats like him, even bought the same kind of shirts that he wore. Perhaps when he got north and settled down he'd get himself a place way out of town and would then never have to worry about talking. Still, Earl did like to listen; if someone were even halfway interesting he could listen for hours. And that's what he missed now. He wanted to listen.

When Grandpa passed away the worst thing about it was that Dad had cried, and that was the one thing Grandpa didn't want. During his long illness, he often made Earl promise that he wouldn't cry. There were so many people there when Dad cried. Everybody got embarrassed and looked away. Dad had buried his face in his handkerchief and sobbed when they took Grandpa out to the hearse. Earl hadn't wept, for he'd promised; Grandpa had always said the most valuable thing a man had was his word. Earl had always wondered if his Dad had promised.

He saw the caribou when he was very tired. They seemed like spirits walking between the trees, and he didn't notice them until he had nearly passed by. He stopped and walked back; there were about seven or eight of them standing among the black spruce. The snow was deep, and they were nearly up to their bellies in the stuff, yet they looked at him confidently, as if they knew he wasn't going to harm them. They weren't like the moose; they had antlers and looked genuine and wild. To Earl, the animals appeared as their kind must have looked to human beings for thousands of years. From the magazine articles he'd read about hunting caribou, he'd imagined them as being very large deer, but they weren't. They looked like the reindeer that pulled Santa's sled every year at the Livestock Association's Christmas party.

He walked back to the truck and looked for a camera he'd brought, but he couldn't locate it. When he got back the caribou were gone; he strained his eyes to peer into the spruce thicket, but they were definitely gone. Earl returned to the truck, amazed at how suddenly the caribou disappeared. It was like they'd not been there at all.

Underway again, Earl realized he didn't feel sleepy, even though he'd been driving well over twenty-four hours. He thought he could see the rising sun. Wondering how far he'd gone, he looked at his odometer and worked the subtraction mentally. When he got the answer, he forgot it. Again he did the calculation, and he read the answer out loud. His voice startled him, and he nearly yanked the pickup off the road. It had sounded foreign to him, like a stranger coming up behind him and asking for directions or a match. He recited his military serial number and this time his voice seemed familiar; then he cursed as he'd forgotten the answer to his mileage question again. He calmed himself, knowing it wasn't important. Whatever the answer was, it wouldn't alter the distance already traveled.

While rounding one of the countless curves he saw an old man hitch-hiking. He swerved away from him and braked to a halt several hundred yards down the road. Looking back he couldn't see him, as he'd rounded the curve too far. Backing, he stopped after going past the place where he'd seen the hitchhiker. He got out of the truck, wondering where the old man had gone. Also, Earl wondered why he'd automatically assumed the man was old; he hadn't seen the man's features at all. He stooped down and scooped up a handful of snow, brushing it over his face. It made his heart jump recalling that his Grandpa had worn a coat similar to that of the hitchhiker. That explained why he thought the man old. He shrugged off the man's abrupt appearance/disappearance and drove on.

Earl took out a small plastic container of honey he'd sneaked out of a cafe. Putting it in his mouth he punctured the pack with his teeth and sucked the honey out until the plastic was a flat wafer pressed between his tongue and palate. Spitting the plastic out, he felt a warmness grab him in the vitals and radiate outward as if he'd spilled hot chocolate down the front of his shirt. It made him feel strong. Earl could definitely do another twenty-four hours.

In the evenings Dad would stay out so late Mom would take the utility tractor and go fetch him. She and he would come in arm in arm, and sometimes she'd have her head on his shoulder, and to Earl he seemed old and quiet. He had grown this way in the four years since Grandpa had passed away, and during the last duck season he hadn't even bothered cleaning his shotgun, let alone using it. He had given Earl permission to use it when he went hunting with his friends, but Earl had been disappointed. His friends, although likable, were noisy and behaved like clowns out on the marshes. In a few days he asked his dad to go, but his dad tapped his pipe and mumbled something about age. On Sundays Dad would sit around with Mom, and if he went out it was to gather mushrooms or just stroll. Three weeks after Earl's high school graduation, his mom told him Dad was sick and needed an operation.

The sun had begun to set when Earl came across a town of fair size. His window thermometer read minus eighteen degrees, and he knew this wasn't too bad; at this time of year it could be much colder. He felt fortunate. In the town he got gas, yet when trying to enter into conversation with the attendant about the weather he seemed to be bothering the fellow. He stopped in a cafe and had a big meal; he hadn't realized how hungry he was, and he abandoned table manners entirely as he chased puddles of gravy around on the dinner platter with a piece of bread.

Quite full, he leaned back in his chair and listened to the jukebox. As each minute went by, he assured himself that he would get to his feet, pay the bill, and start again. The meal had been good, cheap, lots of it, and hot. He wondered what was happening to the jukebox: Someone was turning the volume down so low that he could barely hear it. It was almost inaudible when the waitress shook him; as his vision cleared he looked up into her face and thought of that homely Austrian girl he'd met while he was in the Air Force. She had told him he was intelligent.

He shook his head from side to side and rubbed his hand over his neck; the waitress looked at him oddly and said they rented rooms if he wanted to sack out. But he didn't want to sack out. He wanted to keep going. Paying the bill, he bought a mint and, instead of allowing it to melt slowly, chewed and swallowed it immediately. He got in the pickup, and while waiting for it to warm up, noticed the waitress looking at him from in back of the big window. She was framed by beer advertisements and credit card insignias. Driving away he could just make out the glow of the sun on the southwestern horizon.

He shouldn't have eaten, for Earl felt it impossible to keep awake. His eyelids seemed to lose all strength and droop in spite of his efforts to keep them open. With difficulty, he looked at the speedometer and saw he was going only ten miles an hour; soon, five. Then he stopped.

Lying down on the front seat he barely remembered turning off the ignition.

When he woke it was utterly dark and he was cold. Cold all the way through. He pushed up from the seat and was startled to see his saliva frozen in beads on the seat where his mouth lay open while he slept. He felt his face and it seemed frozen. Punching his legs and abdomen with his hands everything seemed club-like and not him, as if he'd kneaded a sack of grain. Suddenly he was gripped by fear. God, how stupid had he been! More than likely he had been frostbitten badly. Images of his limbless body being wheeled down a hospital corridor horrified him, and he slapped and worked at himself. As rapidly as his stiff and cold joints would allow, he slid out of the truck. He needed heat. Now.

Earl couldn't understand his stupidity in passing up the cafe without taking a room. Goddamnit! He felt the heater grow warm, and he crawled back in the truck. In minutes his entire body tingled, first painfully, like a sleepy limb regaining consciousness; then it returned to full sensitivity.

Almost in panic, he removed his boots and whipped off his socks; he rubbed his toes, and although they felt chilled he could move them freely, and they appeared normal. The rubbing felt good, and he continued until his toes were red and warm. Putting his boots back on, he remembered his panic and the way he'd jumped around. He laughed guiltily as he tied his laces. Earl still felt groggy and wondered how much sleep he'd gotten. But there was no way of knowing. He put the truck in gear and moved on.

He had just graduated from Guidance Systems Training when he learned his dad had passed away. He was granted emergency leave, and when he got home found out that in his last month Dad had sold the ranch to the land cooperative, who in turn sold part of it to the big lumber mill. Earl argued bitterly with his mom, but she told him that it was Dad's land and he could do what he wanted with it. His mother got one half the sale price, and he and his sister had divided the other half. He swore he'd put his share into land, never stupid business investments or bonds, like his dumb sister had; just land. During his last two and a half years in the Air Force he tried not to think of his dad, rather of the land he could buy and what he'd do with it. Late at night in the barracks he'd visualize the ranch house he'd build with the big clapboard barn and the smoke house close by. And he would have a hound, for a guy couldn't get by without a good dog around. He thought about that a lot, and the last two and a half years passed by as if they were yesterday.

It was close to midnight when he saw the white glow over the hills. At first he thought it was another town, but rounding a long curve he could see it was the moon, full and radiant. As it edged up over the horizon, Earl was astounded at its size; the face of it was like a portrait, the continents and seas standing out clearly. But unlike a harvest moon which Earl remembered as being almost angry in oranges and crimsons, this moon glowed with a peaceful phosphorescence and was surrounded gently in its own nimbus. The cold and whiteness of the snowbound country was greatly magnified by the presence of the moon, and this brought a great calm over everything Earl looked out upon.

He could see tall mountains, the rolling hills constructed by two mountain ranges which were drawing closer and closer together and pinching off the monotonous terrain he'd been plagued with for several days. Because of the brilliance of the moon, Earl could see as clearly as if the sun were out.

In a few hours Earl was excited to feel the truck climbing into the mountains and leaving behind the hills with their stubby drab spruce trees. Now he could see the sharpness and smooth texture of the winterbound snow on the summits. His thermometer fell rapidly to minus thirty, and edges of white frost began to encroach upon the transparency of his windshield in spite of the truck's defroster. The road again hugged a mountainside, and driving slowly he suddenly emerged into a wide but precipitous pass at the base of which lay a frozen lake.

The snow on the lake's ice was flat, velvet smooth, and immaculate. The moon now hung directly overhead, and around the edges of the lake were dozens of bands of caribou. He stopped the truck and got out, carefully buttoning his coat up and putting a pair of mittens on over his gloves. Standing at the edge of the road he saw that many of the caribou were moving out onto the lake, and as they did so he could see the vastness of their numbers. What initially appeared to be a few hundred actually was more like thousands. The surface of the lake was littered with columns of caribou, and Earl would see many more emerging from the trees surrounding the lake. He listened, thinking to hear something, but all was silence.

Looking at the opposite mountain, Earl felt his pulse race when he saw the long column of mountain sheep working their way down the face of a cliff towards the lake. His eyes widened at the sight of so many wild creatures; and he doubled his fists in frustration, wishing that Grandpa were with him to see all this. Certainly he'd come far enough north, and Earl felt confident some of this land around the lake must be for sale. He would buy some immediately. Although the deep snow made it difficult to tell, this country looked right for running horses in, so he would have horses, dozens of them.

Nearly forgetting the open expanse of frozen lake, Earl looked back there quickly and was stupefied to see even more caribou, so many in fact they swarmed, defying any estimate or count. The breath vapor from the thousands and thousands of caribou drifted upwards in clean orderly columns, and the moonlight made this appear like the lazy smoke from a million camp fires. Now the sheep pranced out onto the lake with the others, and he smiled just imagining what Grandpa would say. Surely this is what Grandpa's father meant when he talked of the old days.

The sheer number of animals would certainly give them courage to stand their ground, so Earl knew he could walk onto the lake and see the animals close, perhaps walking between the way he walked between the stacks of lumber back home. Yes, and the lake didn't appear that far off. Perhaps a mile, and hell, he could walk a mile without working up a sweat.

Earl looked out again at the frozen scene and saw a half dozen little V's outlined against the face of the moon. Stopping, he craned his neck far back and then saw the V's wheel and turn, descending rapidly. Immediately he knew they were geese, hundreds of graceful white geese outlined perfectly against the face of the icy moon. As the geese grew closer he could see the black tips of their wings held outstretched as the birds glided down, following the moonlight to the lake. Confused, Earl wondered what the geese were doing this far north in the winter. Earl kept going, breaking through the crust and falling in the snow several times, yet it felt good on his face. He wallowed around until he regained his footing.

Sweat poured from him despite the cold and Earl noticed his mittens and gloves had come off. Stumbling through the trees, he emerged onto the edge of the lake, but he snagged his foot on something and fell headlong. He lay exhausted. Rising to an elbow he looked out at the surface of the lake but couldn't see any of the animals. Rubbing his eyes, he looked out upon the lake which gleamed under the full moon. Something seemed very wrong to him, but now Earl was only conscious of being extremely tired. He leaned back in the snow and was pleasantly surprised to find it soft and warm. After all, he was north now, and he would have a lifetime to see as many animals as he wished. Now he just needed rest. Earl decided to sleep awhile and then hike back up to the road and start again. His destination was close, which was good; he was tired of driving and looked forward to a nice warm bed. The coolness on his skin was strange, and Earl wondered if the moon radiated coldness like the sun did warmth. He was in a new, mysterious land now and had to get used to things being different.

Hourglass Lakes

The waters in both lakes were dark and joined by a narrow passage three skiff-widths across. Sitka Spruce grew to the edge along short steep banks whose blackish color was marbled with a whitish-brown layer of volcanic ash. The trees grew densely, standing shoulder to shoulder, and beneath them it was always twilight.

Hiking into the lakes from salt water was not comfortable. Along the narrow path, I had an almost uncontrollable urge to stop and turn, perhaps catching some otherworld creature poised on a log, staring. Decades of winter storms had battered down a hostile tangle of fallen spruce, and this added to the area's sullen presence. Over each windfall, thick moss had grown and long-dead branches stuck out like matted bones.

The closer I drew to Hourglass Lakes, the more suspicious I was that the shadows had been granted temporary reprieve. Now able to leave their dark recesses, they followed single file, silent, bent forward, hermits bound in ancient service.

A Journal from the Bay of Islands

JUNE 23. THE CITY

Today I bought the cannery, surrounding acreage and adjoining buildings for $630,000 cash. At the law firm that represented the previous owners, everyone was shocked, perhaps dismayed, when I walked in with that much cash. They called a security firm and two guards came over immediately. They had nice blue uniforms and guns. They stood over the small satchel containing the money like faithful hounds. I signed papers for two and a half hours.

JUNE 29. THE CANNERY

I arrived yesterday and the watchman showed me around the place. The grounds are strewn with the usual machinery and junk you'd expect to find in a ninety-two-year-old cannery site left in disuse for nearly fifteen years. The watchman asked if he could stay on an extra week to get his things together. He is old and has weak, reddened eyes. I said OK. As long as it is only a week.

After he returns to his place, I'll occupy the big house, where the cannery superintendent used to live. I looked out the window towards the Chinese graveyard. In the first ten years of operation they used imported Chinese labor and some occasionally died in the middle of the season. They'd bury them in back of the Chinese bunkhouse which, they tell me, burned down in 1928. The graves and the grave markings are still there. They're wooden with Chinese markings. The only thing intelligible to me is the year. They used Arabic numbers for that. I can see this graveyard from the window of the house.

In Memory of Hawks

JULY 9. THE CANNERY

The old watchman has gone on a drunk and it was pretty clear he didn't intend to leave. After the week's grace period, I told him he'd have to leave. Actually, I decided to tell him he'd have to leave. I walked down the boardwalk, now overgrown with rainforest moss, and knocked on the door of his small cottage, one of the dozen or so cottages used for cannery management personnel. He couldn't open the door because he was drunk. I walked in and he was lying on his cot.

The interior was rank and nearly sickened me, and anticipating what I was going to say he said, "For Christ's sakes, I don't have anywhere to go. I've looked after this cannery for 23 years. I'm just a wino. This place is 250 acres, I won't bother you."

I said nothing. I left, deciding to think about it. I could call the police, in Alaska they call them troopers, but that is not a good idea.

JULY 23. THE CANNERY

My days are simple here. I rise around 6:00 a.m. and have coffee. I love, yes, love having coffee in the big three-storied superintendent's house and looking out on the small bay the cannery joins at the mouth of the creek. There are salmon going up the creek now and the gulls worry them. An occasional black bear fishes. These all impress me.

There are harbor seal off the mouth of the stream, and they're fishing also. It's quiet at 6:00 a.m. and it's the best time of day, regardless of whether it's raining or fair, though it's frequently raining.

I drink my coffee on the old table and listen to the slow, wet weather seep through the buildings and across the complicated network of boardwalks that are the footpaths between buildings and the beach.

The watchman's cat has abandoned him and joined me. The cat comes and goes via exits and entrances of which I'm not aware. It has the peculiar yellow slit-eyes of all cats and purrs for canned milk I pour into a small bowl which at one time must have belonged to a vast set of china. A tiny member of a frail family, this one bowl is decorated with a single, intricately painted flower. The cat laps milk oblivious to this quiet touch.

After my morning coffee I explored the cannery and adjoining grounds. It is complicated: There seems to be small and large buildings everywhere, and often I find things in these buildings unrecognizable to me. Everything is in poor condition, and getting poorer.

Nicest are the hikes up the old wooden waterline to the lake. This is the cannery water supply. At the lake there is a small punt, and one day I rowed out on the water. There's an island almost precisely in the middle of the lake and it, like all the country around here, is covered with gnarled, elderly Sitka Spruce. The first time I visited the island I was surprised to find white gulls nesting in the trees. I hadn't known gulls nested in trees. They mewed and screeched at me as I explored the small island.

During my second visit I found a gravesite there, a single cross, Russian Orthodox style, its markings rotted away. It could be older than the Chinese gravesites.

The island is my favorite place to sit and look out upon the surrounding mountains that hem in the lake. There's a peace there I have never before experienced. I know that I've come to a place where I'll finally have time.

AUGUST 4. THE CANNERY

The watchman died. I found him stone dead in the cottage. I hadn't seen him in a week. Oddly, the first thing that occurred to me was that I was grateful this was Alaska and not Ecuador. There was no heat in the cottage and the body had remained cool, despite it being midsummer.

From the old cannery office, where the radios are, I called the state troopers. I've grown a beard now, quite a bushy one. When they arrived, neither of the two troopers seemed surprised; one had known the watchman for years and had never seen him sober. "Probably his liver gave out," he guessed, and they left after loading his body aboard their plane. I'm alone now except for the cat.

AUGUST 15. THE CANNERY

Today a woman visited. Her name is Alice. I hadn't seen a sign of anyone in eleven days and was enjoying it. Alice looks like she's about forty, wears jeans, a wool jacket, and an old fishing cap. She's not pretty, but she doesn't talk much. I haven't been with a woman since January in Cuenca. Because of this I wanted her almost at once, somewhat surprising myself. She said something about being my neighbor, but not much else. We had a cup of tea and she didn't ask any questions, rather talked about picking berries and making preserves, and also smoking deer meat. When I told her I hadn't shot any deer or picked berries she seemed surprised. She left in her skiff, an old battered slab of a boat with an ancient outboard motor on it.

Today I discovered the cat had kittens. There is more than one cat around, I assume.

AUGUST 29. THE CANNERY

There're occasional visitors, but they are becoming fewer. It's fishing season and every few days a fishing boat puts in at the old dock. They want to talk but I don't and they soon leave. Others come. Evidently in the next bay there is a logging camp. Often people come from there and ask for a piece of equipment or tool. ne time they used the radio when theirs wasn't working. Like the fishermen, they ask questions and want to talk, but I don't respond much.

The woman—Alice—hasn't been back as of this date.

The weather today was quite normal: Ceiling of 1,500 feet, winds from the northwest at about 10 mph with a visibility of around 4 miles. The bay is calm. A different sort of salmon has appeared at the creek, larger and better tasting. I've taken up fishing, another way of putting off the job of sorting through my Ecuadorian journals.

SEPTEMBER 17. THE CANNERY

Alice, the woman, came again today. Her wrist is broken. But other than that she was the same. I didn't ask how she broke her wrist and she didn't offer an explanation. We had tea again. She talked about canning fish, explaining, "You'll need fish and fish-hash for the winter." After this she simply looked at me. It seemed inappropriate to say that every month a plane brings in a grocery shipment that has everything I need. I have no other needs.

My stereo fascinates her. I played her music, just ordinary stuff you'd hear anywhere. She listened as if she were in a symphony hall. After several cups of tea, she left at mid-afternoon.

The kittens are gone. I don't know what happened to them, probably eaten by something. The cat seems happy.

The weather is brilliant today: Ceiling and visibility unlimited, with hardly any wind. I hiked to the lake and rowed to the island. The lake view from the Russian grave seemed like it had been etched in solid, recently poured crystal. The reflections in the lake joined the skyline in a perfect synchrony.

SEPTEMBER 22. THE CANNERY

Today I saw another deer. I've seen them several times a week. Yet this deer was a large male with antlers. I was sitting in the front room of the house and looking down towards the dock where he emerged from the thick spruce nearby. Though I've shot people I've never shot an animal.

Taking a rifle I opened the window and killed the deer. Somehow, despite never having done it, I dressed the deer and prepared some of the meat. It's delicious. An important discovery, as the meat I get from town is all frozen.

In Ecuador we'd often eat freshly slaughtered llama which is superb. This is nearly as good, though a finer grain.

Today I began my journals from Ecuador. It's a long job. Fourteen years of experiences. Even though I'm not a prolific journal writer, it is still quite a lot. Some are in Spanish, and nearly all of them are in poor condition from mildew and dampness.

SEPTEMBER 24. THE CANNERY

Alice came again and she's interested in me and I in her. Though plain and having hands like an Indian woman in Cuenca, she asks no questions and when she talks it's of practical matters. She showered at the house and in the kitchen I saw that she was actually not as plain as she first appeared. It was late afternoon and she sat at the table drinking tea. I considered how to manage all the necessary moves required for this situation, and she made things more difficult by giving me no signs. Taking a chance I walked to her side of the table and put my arms around her and she was very easy and open to that.

It is getting light later now, at about 8:00 a.m. She left at the first sign of light. I think it had been a long time for both of us, but of course I can't be sure about her as women are natural dissemblers.

OCTOBER 4. THE CANNERY

In my journals I came across the entry concerning Rio. Fuentes and I went there for business, then later simply for relaxation. Fuentes knew of several high-priced pleasure palaces. In one, which we finally stayed at, it was like old times in Thailand and Laos.

You bought sex like frozen dinners. Any woman was available, some of the most beautiful and picturesque women I've ever seen. My journal entry was unusually long.

Fuentes, of course, was above this: He would hold court at a table adjacent to the main casino and recite poetry and get drunker and drunker. The whores and casino workers didn't know what to make of him, but he spent money easily and in great quantities.

Alice hasn't been back since the 24th of September. I thought she'd be back before this. I know nothing of her except that she lives on an island in the next bay.

It surprises me that she hasn't been back, and it annoys me. She's a plain-looking woman and almost more muscular than I am. I like it here, but I really would like a woman to be with me. Then sometimes I don't want a woman to be with me. In Ecuador I became spoiled. There were always women, more than I wanted. With the Indian women, sex was like any other body function. I'm definitely back in North America.

The weather today was quite bad: Ceiling was below 400 feet most of the day, and visibility varied from between a mile to less than a quarter mile. The winds were gusting and southerly. Lots of rain. But I'm used to rain.

At night, it's getting colder. The boardwalks are wet during the day, then glaze at night with a fine crystalline skin of ice, making them treacherous. All the swallows are gone. I liked the swallows, though I haven't written about them.

OCTOBER 18. THE CANNERY
Alice has not been back, and I've given up. Today an owl flew into the side of the old store and broke his (her?) neck. It was probably pursuing a weasel or squirrel. It's the first owl I've seen. The squirrels around the cannery are rusty red and noisy, cursing the cat every time they see it.

I'm not even a tenth of the way through my Ecuadorian journals.

OCTOBER 28. THE CANNERY
Today Alice reappeared. She simply tied up her skiff to the old dock, walked up to the house, and presented me with three dozen chocolate chip cookies. While I made tea and ate cookies, she explained to me the importance of good nutrition. Especially vitamins.

She talked like we'd just been together several days ago, though it has been five weeks.

After tea and cookies she took a shower and it was much like before, except that it is getting light much later in the morning now. She left me a large bottle of vitamins.

NOVEMBER 12. THE CANNERY
I've decided that I resent a woman who takes or leaves me at her whim, and I've decided to distance myself from Alice the next time she decides to reappear.

My Ecuadorian journals are intriguing. Today I went over the entry when Fuentes killed the two customs agents: We haggled and haggled with them over the amount they demanded until finally Fuentes exclaimed in Portuguese, "This is stupid," and swiftly pulled out his old Luger and killed one. Then while the other scrambled in a death-panic for the door, he killed him.

As we returned to the airfield he kept muttering, "In heaven I'll be free from petty corruption."

I can only hope he is.

NOVEMBER 14. THE CANNERY
It was quite cold today. While having my morning coffee I noticed there was skim ice on the shores of the bay, though it was soon broken up by tide and wind. I suppose this results from the freshwater influence of the creek.

The ravens, huge and black, stay huddled on the eaves of the old store. The old store is interesting: Inside is a complete post office, including old rubber stamps and such. There is a massive upright safe in the old store and the combination to it was written on the back of the entry door to the store. In it were dozens of boxes of business records and various other papers. I've been sorting through these.

Today I thought of Alice and how I wanted her. Still, I'm considering how to arrange for a dependable woman who will stay with me. After twenty years, it's difficult caring for myself in the routine ways. And then there is the obvious luxury of regular sex.

NOVEMBER 27. THE CANNERY

There is snow now. The spruce are bent low with it, but in the daytime it begins to melt and gobs of sticky snow fall to the ground. When the snow is freshly fallen it is beautiful, a thick blanket of stillness that I find especially comforting during the early hours when I drink coffee and study the bay. The cat stays in all the time now. She sleeps on the back of an overstuffed chair, her paws scrunched under her body. Slowly I've worked a third of the way through my journals. An entry from six years, seven months ago:

Fuentes came to my hotel in a three-piece suit exclaiming, "There is no reason for men to live in rags." It was a specially tailored suit made in Quito. He urged me to fly in next weekend and use the same tailor. "In buying nice quality things, there is something good and opulent in it for men that is wasted on women."

The bay is frozen halfway out, with strange almost plastic ice. High in the Andes I saw much ice, but not like this. My supply plane had to land far out in the bay, and it took me the full day to backpack everything in.

The woman, Alice, would be a welcome sight, as during the past two weeks I've wanted to get laid very badly. Yet she stays away, and despite my decision to have nothing to do with her, if she returned I would. Somehow, this weakness in resolve bothers me.

DECEMBER 21. THE CANNERY

It has been awhile since I've written anything. The weather through November and into December became colder, yet with frequent thaws and winds. As the almanac said, the temperatures aren't like everyone thinks of Alaska; most days it gets above freezing, and the moisture and chill are far more of an annoyance than extreme frosts.

Yesterday I was working one of the massive generators, and I had really gotten involved with the work, as I'm in my element with machinery. I was just beginning to rig up a block and tackle to remove a part when I heard ravens clucking, much like they did when bear were in the creek last summer. The door to the generator house opened, scaring the hell out of me. Alice stood there with a small backpack. Seeing that I was startled she said, "It's just me. Merry Christmas."

Oddly I wasn't cheerful. Lately, meaning in the past month, I've been plagued with hordes of erotic dreams, caused by memories of years ago. I lowered a block to the floor and muttered something about a surprise visit. "Another surprise visit," is what I said. She answered that if I was going to be grumpy, she'd leave. I said that was all right, and she closed the door, and I heard her walking away.

I stood holding a wrench, listening to her footfalls recede on the boardwalk. My stomach sank. I became angry, humiliated.

Soon I could no longer hear her.

I've become knowledgeable regarding the terrain surrounding the cannery, and I felt certain that with the bay frozen, she'd hiked in from where my supply plane beached. I knew of a faster way there than the path that dawdled along the shoreline.

I could catch her if I took it, but this idea didn't appeal to me. What had happened to her was proper. She'd arrived and I was evidently supposed to smile and greet her like she was royalty. I've had better looking women hauling my excrement out the back door. I threw the wrench down, and it is unlike me to misuse tools.

Quickly I took the path, and it was as I'd anticipated. I arrived where she'd outhauled her skiff before she did. I said nothing initially. We simply confronted each other until I finally said, "You caught me by surprise."

It is evening as I make this entry. She left two hours before sunset, leaving a knit sweater as a Christmas present. Against my better judgment, I asked her to stay another night, but she wouldn't and I felt humiliated in asking.

Sun comes up about 10 a.m., perhaps later. This morning she was asleep on the giant bed which is the centerpiece of the master bedroom which takes up almost all of the third floor. The frame of the bed is deeply and beautifully stained oak, with heavy legs shaped like carved lion's paws. I put on a robe and sat on the linen bin covers in front of the windows that look out on the bay.

These windows look straight southeast. When the sun rose in the extreme southeast, the light filtered through the curtains of the windows and fell across her leg and thigh which protruded from under the goose down comforter. In the corner of the bedroom the fireplace, mostly decorative since the house is oil-heated, burned quietly, a large hemlock log lying in its heart. Her breathing moved the comforter easily up and down, and in the growing light through the window I studied her leg and thigh, then her neck and face.

I sat like this until the sun cleared the southeastern horizon. When I got in beside her, I sank deep into the mattress, my bare shoulder resting against her breasts.

JANUARY 18. THE CANNERY

Today I was again sorting through the various papers and records that were kept in the old safe in the cannery post office. Most of them are of no interest, having to do with business. Yet I found an intriguing entry in the cannery watchman's "daily transaction log," as it was called. Usually the log is filled with routine matters of maintenance and weather. I'd just about decided to give up my perusal of the log when I found the September 23, 1909, entry which read, "I'm so awfully, awfully miserable, and it's only September." And that was it. There is no hiatus in the log, rather it continued in the same handwriting through that fall and winter.

There is some uneasiness for me in the situation that has developed with Alice. I think of her too often, and it isn't fruitful or satisfying, and by satisfying I mean tranquil. Of all things, I want tranquillity.

This is the new year. And while considering what is ahead I slowly and routinely sort through my journals looking back at other years. I found an entry from eight years ago when Fuentes and I had been temporarily jailed in Columbia

Fuentes looked at me over his glasses and said, "You are intelligent, but sadly you are too sensitive and there is an odd carelessness in you with women. Women are beneficial to men in providing them with heirs, sons. To spread your seed without caution is not good."

At the time, I'd put the remarks off as simply the moralistic Fuentes, a typical *maricon*. But when I re-read the entry this evening I thought about numerous things which seem to enhance the content of his words.

The snow is very deep now, and the thaws are fewer and far between. In the mornings, resting in the pathway I've cleared between the superintendent's house and the old dock and store, I find hapless deer.

Tired and unable to feed because of the deep snow, they've come here. Most can't walk, and often hardly react to me. They're near death. The first time it happened I waited for three days, then went to the bedroom and dug out my duffel bag containing my .45. I removed it from the case, unwrapped it from the chamois cloth, then worked the bolt several times, inserting a clip.

Being careful not to slip as I walked down the walkway towards the deer I came to them and put a bullet in each deer's brain. It was all I could do at that point.

JANUARY 27. THE CANNERY

I've not worked on my journals for a time now. Why do I work on my journals? What I read in them, often, is unpleasant. Some things I'd rather leave forgotten, which means I'd dulled the edges of the harder, harsher(?) stuff. Frankly, some things I've forgotten entirely.

More rarely, there are a few incidents I'm able to recall almost as precisely as I narrated them in my journal.

In any event, often what I read in them is unpleasant. But there must be a central meaning somewhere within them, and that is what I intend to find and someday, hopefully soon, retell in something that will make a continuity from all the conflict. Mostly conflict.

Who will I tell? What would I tell?

I think I would begin by saying that I am not a bad man. I've been called a bad man, but mostly by bad men. Very bad men.

There were times when I was feared almost as much as Fuentes. But that sounds melodramatic.

It is very cold now, colder than my almanac says it should get. Also, I think there is more snow than normal. I ordered a model ship kit from Italy, and two days ago it arrived in the mail plane. I now assemble it plank by plank. When finished, it'll be a sleek schooner with full sails. The cat watches me, nodding off and waiting for spring.

FEBRUARY 4. THE CANNERY

Alice returned again. I made strong coffee, Ecuadorian style. We sat and ate some of her cookies with centers made from her own preserves. They remind me of a long, long time ago. She'd brought several dozen of these in an old tin cigar box lined with a clean, white linen cloth. She chatted about her visit to town, though she didn't say precisely when she'd made it. She said she enjoyed town, but mostly that it was nice to get back to her home. Simple things.

She went up to the shower and I studied the ceiling where I could hear her footfalls. Her boots fell to the floor, and for several minutes I could hear the water running down the drain.

Then I did a surprising thing. For me.

I quickly took the stairs three at a time, then pushed open the old wooden door of the bathroom. She had just stepped from the shower. Similar to my bedroom, one wall of the bathroom is lined with spacious linen bins which are constructed before a dormer window, and these serve nicely as sitting benches. I took her roughly, not nicely, and swung her from the floor still wet, throwing aside her towel. I put her on top of the linen bins and we then described a primitive and unruly version of fucking that ended with incredibly intense orgasms, the mutual intensities of which elude any words I might enter here.

She somehow remained sprawled atop the bins, while I had slipped to the floor where I lay on the damp parquet. Through the heat and steam I heard her say, "I didn't mind that; it was different. It takes the civilization from it."

All that night and into the next day we made love constantly. As I have grown to expect, there is an urgency and vitality in her I find new and that I enjoy. There is an electrical current that sweeps me along, carrying me. Sometime past noon of the next day (I can't be sure of the time) she left the bed and woke me, saying a quiet good-bye. I remained there, dozing. I woke in time to hear her ancient outboard motor as she departed the bay. After that I slept.

This situation with the woman is distracting.

FEBRUARY 8. THE CANNERY

I have not written about the mountains. This is because I lived in the Andes for so long that perhaps I've become jaded with mountains. The lake is frozen now, and you can walk to the Russian grave site. There you can look out upon these mountains that are earth twins, except they are mirror images. According to my map, they are just over 3000 feet in elevation. In the summer their summits are sharp and unfriendly; now they are covered with snow, which the wind brushes hundreds of feet into the air. These form icy gyres that move with the wind.

On some days, when the northerlies are strong, I fill the thermos of coffee and come to the Russian grave. Today I did this, taking the last of her cookies with me. The grave marker is buried, as it has been every winter for perhaps a hundred winters.

I worked from the early morning on the journals, the first time since mid-January. An entry from three years, two months ago:

Fuentes and I met the Minister and his aides. We rented the entire Presidential Ballroom at the Hotel El Camino. There was much expensive food, including Russian black caviar stuffed inside giant prawns. Fuentes told me, 'Don't worry about this Minister. He is a kindred spirit.' I knew what he meant when he had young Eduardo serve the champagne. Eduardo's eyes are as large as a llama's, and he wore svelte leather trousers that I recall Fuentes had tailored for him in Panama. The Minister watched Eduardo all evening, his eyes half closed and knowing.

A strange thing happened to me as I was transcribing this passage (many of the journals are nearly illegible due to the ubiquitous rot): I heard Fuentes only for a moment. His voice seemed to be in the wind, but I know it's not; rather it's only in my imagination. I can still see Fuentes beside the airplane, looking up, his sunglasses pushed up on his forehead. He was calm despite the fact that his moment had come.

FEBRUARY 12. THE CANNERY

I was surprised today when Alice returned. This is the shortest period she has allowed herself between visits. I was in the warehouse restoring an ancient truck, evidently used to haul nets between the dock and gear lofts. This time I heard her outboard motor, for there is no mistaking it.

Since fresh snow fell the evening before, she followed my tracks to the warehouse, opened the door, and peeked in. While I worked she talked about salmon canneries: how she'd worked in dozens of them. In fact, she surprised me by saying she'd worked in this cannery as a young woman. It was the first thing she'd told me about herself.

This visit went much like it did the time before, with the exception of the scene in the bathroom and the situation I'm about to narrate: Early the next day (it is getting light earlier now, noticeably earlier) I asked her what it would take for her to move in with me. She looked at me with (what I thought was) a smile. In any case she answered, "A miracle." Then she laughed.

I didn't think it was a situation that warranted humor, and I told her only a stupid woman would react that way. It was early morning and ordinarily we would have spent more time together prior to her departure, but I walked out and returned to the warehouse. When I returned in the early afternoon she was, of course, gone. I hope I never see her again, and I must do something about getting a dependable woman out here.

I think of my old haunts to the south.

My humiliation over Alice would have rendered considerable humor to Fuentes. It would have confirmed theories he'd espoused on the subject of men and women. But of course he's not able to enjoy the comical plight of men and women any longer. This is the final humor.

FEBRUARY 23. THE CANNERY

Today was the worst storm of the winter. Winds northeasterly, steady at 60 mph, with gusts higher. Temperatures under freezing, and towards noon one of the cottages simply blew apart like soggy gingerbread. Water from the bay was whipped into a white mist which girds the dock, weathered piles, and plank decks with a thick armor of cloud-white sea ice.

The house holds against the storm.

The cat sits in the window looking out, eyes wide, occasionally turning towards me, as if wondering when it'll all pass. The force of the wind is like many dangerous things: beautiful.

A strange hawk, a type I haven't noticed here, sits atop the water tank in the lee of the old store waiting for the storm to end. It is very small and slate gray with a strong, hooked beak. Its talons are tiny but clearly powerful. Occasionally a gust would force its way around the old store making the hawk cling grimly to the water tank.

How many storms has it experienced? The spruce and hemlock groan and thrash chaotically in the storm.

MARCH 16. THE CANNERY

I have not written about the oldness of the cannery and how it affects me:

Often, with little purpose, I wander among the old buildings and I'm able to feel them sing stories through me, or somehow feel them narrate the countless summer nights when steam cookers sealed cans deep into men's and women's souls, and boat keels pierced bay water skimmed with fish oil and feeding gulls.

There is a pattern in the ancient exposed grain of the boardwalks that is like the markings on Inca cenotaphs along the high Andes trails.

I continue to work on my journals. An entry from two years ago:

The three Indians waited in the rain, their large eyes unblinking, heads bent. Fuentes borrowed my .45 and looked curiously at one of the guards when the guard said, "Look at them. Like docile goats." Despite the Indian's betrayal, Fuentes looked at the man and said, "Esos no son cabras, son hombres." Fuentes then stepped into the rain and told the Indians, "If you like, you may pray." They did, on their knees in the mountain mud, lips moving, the rain dripping from their cloth hats.

I studied this passage for a long time, but despite the thought I've generated from the quiet of this place, there is yet no sense of tragedy or cruelty in this account for me.

It is interesting to see that I lied to this journal. While re-reading the entry of February 12, I saw this was the case. On that date, when Alice laughed at me, I indeed said, "Only a stupid woman would react so." But I had actually added, "I have no use for a wise-ass cunt."

Why did I couch my original words?

This scene took place over a month ago. I can still taste the sex I had with her. I wish I hadn't said what I did, yet I'm sure my reaction was warranted. It simply wasn't politic.

There is now nearly 12 hours of daylight again. My almanac says that with the equinox will come spring windstorms. Towards nightfall, I repaired a small section of roof on the old store.

MARCH 20. THE CANNERY

Today is the vernal equinox, the first day of spring. The planet, at least the portion I occupy, seemed unaware or unconcerned about this phenomenon: The sea ducks in the bay feed in flocks approaching an acre in size, the winds blow from the sea, and cold rains fall upon the moss-covered roofs of the cannery. These shed the water in gray steady rivulets that years ago rusted away the gutters and pipes.

I sit in the kitchen drinking coffee and watch the sunlight grow brighter as the morning wears on. But it is quite overcast, and the sun eventually becomes a brilliant glow above the low-lying rain clouds.

The calls of the feeding ducks in the bay are soothing and convey contentment with the way things are and will be.

MARCH 30. THE CANNERY

Awoke this morning at 2:00 a.m. Though I didn't know what woke me, I knew it wasn't a dream or my imagination. Without turning on the lights I slipped on some clothes and picked up the rifle. The latter was in the event it was a marauding bear, for it is now past the equinox.

In the distance I heard the small generator which I run at night. Looking out the kitchen window I could see the wind had created a small surf on the beach. The string of lights stretching from here to the old store swayed in pendulum-like motions, casting mobile shadows upon the old walls and boardwalks.

Watching this I was struck with a strange fear, a terrible anticipation. This caused me to quickly strap on the holster containing my .45. Quickly I inserted a clip. As I loaded the round into the chamber, the weapon's sound seemed out of place in the old house.

Despite months of peace since I left Fuentes in the Valle del Fuego, nothing is lost in the swiftness and ease of my fears. The cat, who has taken to trailing me, hopped sleepily down the stairs and threaded its way between my feet, rubbing and purring.

Outside was quiet except for the steady wind. As I prepared to walk downhill towards the dock, almost of its own volition the pistol was out and tracking a shadowy figure's torso. My finger began a familiar caress of the trigger. Whoever it was carried something over its shoulder, and staggered up from the dock. I put the .45 away.

It was Alice.

When I met her she put the outboard down and said, "I rowed 14 miles before I stopped here. I'm frozen stiff and beat. My motor. It just quit, and I sold my spare sometime ago. In the morning I'd like to use your radio to call a plane. The logging camp is closed now. It's another dozen miles to home. I couldn't have made it. I'll bunk in the warehouse, OK?"

I nodded, and she resisted me taking the motor from her as she struggled towards the warehouse. In the light I could see she was a mess, and exhausted. When I pointed out there were several extra bedrooms in the house she answered, "No, the warehouse is fine."

I left her to her own devices.

At 6:30 that morning I had coffee, worked through a few journal entries, and walked down to the warehouse. Her outboard lay before the warehouse entrance. I took it down to the shop where the cannery's half dozen outboard motors are stored. Though all these parts are old, it suited her motor well. I had it going before 10 a.m. I was standing there testing it in a large wooden barrel when she opened the shop door and said, almost as an accusation, "You fixed it?"

While she carried it to her skiff I saw that her hands were badly blistered, which considering their toughness, testified to the many miles of rowing. I told her that I had many outboards in the shop. She could take one as a spare, and that her motor belonged in a trade museum.

She didn't reply, and I was beginning to become annoyed when she turned and said, "I haven't eaten for two days."

Controlling an immediate urge to be sarcastic, I offered breakfast.

I knew she didn't want to enter the house, yet hunger overrode this. We walked up, and I prepared a large breakfast which she devoured with fervor.

Throwing down a last cup of coffee, she began to mutter what might have been a thank you but stifled it. When we returned to the dock she simply got in her skiff and prepared to shove off. There had been no recognizable thank you for the repair work, shelter or food. After she cast off, she looked at me as the skiff drifted slowly away. At this point I thought she was, logically, considering some form of thank you; but looking at her eyes, I could see she was furious in a strange, quiet way I hadn't noticed.

With the skiff drifting farther away from the dock, we stared at each other, and I thought, 'I'll be damned if I'll be stared down by this Amazon,' and I maintained my scrutiny. Yet a spontaneous action, a reflex, moved upwards, seizing hold of me from inside, as if I were a hand puppet. Whatever it was compelled movement in my mouth and lips:

"I'm sorry."

She gave no sign of accepting this, rather she stepped to the stern and while gripping the pull cord began to say something, thought better of it, then did say, "I don't care how big you are, if you call me anything like that again, I'll fight you."

She meant it. She then started the outboard and steered her skiff out of the bay, parting the flocks of feeding ducks as she went.

Afterwards I returned to the house, made a cup of coffee, and added a touch of Irish whisky. I had never apologized to anyone in my life.

I don't view it as an improvement.

APRIL 6. THE CANNERY

It is hard work to concentrate on my journals, for my mind drifts; I think of Alice and more specifically of being upon the large bed upstairs inside her. This is the essence of drifting.

In my journals I'm within six months of the incident at Valle del Fuego. I've never re-read that entry since I wrote it 11 months ago. As I grow closer to it I wonder if I'll discover some detail, some mitigating fact, which I've allowed to slip into a fiction to forget and ignore. This possibility makes me uncomfortable. He could not have survived.

I notice different sorts of birds around the cannery, mostly songbirds, and certainly different varieties of ducks, also a pair of large cranes or storks which perhaps are looking over the lake as future nesting grounds.

Yet it is chilly and rainy, hardly seeming like spring.

APRIL 7. THE CANNERY

I hiked up the waterline to the lake. The cranes are indeed there. They are large, slate gray, and silent. Laboring to make flight, their legs hang straight behind, with dagger-like beaks thrust into the air ahead.

I can't hike to the island because the ice is quite rotten, but I still can't use the punt. I wonder if the marker on the Russian grave is visible now that the snow cover is thinning. The weather has improved: Winds calm, partially blue skies with visibility as far as the terrain and horizon will allow. The willows have tiny buds.

These must be good signs.

Out on the bay, the waters are calm and quite navigable. I spent a restless night and as I write this I'm very tired.

APRIL 14. THE CANNERY

Alice left after spending two and a half days.

Our silences were comfortable. For the first time we simply sat together, and I even worked on my journals with her present. She had brought a set of pencils and sketch paper, and drew the water tank.

Then me.

She is a superb artist, working quickly and with a sly smile as she peeks over the pad at what she draws. Her drawing of the water tank wasn't like a photograph but better. Somehow it was better. Certainly this skill isn't self-learned.

She found the wide belt Jesus Brocza made for me and fell to studying the intricate art work. It is more a mural than a belt.

Jesus's carvings are magnificently crafted, and indeed he was famous throughout the Zuay Province, coming from generations of leather workers. The art work on the belt can hold someone's interest for a long time, and she ran it across her fingers, studying the thick, rich cowhide.

She handed it back to me praising the high degree of craftsmanship. I simply draped it around her hips and said, "I would like for you to have this," and I was pleased to encounter little resistance.

After she accepted I was somewhat afraid she'd ask what had become of Brocza. How would she react when I answered, "I killed him"? Yet neither of us asks questions of the other. We made love like impulsive teenagers throughout her visit.

APRIL 21. THE CANNERY

Now little time passes before I miss Alice and it is a struggle to regain my routine. I can't, or won't, decide if she has become a weakness; I cannot stand weakness in myself and it disgusts me in others. Yet I miss her.

I am now organizing my journals since during the transcription process they've gotten out of order. The memory of Brocza's belt prompted me to re-read the entry from seven years and eight months before:

When I returned from Guayaquil things were different at the hacienda. Finally my housekeeper said, "Pia sleeps with the leather carver." I laughed, understanding why everyone was so subdued. I had bought her from an Indian family and she was the most beautiful Indian woman I had ever seen, though lukewarm in bed and an unwilling learner. Two evenings later Fuentes returned from Havana and as was our custom we sat on the verandah while Mara served drinks. Looking out over the plateau, Fuentes fed his pet rheas, smoked a Cuban cigar, and then said, "You'll kill the leather carver of course. Our reputations are crucial and a muy malo hombre like yourself can't allow a simple artisan fertilizing your woman." Mara, hearing this, remarked "Men are pigs," and Fuentes chuckled and remarked, "Perhaps, Mara, but here men rule."

Towards midday, a small tanker pulled into the bay and, after considerable maneuvering, managed to tie alongside the dock and deliver the annual supply of fuel.

The captain of the tanker came up to the house with the necessary bookwork and while drinking a cup of coffee glanced about the house but, unlike most, asked no questions. Feeling there was something unusual about him, I asked if he'd ever been here before. He looked over at me, stroked the cat as it jumped into his lap, and replied, "I was born here 63 years ago."

I was surprised, but probably a number of people have been born here. Certainly they've died here. The graves tell those stories.

MAY 9. THE CANNERY

There is now a solid sense and feel of spring in the onshore winds. The snow is gone and I took the punt out on the lake last week for the first time since fall.

The water of the lake was dark, full of runoff which pours down from the mountains. A cupful of this water is like a strong tea. The swallows' return is the brightest event: They cut accurate swaths through the air, soaring up then suddenly whirling down, hunting bugs. Often upon the rise they stall, sometimes only a dozen feet above the ground; yet they simply twist about in midair, open their wings and regain flight, skimming just above the ground as they fly off. I've worked and operated on hundreds of diverse flying machines yet I'll never touch or see one that is the equal of a swallow.

Alice stayed with me since yesterday and departed after dinner. This time she brought several loaves of heavy brown bread and a toy mouse filled with catnip for the cat. After heating the bread, we sat at the table and buttered slabs of it, devouring it with great relish.

"Pigging out" is the expression she used. She laughed when I found the expression novel, and I confessed that my American idiom is over 20 years out of date.

In the morning she said, "I won't be back until July. During the spring and summer I go off and fish commercially. At least this year I must."

I was sad, yet couldn't help note it was the first thing she'd said about herself, her future activities. At least it is a sign of politeness. Still, I'm uneasy thinking she might perceive that I am dependent on her visits, as intermittent as they are. This would be a sign of weakness and in the perception of weakness there is certain decay in the way people view and respond towards others. This is the most reliable fact concerning my fellow humans I've learned in 40 years.

Today when she left I thanked her for the bread and allowed that I would be looking forward to her return in midsummer. She smiled and said she would also.

On the old cannery dock I looked at the wake as it radiated from the cut of her skiff through the water: The ripples were tiny mounds that glossed across the surface, gradually growing farther and farther apart until spent against opposing shores of the bay. This ordinary phenomenon reminded me of the giant rollers which ambled in from the South Pacific; when I flew over the Golfo de Guayaquil they would pass in endless numbers, the weight of each exceeding all the armies of the world.

MAY 14. THE CANNERY

Yesterday I transcribed the incident at Valle del Fuego from my journals. I read it over several times, each time with the familiar fear. Yet the details were like I remember them. I quote from my journals of 12 months, 3 days ago, omitting some details that are not central:

Considering the hundreds of close calls involving escapes under fire and such, there is irony in the fact that a mechanical failure caused Fuentes to make a forced landing.... He put down in a cleared field in the Valle del Fuego close to the village of Los Banos where we've had dozens of dealings which left some of the residents poorer or dead.... I was following in the Alouette probably 25 miles behind the fixed-wing craft when I heard Fuentes' distress call. We'd just completed a larger-than-usual transaction in Columbia and the money was hidden in the shaft alley of the turbocharger, four and a half million dollars American.... I circled above him, the chopper laboring in the high altitude.

To the north from Los Banos I could see 3 jalopy-loads of villagers heading in Fuentes' direction; within a few minutes and to the south, an Army truck with a jeep preceding it roared towards the field.... His complicity in the assassination of General Breones dooms Fuentes with the military forces in this province. Instead of picking him up, which I had plenty of time to do, I circled 2,000 feet above him until finally Fuentes walked back over to the plane and I heard his voice on the VHF, "I hear you thinking." Then he stood there, looking. I circled several more times. Then he broadcast, "I know you and I'll find you." I switched off the VHF and left him there standing on the wing of the Navajo holding the microphone and looking up.... I was so tired of what I was. The world will not miss Fuentes, nor in time me. I returned to the airfield at Cuenca, told everyone complications had necessitated Fuentes' remaining in Bogota, which is not unusual. Telling Mara and his eldest son that he needed the Lear, I loaded everything and departed.

In Port-of-Spain I bought a plane ticket for Paris then slipped away and took a taxi back to the steamer dock. There's humor in using an old slow steamer to make a quick escape.... I write these words in a large stateroom elaborately crafted with teak and mahogany complete with shaded lamps and a rolltop writing desk. The old ship sways steadily with the sea as we steam towards the north.

MAY 28. THE CANNERY

I have fallen into a depression. I do little or nothing. Several nights ago I became drunk and slept in one of the cottages. The next morning I was wet and cold, but the cat found me, curled next to me. It hadn't been cold at all.

Perhaps it was the completion of the journals and re-reading the entry from the Valle del Fuego.

Yesterday I abruptly wept. I don't know why, just as I don't know why I've fallen into a depression.

It was 23 years ago I left the United States in an Army transport for Southeast Asia. I deserted within two months. I wrote home and my stepfather reported my address to the Army Police. Yet it was my mother in their last letter who wrote, "For us, you died."

I am somewhat weak from my drinking bout.

In the bathroom while drunk I'd written in Spanish, "You can't ever remove yourself from what you really are." It sounds anemic in English.

JUNE 11. THE CANNERY

These days aren't really summer days. It rains frequently, and though the temperatures have risen (it was 52 degrees yesterday) there is not a feeling of summer in the air. Nor will there be.

It rains, seemingly, with no end; this has done little to elevate my mood. I've had to do that somewhat artificially, which is reminiscent of my days in Laos. I hated Laos.

In Laos there were phenomenally large lizards that would spring out of nowhere and scare the hell out of me. That is one thing about the high altitudes of Ecuador. There were far fewer snakes and lizards than in southeast Asia. There are no snakes and lizards here, but much water.

My hours are spent wandering both actually and mentally. In the morning I watch the swallows and the cat at war, the swallows always winning except on rare occasions when the cat manages to snag one, crunching it noisily between sharp teeth.

I take long walks towards the lake, and follow deer trails off into nowhere. I think of many things on these walks.

I was going to say I'm not ordinarily reflective, yet I am; hence of late I've been even more reflective.

JUNE 13. THE CANNERY

Today the supply plane arrived. I thought they'd forgotten me, as I haven't had a supply plane in over six weeks. In it was personal mail which initially astounded me. Who in hell would send me mail? No one should know I'm here, let alone write me.

It was a single, large official envelope from the postmistress which the pilot handed over to me. I made coffee and studied the envelope. Then I opened it and saw that it contained a single letter from Alice. It contained a package of alfalfa seeds with printed instructions; on this package was scrawled, "You won't keep a garden. Follow the instructions and eat them at least three times a week."

Also was a notebook-sized piece of paper with more scrawl saying, "Fishing is poor and so is the weather. How is your cat? If she is eating swallows stop her by attaching a bell."

Then she signed her name. Thinking of this morning, during which the cat had been particularly effective, I smiled and examined the packet of seeds.

I moved the supplies up from the beach to the house and though I've never seen the sense in raising or eating sprouts, I was re-reading the instructions when I accidentally turned over the paper on which she'd written and saw there was a P.S. I hadn't noticed: "P.S. I'm pregnant."

I made more coffee and wondered about this, as anyone would. I've never been one for quick assumptions, never. I know nothing of Alice and if she is pregnant clearly she could be so by anybody.

Yet I find it strange that except for the fact she informed me of the need to go fishing, she was careful never to tell me anything personal about herself. Since this new information is personal it is really out of character and it is only logical to think that it doesn't concern me.

Somehow Alice manages to disrupt the normal order of events. Yet as I write this, the news is still novel and the matter will take further consideration. I've had several women lie to me about that, or simply be mistaken.

It is just that I don't want to be faced with any sort of tension or awake each morning to unanswered questions.

It wasn't until a few minutes before entering this in my journal that the irony between the outlandish "P.S." and the alfalfa seeds occurred to me. But this is accidental, for Alice has always seemed anything but a complicated woman.

JUNE 18. THE CANNERY

I have decided that the information about her pregnancy is meant to convey the fact that she'll be unable to return for a visit again. This makes the P.S. far more understandable. In any event, the unpredictability and threat of a growing dependency on her visits were undeniable disruptions. I noticed that on the envelope was an address, a post office box in town. I was going to write, but I thought she'd be away in any event.

Often women who I had regular sexual contact with would claim pregnancy or actually become pregnant. Generally they were ignorant women from native stock and either illiterate or close to it. I would always see to it that such pregnancies were terminated early-on. Over 17 years ago a white woman, a bothersome yet sexually interesting French woman, the wife of a Consulate, became pregnant by me, but she was killed in a car bomb explosion. At the funeral I held the husband tightly around the waist to keep him from collapsing with grief. For months after she and I began having relations she'd say the same words in French each time I penetrated her. One day I discovered that it meant, "Thank God, at last." I thought of those words as we followed the small station wagon carrying her remains to the cemetery. I was only 24 years old then.

This business with the letter has genuinely upset me.

JUNE 22. THE CANNERY

Perhaps many animals have a drive to become individual, no matter how regimented or anonymous their daily survival becomes. Take the swallows: There must be hundreds of swallows around the cannery grounds nesting in the deep eaves of the dozens of old buildings, yet I am able to recognize individual birds. It is something in the way they call, perhaps the manner in which they react to the cat who now pursues them relentlessly. So those few, despite the hundreds of swallows, I can readily identify. They have become individually significant despite this mass of similar appearing birds.

Also the squirrels: Small, noisy squirrels have again taken up residence all around the cannery, yet there are a few who make themselves quite identifiable. One has a way of holding its tail lower than the others. This squirrel has the odd capacity for running up the sheer walls of wooden buildings. None of the other squirrels either can or choose to do this.

Individuality makes itself very clear in ravens: About a dozen ravens hang about the cannery, but one is different from the others; his vocalizations are even stranger than ordinary ravens, which is no mean accomplishment as ravens have an unearthly repertoire of calls and croaks.

It is because of this drive for individuality that I know it was Fuentes yesterday who flew over the cannery in the red and white Cessna 206 on pontoons, or floats as they call them in Alaska. How many times did I watch Fuentes fly aircraft? Ten thousand? Twenty thousand? Though pilots' techniques vary considerably, and at a distance most people cannot discern one pilot from another in the way they handle an aircraft. I knew: It was Fuentes.

When turning, and especially when he was simply surveying the countryside without intention of landing, Fuentes had a curious "twitch" prior to banking right or left. It was a signature, or it is his signature.

The plane flew over just after noon yesterday; it was very low and just above stall speed. It made several passes before I took notice, as many planes come over here. I could see that it contained at least four passengers; yes, I'm sure it was four passengers. When I saw the plane bank for its last turn around, I scrambled back to the house for the binoculars, but I was too late. It flew over and then disappeared.

But it'll be back.

There is no point in wondering how he survived the impossible situation in Valle del Fuego. Obviously he has.

JULY 23. THE CANNERY

I did not sleep, but maintained a curious vigil all night. Through the night I kept telling myself to open the steamer trunk which contains my arsenal, but I didn't. While I waited, looking out the window, I meant to go upstairs to my bedroom and at least fetch my .45 which is on the bed stand. But I didn't. Rather than this, I drank coffee after coffee and looked and listened to the passage of things in the short night.

In abandoning Fuentes in the Valle del Fuego there was a desire to be shut of violence. I have resisted considering myself moralistic about the violence, or reacting to it out of conscience. I simply don't consider violence immoral, no more than I would consider the cat's assault upon the swallows immoral.

Rather, my adverse reaction to violence was its strife and noise: The gunfire, the screams and howls. Violence wasn't like that portrayed in the movies when I was young. Even prior to Ecuador I observed that when humans die, or are dying, they don't behave as they do in the movies. Instead they scream, plead, betray husband, wife, or offspring, mother, father, sibling. Anything to live. And when the violence is actually done to them, when they know it's too late, they are quite unlike oxen or llamas; instead they emit shattering vocalizations which both English and Spanish lack precise words for. This is not to speak of the half dozen physical manifestations (such as defecation) which are never worthy of the movies and certainly television.

Fuentes and I talked of this. The violence. My Ecuadorian journals are now bound in a dozen thick volumes. I looked through them for nearly two hours before finding the following entry from three years, two months ago:

Today I told Fuentes I was weary of the violence, despite the fact it isn't that frequent anymore. He smoked a cigar and nodded, tapping the ash from the smoldering tip with his eyes half closed while Mara rubbed his bare feet. Finally he declared, "You have the poet's tendency to become maudlin and introspective, and this is your weakness. You see, you are not a violent man. You've done what was necessary to survive and even those you've killed wouldn't find fault with that."

JUNE 24. THE CANNERY

Towards the morning I slept. The *soldados* whom Fuentes has with him must be receiving much, for if I had resisted most would die. But not Fuentes; I have seen too much to deceive myself. No, my final opportunity was in the Valle del Fuego, and I've missed that. I sit in the living room drinking coffee, occasionally adding a touch of whisky, and writing.

Somewhat past noon the plane flew over again. From my vantage point I could see there was only a single person, the pilot. It circled once at an altitude just above effective small arms range. Then he changed pitch suddenly on the prop, which is Fuentes' way of informing me of an impending message drop. Soon a small bundle was tossed out with a long plastic ribbon tied to it. Almost floating down, the ribbon fluttered behind the wad of cloth, drifting then landing between the old store and the water tank.

I left the house and fetched it.

Contained in the cloth was a note wrapped around a dozen Ecuadorian *sucre* pieces for weight. I walked out upon the end of the dock, accepting the fact that riflemen could have already been in place around the bay. But nothing happened.

As Fuentes circled at 5,000 feet, I pocketed the coins and read the note which read simply in English, "It isn't the money, it is the betrayal." Then in Spanish, "You can never remove yourself from what you really are."

Seeing that I had the note, he flew off, the wings dipping a gentle salute.

JUNE 25. THE CANNERY

I have taken all my Ecuadorian journals, also I will include these, and put them in a waterproof container and place them in the safe at the old store. In several days, at the most a week, I'll be dead. I will carry on my regular routine. The reason I won't resist is because I have become tired of the strife and violence. I've discussed this earlier. There is no time to repeat things.

Typically, Fuentes eliminates the sons of his more formidable enemies, claiming a traditional tie with the ancient Indian cultures in doing this. "You don't want avenging sons surviving," and he would do away with the sons of truly deadly enemies. If his enemy's woman were pregnant, he would maintain her until he saw whether she gave birth to a son or daughter. When Mara would argue about the cruelty of this he would only nod and repeat, "You don't want avenging sons surviving." So, there is a benefit to Fuentes' not knowing about Alice. I've been tempted to write her, to call a plane out especially to take the letter to town. I even thought of sending her the journals. But I dismissed these ideas entirely.

I was looking forward to her visits after she returned, if indeed there were going to be others. But those possibilities have ended now. It is night while I write this. The cat brought in a strange kind of mouse that was still alive; it simply let it free in the kitchen, padded into the living room and settled onto the back of the easy chair. It was no longer concerned about the mouse. The cat will survive here at the cannery.

Suddenly I've recalled the time last June when my lawyer pushed the beneficiary card at me. I thought for 15 minutes and finally said, "There's no one." She looked at me and said, "There must be someone. There is a matter of $3.5 million dollars and the cannery."

Finally we settled on an assortment of charities, and I agreed to this only for expediency's sake. The issue was mundane to me.

Just this instant I saw a flash of light in the forest towards the point where the jaws of the bay draw close together. It lasted for a second or two, probably a nervous bump of a flashlight, yet I saw it immediately. This was careless. Yet Fuentes always sends in his less skillful *soldados* first, for they are less valuable to him.

I had better take these journals, along with the others, down to the safe, for it is nearly two in the morning and it's getting somewhat light in the east. I genuinely resent dying now, for the quiet and gentleness of the morning has always been special to me no matter where I was.

Fuentes, Fuentes, goddamn you. I thought you were dead.

Statements About Edward (An Obituary in Progress)

"*E*dward often lost track of where he was."
-Lt. Culbertson, Anchorage Police Dept., Shift Commander
He was reported missing at 10:30 p.m. The patrolmen followed Edward's tracks in the snow right to the bench. By that time, though, he had been dead for several hours. It hadn't been much of an escape: He evidently found the back door of the Care Center open and walked out into the January weather as he was, in pajamas and slippers. The cause of death was hypothermia.

"*Edward liked it in the park.*"
-Jean Parks, Care Worker, Pioneer House
All night the temperatures had been in the twenties with a stiff wind coming off Cook Inlet. We found out later that Edward had plodded through the deep snow over to the bench and sat down. By this time, he'd lost his slippers in the snow and was barefooted.

"*He told me he'd been the United States Marshal at Nome.*"
-Fred Sidell, Barber, Pioneer House
Edward was eighty-nine years old, didn't have any relatives or in fact any visitors during his last ten years at the Care Center. Eighty-nine years was a lot to forget, but Edward had. Only twice, that I heard of, did he allude to biographical fact: Once to Fred, who cut hair at the Care Center, and the second

192

time to a nurse's aide. Edward had transferred in to Pioneer House a decade before from a nursing home that had gone bankrupt. No one knew anything about him.

"He looked up at me and told me he'd found Wily Post and Will Rogers."
-Anna Murphy, Nurse's Aide, Pioneer House

He'd announced this during his last Thanksgiving program two months before; maybe one of the skits had stirred his memory. When someone asked him who Wily Post and Will Rogers were, the volunteers had already begun serving ice cream and Edward had lost interest in such matters.

When I dropped off a hitchhiker across from the park, he was just sitting there staring off across the water. I was in a hurry and drove on, but I can guess what happened:

At the tide's ebb, Edward walked to the inlet's muddy edge, picking his way around chunks of ice grounded on a previous higher tide. His knees and back, plagued for years by arthritis, worked smoothly. For a second, he allowed himself a look back: He saw an Anchorage now noisy and gigantic by comparison to the smallish town he'd first seen in 1927. Then he saw the ancient on the bench, and he recognized himself and reflected how strange it was to live so long. Everyone else he knew hadn't.

He must have known that longevity had marooned him on an island where he no longer belonged. Best thing was to move on.

So Edward would have turned and struck out towards this hunter's moon. It was just like the King Islanders used to say: Winter moons served as beacons, guiding Inipuit to lands rich in seal, where men and women dance to the old, true stories sung by the voices of drums.

Along the 70th Parallel

I.

"We are normal people"
Wilton Kellogg, Jr.

Today Eskimo Pete showed up with the mail and instructed that from hereafter, we will refer to him as Inipuit Pete. Also Katy, Piccolo Jane, and PeekyBo will be called by their Inipuit names; furthermore, their Friday visits to Gabriel Tracking Site will be five hundred dollars a visit, up front. He said it was all a part of the sovereignty movement whose central premise is pride in one's heritage.

After this, Pete visited me in the bunker. We talked, mostly about the old times, and as usual Pete listened to several phone conversations I'd recorded last week. Hethen returned to Gabriel Village with piles of magazines, two computer-enhanced Jane Fonda exercise videos, three lids of so/so dope Buffalo Jim had knocking around in his drawer, a few amyls of smelling salts, and two quarts of ethanol extracted from discarded Long Range Converter Units. Over the years, Pete has developed some self-destructive practices.

Wilt theorizes that Pete's actions were a temporary phase resulting from his attending the circumpolar conference in Copenhagen. "It's those Greenland Eskimos," Wilt claims, "they always make trouble. I remember that from my Army days."

Spike O'Flaherty, the station's computer jock who keeps our old mainframe up and running, is not pleased. He says that the day he'll pay five hundred dollars for the likes of Katy, Piccolo Jane, and PeekyBo, is the day he'll caponize himself.

The five of them—Billy, Spike, Overout, Buffalo and Wilt—had a rare staff meeting after Pete's visit—to strike a group stance about this business, as Buffalo says. Ultimately, Wilt Kellogg, Supervisor of Gabriel Tracking Facility, decided. "Listen, in the final analysis, we are normal people who just want to be happy. It's not like we can't afford it."

I had been invited to the meeting but stayed in my bunker.

From my archives: A Christmas telephone conversation, 12/25/69:

"I love you so much, honey. What do you do over there, anyway?"
"I'm in the infantry, Sweetie. That's what I do over here."
"I bet you're doing it with all those German girls."
"No, Sweetie. I'm saving it all for you."
"God, that's so nice to hear."
"I know Sweetie. Being away from you, well, it's just like walking around
without any pants on."

I have been here the longest—since 1968 when Gabriel Tracking was still under the Air Force. In those days, it was a more dramatic place to work. The Soviets were only eighteen miles from Cape Whisky on the northwest end of Gabriel Island, and our every move was scrutinized from their massive station at Cape Goloduff. Gabriel Village's people were still much like they were at the turn of the century, and some of the old women had chin tattoos and smoked plug in clay pipes. A few of them could even remember the old steam whalers that came north hunting bowhead. And of course, the whisky runners.

Eskimo Pete was young then—same age as me, born in 1941—and was a pretty optimistic sort of guy. He wanted to be a movie star.

How many Eskimos do they have in Hollywood? Well, not many.

So, he was going to Hollywood. Major Lowenstein was the CO when I came on for ACR, and he resented me—out of the forty-seven people at Gabriel Tracking, I was the only civilian. Back then I was the janitor; now I am called the maintenance engineer, and next year I've got to retire. That's a major issue.

II.
"People cannot be civilized without the concept of money."
Buffalo Jim Wilcoxen

Buffalo is dedicated to the idea of strengthening the local economy. Every week, he gets into the site half-track, and—regardless of the season—motors down the eight-mile road into Gabriel Village to teach basic accounting.

How else will these people ever advance? We owe it to them.

Buffalo is convinced that there is great economic potential for the Eskimos of Gabriel Village in the domestication of the walrus.

"A walrus? What do they need?" asks Buffalo, to just about anyone who questions his idea. "Some clam necks, a place to haul out, and every year or so, some poongtang. The rest, well, it takes care of itself."

Once domesticated, the walrus can be herded up; then, after the walrus have grown tusks of appreciable size, herdsmen can cut them off and allow local carvers to craft them into cribbage boards, kayaks, and retro-scrimshaw. The income would be steady. The walrus needn't be killed for their ivory; eco-tourists might fly in to see genuine herds of Bering Sea walrus, and Eskimo carvers, in the end, would benefit.

"It is what is known as a Closed Economic System," Buffalo wrote in his seed grant application to the Anchorage Economic Consortium. Buffalo's entire premise is based on the sure knowledge that in the 21st Century, a people cannot be civilized without the concept of money.

From my archives: A telephone conversation, 1/18/74:

"Sometimes I wake up in the middle of the night, and there are huge lizards crawling on the ceiling."

"Oh, God, Son. That's awful."

"I went to the Chaplain, but he was shipping back home the next day, and didn't have much time."

"Is he Christian?"

"Yes. Oh yes. He was a Baptist, even."

"Well then, Son, what did he say about the lizards?"

"He said that in Vietnam, there are lizards everywhere."

Since I am the maintenance man, no one was even aware of my bunker until 1969, and by then I was down twenty-eight feet. Once below the permafrost, it was easy going, except, ironically enough, for ground water.

"Listen, Spellman, you just can't dig a hole straight down into the planet. It worries hell out of people, plus this is government property, and there are regulations."

Captain Wilson succeeded Major Lowenstein as CO, but as the result of a B-52 shootdown over Vietnam, the Captain had only one eye. Still, regardless of their respective number of eyes, Wilson was a vast improvement over Lowenstein.

"And another thing, Spellman: The Soviets have birds that strike their target, burrow down seventy-five feet like giant ticks, and turn everything within ten miles to molten oblivion. So, get back to me on this, OK?"

Captain Wilson ended every official conversation the same way; perhaps it was his management method of trying to make orders seem like group consultation. Yet, because of it, few ever did what he asked.

I was the one who acted as intermediary between Captain Wilson and Blazo. Despite Blazo's being a Friday girl, she fell for Captain Wilson completely and became pregnant, viewing that as a way of affirming their tie. The Captain was a gallant sort, bought her jujubees and caramel corn on movie nights, and they would hold hands through almost the entire feature. Friday girls didn't ordinarily get that kind of treatment.

But Captain Wilson was married, plus thirty-two years older than Blazo, and it was completely impossible. Blazo was devastated. She was sent away to boarding school in New York State and never returned to Gabriel Village. Soon the Captain was gone also—retiring from the Air Force.

But this has gotten me away from the matter of my bunker. For it was my talk with Captain Wilson—a person knowledgeable about modern weaponry—that made me aware that I must dig deeper than I had initially planned. Far deeper.

III.
"There is such a thing as moral entrapment through dumb fate."
Billy Conklin.

It was almost four years before we all realized that Wilt Kellogg truly believed that on Friday, Gabriel Village girls came up here to clean rooms and do laundry. I remember Billy's absolute disbelief when I told him.

Nobody can possibly be that naive. Jesus.

But Wilt was that naive. He was a family man, believed in the power of prayer and in the national revitalization of family values. Becoming routinely immersed in moral turpitude every Friday night (to offer a bit of site talk) wasn't something that raised much of a blip on Wilt's radar.

Billy Conklin was the last regular visitor to my bunker. We would watch one of the movies from the hundred-plus old sixteen-mm films I have, and then afterwards sit around and talk. My living quarters are at eighty-five feet, and even if it's minus fifty and blowing thirty knots outside, it's always sixty degrees at the eighty-five-foot level.

Billy likes the way I've deceived the elements. He claims it is a metaphor for "the traditional disparity between what's real and what's not," as he put it. Billy is full of gibberish like that since he considers himself a philosopher.

"I majored in philosophy," he says, "but my wife got pregnant, and I went into electronics."

He and his wife hate each other, but they don't get divorced because he's gone most the time anyway, and they would take a terrible tax loss if they did. Both of their children—now in college—are spoiled geniuses. Buffalo claims that after their parents are gone, both will spend their lives in jail or hooked up to electroshock therapy machines.

Billy prides himself about his knowledge in the study of ethics. In fact, Billy is the only tech at Gabriel Tracking who has questioned out loud the Friday visits by the girls. I don't partake of Friday night activities—never have. If someone wanted an explanation, I just told them—well, I told them I didn't need to explain anything, especially to them.

(People respect someone digging a hole into the earth, so when I say something, it usually ends further inquiry.)

But Billy was more patient and crafty. For three years he hinted around for my *real* reasons. Finally—probably worn down from having to dodge the matter—I said that in my view, I didn't think it right.

Never did.

"Well I do, and so do the others, except Wilt, who probably sleeps with his hands taped to the bedposts. But I think my decision is based damned firmly in logic and ethno-historical considerations. So, I'm interested—why don't you think it right, Digger? You and I are always frank with each other, and Lord knows I respect all views, especially those based in ethical reasoning."

Instinct told me to demur. One of the principal tenets of getting along in remote locales is never bringing up what you think are deficiencies in co-workers. But Billy was a thinking person, different than almost any who worked at Gabriel Tracking. So, I broke this long-held tenet. I lifted my hand and counted my objections finger by finger, stopping at the thumb.

"One: It is a felony in Alaska to have sex with girls under sixteen. Two: It takes further advantage of people who have been preyed on by Europeans for over a century. Three: To buy someone's body for sex is to practice a form of slavery. Four: To solicit or accept sex for money is against the law. Five: It is contrary to ACR's community relations policy."

Billy Conklin thought about this—sipping his bourbon, nodding—for we always imbibe lightly during our after-movie talks. I was relieved to see that he wasn't angry; instead he finished his drink, stood and said, "I think what society has overlooked is that there is such a thing as moral entrapment through dumb fate."

He excused himself, thanked me for the movie and liquor, and as he climbed the first rung to the station, he added, "And I'm really disappointed how you've failed to see that, Digger. I thought you were of a more sophisticated nature."

And, of course, Billy Conklin never came down into my bunker again. What this demonstrated is that once you have a central tenet, you shouldn't break it. Absolutely never.

From my archives: A phone conversation, 9/23/91:

"Yesterday, they cut off somebody's head."
"What!? Why?"
"For Blasphemy. Against Allah."
"And to think, we support those people."
"Last week, they stoned a woman to death for prostitution."
"Oh my God! Have you gone on a camel ride yet?"
"No, not yet. But it's on the top of my list."

I consider my habit of eavesdropping on phone calls something like succombing to combat fatigue. Most at Gabriel Tracking, in fact along the entire system, do it. That doesn't make it right, and let me declare up front that it is against ACR company policy.

Most calls relayed are to or from military personnel and dependents back in the states. All of the links are unsecured, so it's not like we're picking up secret information.

Phone sex is the favored target of eavesdropping, with vituperative husband/wife arguments second. Then there's the combination of both. Some of the more lurid calls are put on the speaker system, especially if Wilt is not here, or in his room. I think phone sex *began* over the overseas military links, especially the ones reserved for the Red Cross.

But this is not what I collect because, ultimately, it is a degenerate habit to listen to such calls and does little to bolster one's opinion of human dignity. The only person I know who also isn't interested in these is Pete. I like ironic calls, and so does Pete.

Spike and Overout shake their head and declare my tapes the most mundane collection possible—a waste of time and resources. Spike and Overout are not what you'd consider a litmus test of taste and humanity, though.

Early in life, I learned the difference between what is coarse and what is colorful. And what is decent.

Before her disappearance, my mother taught me the value of decency. Even drunk, my mother was a strong believer in "civilized conduct," as she put it. She disliked coarseness. I suppose many would think that's contradictory in a person so outwardly flawed. I didn't and still don't.

I admired that aspect of my mother more than anything, that and her endless ability to imagine things, a quality I wish I would have inherited—or inherited more. Though most looked down on my mother, they didn't know her. So, my approach to the phone conversations at Gabriel Tracking follows the precepts I learned and appreciated when young. I'm adamant that it should never turn into a prurient habit. I'm always looking for something different—wisps of conversation that to me point out how paradoxical human nature is.

Like my mother—especially the way she was taken from me.

IV.
"I wish there was a Santa Claus. I'd bring him down with the .375 mag."
Overout Karl Coverdale

Overout is an artifact from full-time days.

He is cynical, foul, obscene and beyond raunchy. A sentence doesn't pass that the *f*-word isn't stuffed in somewhere. In Overout's view of the world, wars are good because they rid the planet of useless *f-ing* bastards; an election that doesn't turn out an incumbent is *f-ing* rigged; soup kitchens and homeless shelters wouldn't be *f-ing* necessary if *f-ing* politicians and administrators had to eat and sleep there every night, and organized *f-ing* religions are backwaters where the gullible and dogbrained of society are clumped together into a *f-ing* scummy flotsam.

"Show me a *f-ing* Skypilot, and I'll show you someone who'd drink from a *f-ing* toilet bowl and smile," he said once.

No one at the site now ever was a full-timer except Overout and myself. For the first twenty years, personnel lived at Gabriel site full time, except for vacations. But ACR went to a fortnight-on/ten-days-off schedule after several suicides and a long series of nervous collapses. And everyone preferred this except me—and possibly Overout, who always has a marriage failing somewhere on the mainland. I'm still full time, because I sued. When I was hired, being full-time was in my contract. My original contract.

The ACR psychologist uses me as an example to new hires during company orientation.

"Isolation is not something to take lightly," he tells them. "To see what isolation can do, just take the case of Digger Spellman at Gabriel Tracking."

I am the only full-timer now in the fifty-six-station system run by ACR—a system stretching from Siberia to Spitzbergen. But because of his years as a full-timer, Overout still has retained characteristics—one might say, "personality residue"—from those days.

For one, you don't want to be anywhere close to Overout during the holiday season. No Christmas talk! If someone puts up a holiday decoration, he takes it down; and if one were to put it back up, he'd skin them alive.

He has children and grandchildren spread out over both hemispheres. At holiday time he volunteers to spend an extra fortnight at the station because it keeps him from home and all the trappings of Christmas. Also, he makes double-time, minimum.

There are things mysterious about Overout. For one, he could give somebody a haircut with a rifle.

On most winters, polar bears usually wander in over the pack ice, and, finding lots of garbage and diverse points-of-interest, stick around after the ice recedes. Then the beasts cause all sorts of problems both at the village and tracking site.

Polar bears are fearless, intense customers. And years ago, it fell to Overout to do the honors with the elephant rifle kept in the security locker for that purpose. Without much pause, he aimed and shot one such creature through the eye. It folded into a pile of fur and viscera, and that did that.

He can disassemble and reassemble any rifle in seconds, and can recite ballistic information out to one thousand yards for dozens of calibers with diverse loading information.

He never hunts, does not own a gun and avoids any outdoor activity. When asked why and where he came by his skill with firearms, he answers, "Same way I did old Roscoe: I was born with it."

Many winters ago, several techs were teasing Overout about his disdain of Christmas. "Bet you'd sing a different story if you saw old Saint Nick come flying over the antennae field Christmas eve!"

Overout, a devotee of vintage girlie magazines, looked up sharply from a stack of French classics—Santa Claus wasn't a topic he even liked to kid about. The glow in his eyes was identical to when he raised the rifle to his shoulder to blow away marauding bears.

"I wish there *was* a *f*-ing Santa Claus, I'd bring him down with the *f*-ing .375 mag. And I'd dance on his *f*-ing carcass."

They began to laugh, but Overout just continued to scowl at them until their laughter fell away to a nervous patter.

From my archives: A phone conversation, 7/23/77:

"Three days ago President Carter gave a speech at base HQ. God, he's an embarrassment."

"Sonny was caught in school again with blasting caps."

"Jesus. Well, tell Grandpa Felton that I still haven't received any issues of

Shotgun News *yet. The Sarge gets it, but hogs it.*"

"*Grandma Felton keeps asking why the Army is in Korea, because the war has been over for years.*"

"*You tell Sonny to get his shit together, or Ill kick his butt a good one when I rotate out of this damned place.*"

"*Megs wants to play little league baseball.*"

"*I keep writing Grandma Felton over and over again about Korea. It doesnt do any good. Meg's gotta learn she's a damn girl.*"

"*God, I miss you, Hon.*"

"*I know. I know.*"

When I'm feeling low, I watch the movie *Brigadoon*. I go into the movie locker at the forty-five-foot level, get it out and thread it onto the projector. Just this—before even showing it—settles me out. But watching it really does it.

I was twelve years old when *Brigadoon* came out, and my mother and I saw it together at least twenty times. She thought the idea of a magical village appearing every hundred years—to disappear in the mist and heather for another hundred—was unbelievably magical. "Like all the ugliness in life, Junior," she said to me. "A girl has to believe in that—that allthis ugliness will just vanish, all go away, leaving just the nice things."

Though I never liked smaltzy musicals, I like *Brigadoon* because of seeing it with her. Initially, we went to the neighborhood movie house; then it moved out to the drive-ins, and we'd head out there in the old Nash, recline the seats back, and watch. Mom would sing along with her favorite numbers and I'd hold a big tub of popcorn in my lap and try and ignore her pouring Dixie Tall Girls out from her Stanley thermos every ten minutes or so.

Driving back to town with Mom after she had imbibed a thermos of Dixie Tall Girls was a pretty scary proposition, and that's why and when I learned to drive, coming in from the drive-in after watching *Brigadoon*.

When the musical score came out on new long-play records, we bought a record player, and Mom would play the music and dance along with it. She was a pretty woman, actually having long beautiful legs like Cyd Charisse in the movie, and sometimes I'd dance the Gene Kelly part—jumping from the couch over to the Hanson bed, back to the couch, up onto the kitchen table. We'd go on like that until Mrs. Gruder below would start banging on the ceiling with a broom.

I never begrudged Mom the pleasure of her *Brigadoon* antics because at that time she was double-shifting at the Streetcar Grubstead and waitressing was wearing her down fast. On days off, or when she got home, she'd page through magazines and drink Dixie Tall Girls. She'd dream of being someplace—doing something—other than serving Mr. Baker omelets and getting a hand up her skirt if she didn't watch out.

So down at the forty-five-foot level, I watch Gene Kelly and Cyd Charisse going through the "Heather on the Mist" dance number, and I think of Mom and me back in the apartment above old Mrs. Gruder's—dancing around like a couple of nitwits.

And I sip bourbon, zone out, and sometimes wake with one of the reels flopping around on the projector and the light glaring off the wall. It is actually owning *Brigadoon,* watching it any time I want—especially when site tedium gets bad—that makes me appreciate how lucky I am. And because of this, I'm in good shape head-wise compared to so many others, even those who were never full-timers.

And it is all a part of my Mom's legacy; and no matter what was later said about her, no mother can do better than that.

V.

"The cold and wind are always waiting. Time is on their side, not ours."
Spike O'Flaherty

Spike is much better now. This is his second time at Gabriel Tracking, and the management is keeping a close eye on him. His first tour was a catastrophe. It all happened because Spike, unlike all the others here—maybe even myself—is unable to separate the station environment from that outside. Yet the capacious salary and benefit package are Spike's sirens.

Now he checks the weather station readouts only once a day, where before he began by checking them two or three times in the morning and afternoon, then more often, until it became bad. Obsessive, is how they termed it.

Since I'm the maintenance man, I handle all the routine physical plant stuff. Gabriel Tracking is a carefully engineered and controlled environment supported by boilers, circulating pumps, blowers, fuel pumps, fuel lines. The lot.

And that's not even mentioning the mission-oriented stuff, the electronics, the outdoor antennae field, the big radar dome on top of the station—and all the motors, gears, lifters and sensors that go into their operation—all that is the technician's world.

So when we're inside enjoying lobster and steak night, Gabriel Tracking is operating pretty much in a never-never-land of technology supported by the arrival of supply barges during the fleeting summer, and the tenuous supply flights the rest of the year.

Spike is aware of how delicate this balance is; and the first time out, his incessant worry about it all just dissolved, slipped right away from him. He kept constant scrutiny of the weather, the ice conditions. He became a menace to me, asking if I'd done the annual maintenance inspection of this, that—it was just all craziness. Eventually, they carried him out of here in restraints.

Even now, ten years after his first tour, he notices seasonal events—you'd say, almost depends on them emotionally.

The most anticipated event is spring breakup. "The thaw," as Spike puts it.

If it's late, Spike still worries, despite my assurance that in all of human history, spring and summer have always arrived. Yet an early thaw makes him unsettled: Will the coming winter be early?

As the thaw progresses, he views the arrival of each summer visitor with great relief. His favorites are the Lapland Longspurs and the Wheatears, little birds few notice. In fact, I really didn't know their names until Spike pointed them out in his bird book. To Spike, they're messengers of joy.

"I know that if these little fellows show up, then the weather will be survivable, because—instinct. They know."

Then as the ice recedes from the tundra ponds and lakes, the waterfowl arrive in countless aerial wedges, cackling jubilantly—descending unevenly through layers of cold and warm air as they glide towards the tundra. Most are snow geese, white-bodied, with ink-dipped wingtips that flash in the arctic sun.

With their arrival, Spike knows he will have at least sixty days worry-free.

"Geese know about winds and weather, more than anything."

Spike is no longer teased by others, and we all hope he'll keep it together. For myself, I'm more grateful to Spike than anyone else because he's taught me that this stack of concrete is nothing but the most fragile of fortresses opposing the elements.

We are (by our nature) frail and temporary visitors to this enigmatic land of ocean, tundra, and boundless skies.

As the days grow shorter, Spike tightens up emotionally. By the first of September, we're getting true nights, and temperatures fall below freezing. There's really no autumn, and winter comes upon us swiftly. Spike knows there is never a guarantee this winter will be as survivable as the former, nor that the equipment needed to survive will function as well as it did last winter.

"Spike, don't worry. It's always sixty degrees in my bunker."

This offers only a minimum of comfort to him, and as the winter solstice approaches—always his worst day—Spike looks up miserably and says, "Can't you hear it out there? The wind and cold are always waiting. Time is on their side, not ours."

And I do hear it out there. In fact, when we get a powerful winter northwester' from the Gulf of Anadyr, it will pick up ice and snow, hurling it over the entire station. After such a storm, if there's a full moon, the station looms atop the mountain, chiseled against the sky, bloodless white and quiet. During midday chores, "day" in name only, I take a long look at this and think a powerful sorcerer has made Gabriel Tracking materialize from the land itself; and with a wave of his wand, he could well make it vanish.

From my archives: A phone conversation, 2/15/90:

"Well, he lived alone on the river. He was a river rat."
"So, they didn't find him for a while?"
"That's right. It was three or four days, they figure."
"He was my favorite uncle. I thought he'd live forever."
"Well, he smoked, drank and Lord knows what else, in his day."
"I know. He did it all. He truly did."
"There was a time we thought you'd turn out like he did. Thank God for the Navy."
"Did he always live alone? I never asked him that."
"Always. Since he was sixteen. Don't know if he wanted to be alone, but that's how he got it."

My mother went away for the long weekend to see a friend in the city and never came back. I walked with her to the Greyhound; she got on the local because we had been late for the express. At the station, I helped her pick out some magazines. She kissed me, gave me a wink, and I never saw her again. I was thirteen.

I knew her friend a little; she had waitressed with my mom. A visit with her meant they'd drink pretty hard. Mom would have never just deserted me, but that's what everybody thought even though to my face they'd say she probably met with foul play. With the help of my Social studies teacher, I filed a missing person report; but they found nothing out except Mom and the friend had gotten in a car and headed for Mexico.

At least that's what they wrote in the letter.

I had no relatives, didn't know who my father was—at least never was told. Mom mentioned several times that she had an older brother but hadn't seen or heard of him since the Depression. The police tried to find him, but couldn't.

So I was put into foster care and the less said about that the better.

Some people are just naturally mean-spirited and never say anything good about anyone, especially those who aren't there to defend themselves.

I ran away when I was sixteen, and even at that, I waited too long.

In the last thirty years, I've spent a lot of money on private investigators, plus many weeks of my vacation trying to find out what happened to Mom. Despite this, turning up any information has been like trying to bite into rock. The only thing I've found out for sure is that in the year following her disappearance, the police never even looked. The part about Mexico was not true. I don't know who made it up, the police or my foster parents.

So, in three months, when I reach my thirtieth year in the service, I've got to retire. Until a few years ago, I always intended to look for her full time—throw all resources available into the effort until I found out what happened.

But in the last five years, there have been no leads at all; so I'm falling back on what I've called Plan B. Three years ago, somebody purchased the Seventh Day Adventist mission and adjoining property in Gabriel Village. Despite efforts, all anyone could find out was it had been purchased through an Anchorage law firm. The mystery is still the talk of the village, but the answer to that mystery is my Plan B.

Actually, when they find out, villagers will laugh, for I'm rather considered like—well, they call me "the old man in the mountain," though I guess in Eskimo—I should say Inipuit—it mean something more along the lines of "old spirit under the earth." Either way, I like the nickname, and I'll leave my bunker and Gabriel Tracking without a thought (or at least without remorse). I know quite a few people in the village, and I'll be left in peace.

The old mission has a meeting area, and I'll open up a small movie theater there, even though the villagers have VCRs. Still, most remember the lively society that went along with a real movie, so I'll get a few customers. That's enough—wouldn't want a crowd anyway.

It doesn't take a Sherlock Holmes to know what happened to my mother. Yet I shouldn't get cocky about it because, frankly, the answer didn't occur to me until several years ago. So here's the answer, the way I figure it:

Mom and her friend were just like the two hunters in Scotland who stumble across Auld Brig O'Doon—the village's real name in old time folklore. Though what Mom discovered might not *be* Auld Brig O'Doon, it has the same spirit.

And I know she deserved that.

Whatever superior power there is wouldn't let my Mom's hard life go unrewarded. To think of all those thousands of hours of waitressing—and nothing? You mean that was all the reward she would get? That just *couldn't* be the case.

So her magic village appeared, its gardens lush with flowers and everyone strong and proud. The houses were solid and warm, people were never alone, and there was always music and dance; and Mom would fit right in. And even though it will reappear again in about sixty years, I hope Mom will stay. For she's got to know I'm all right—that I made it through, that I also found my Brigadoon and that it too will soon return to its ancient home along northern seas where bowheads feed. This is the place the Old Ones talk about when they tell how the polar star and the solitary cry of the arctic loon joined in love. This union gave birth to Magic, the most wonderful realm we have on this earth.

About the Author

Irving Warner lived and worked in Alaska from 1965 until 1995, both as a fish and game employee and as a professor of English at Kodiak College. Born in California, he was a competitive chess player prior to moving to Alaska. He earned a BS in biology at the University of Alaska and an MA in English at the University of Maine. He writes poetry, screenplays, novels, and essays, as well as short fiction. In 1985 his radio play based on the Japanese occupation of Attu Island was presented on Alaska Public Radio. His first book of short fiction, *In the Islands of the Four Mountains,* was published in 1977. He won an Alaska State Arts Foundation Award in 1985 and a National Endowment for the Arts Fellowship in Short Fiction in 1989. Warner now lives in Port Angeles, Washington, and takes care of his geese, chickens, and rabbits when he's not writing or teaching harmonica classes.

Other Pleasure Boat Studio Books:

William Slaughter, *The Politics of My Heart*
(ISBN 0-9651413-0-6)

Frances Driscoll, *The Rape Poems*
(ISBN 0-9651413-1-4)

Michael Blumenthal, *When History Enters the House:*
Essays from Central Europe
(ISBN 0-9651413-2-2)

Tung Nien, *Setting Out: The Education of Li-li,*
translated from the Chinese by Mike OConnor
(ISBN 0-9651413-3-0)

from *Pleasure Boat Studio*

an essay written by Ouyang Xiu,
Song Dynasty poet, essayist, and scholar,
on the twelfth day of the twelfth month
in the *renwu* year (January 25, 1043)

I have heard of men of antiquity who fled from the world to distant rivers and lakes and refused to their dying day to return. They must have found some source of pleasure there. If one is not anxious for profit, even at the risk of danger, or is not convicted of a crime and forced to embark; rather, if one has a favorable breeze and gentle seas and is able to rest comfortably on a pillow and mat, sailing several hundred miles in a single day, then is boat travel not enjoyable? Of course, I have no time for such diversions. But since 'pleasure boat' is the designation of boats used for such pastimes, I have now adopted it as the name of my studio. Is there anything wrong with that?

Translated by Ronald Egan
The Literary Works of Ou-yang Hsiu
Cambridge University Press
New York 1984